Playing for First

BLUE FEATHER BOOKS, LTD.

*To my Little Phyllis Valentine, with all my love.
Thank you for believing in me.*

Playing for First

A BLUE FEATHER BOOK

by
Chris Paynter

This is a work of fiction. All characters, locales and events are either products of the author's imagination or are used fictitiously.

PLAYING FOR FIRST

Cover design by Ann Phillips

A Blue Feather Book
Published by Blue Feather Books, Ltd.

www.bluefeatherbooks.com

ISBN: 978-0-9822858-3-1

First edition: June, 2009

Printed in the United States of America and in the United Kingdom.

Acknowledgements

Thank you to Emily Reed and everyone at Blue Feather Books for welcoming me into the fold. I could not have asked for a better publisher. I believe God leads me exactly where I need to be, and I feel like I am home.

I want to thank my editor, Jane Vollbrecht, for her exhaustive work with *Playing for First*. I especially thank her for her patience with this newbie author. She is a true mentor and friend.

Thank you to my parents, Nancy and Morris, my brother, David, my sister-in-law, Grace, and my niece, Cassie, for their love, acceptance, and support throughout the years.

And last to mention, but first in my heart, thank you to my wife, Phyllis. Without her constant encouragement, this book would still be tucked away as a file on my computer. I thank her for giving me the strength to keep writing and to take that leap of faith.

Chapter 1

"What'd I tell you boys about finishing off a tackle?"

The players stared at their feet.

"Look at me!" the coach screamed.

All but one of the players' heads snapped up. The coach, dressed in baggy purple shorts and a gray T-shirt emblazoned with the school's mascot, stalked back and forth in front of them. The muscles in his legs rippled with each step.

He stomped over to the one player still staring at his cleats. The coach grabbed a handful of jersey and jerked the kid forward. "I said look at me."

The kid raised his head.

"Ellis, you're the worst of the bunch. Hell, you couldn't tackle my mother. No, check that. You couldn't even tackle my grandmother. Do you know how old she is?"

The kid mumbled, "No."

"What was that? I can't hear you."

"No, Coach!"

"She's eighty-five and has a bad hip. I can see her now, hobbling down the sideline, scoring a touchdown because you"—he poked a finger in the kid's chest—"couldn't wrap her up."

Lisa watched the scene unfold below her. She'd set aside her reporter's notebook when she settled onto the metal bleachers halfway up from the football field. She'd heard this new high school coach was a hard-ass, and now she was getting a firsthand view. She wondered if some of the theatrics were only for her benefit.

"Brad!" he shouted at his defensive coach.

"Yeah, Coach?"

"I expect these boys to be in shape before Friday's game. If that means they all have to run laps around this field every time one of them misses a tackle, then do it. Which, by the way, is a good idea. Move it. Five laps in full gear." He motioned them away as if swatting at a fly.

1

The coach retrieved his playbook from where he'd tossed it on the ground two minutes earlier. He flipped through it before acknowledging Lisa in the bleachers.

"Didn't see you join us," he said.

Sure you didn't. Lisa rose with her notebook in hand and tromped down the bleachers to stand in front of him.

"Coach Billups, I'm Lisa Collins with the *Indianapolis Gazette*." She offered her hand. He gave it a half-hearted shake. "I'm covering your game Friday night. I wondered if we could chat about your team."

His eyes narrowed. "Chat? I don't know anything about chatting, but we can discuss my team."

Lisa didn't let on that the coach's patronizing attitude had hit its mark. She flipped her notebook open and talked with him for the next twenty minutes about the team's strengths and weaknesses and his take on the competition.

She finished with her questions and offered her hand to him again. This time, she took the initiative and gripped his hand firmly.

"This'll be in tomorrow's paper, if you're interested." She squeezed his hand again before letting go. "Good luck, Coach. I'll see you Friday night."

Heading to her Toyota, Lisa resisted the urge to mutter "jerk" under her breath. She glanced at her watch. Good. She had plenty of time to drive to the newspaper office, file her article, and then drop by Frankie's.

* * *

Lisa pulled into the nearly empty lot at Frankie's Watering Hole. Since it wasn't that cool yet, she left her IU jacket in the backseat. She stepped up to the front door and checked out her short, blonde hair one last time in the chrome facing of the entryway.

It was a Tuesday night, which meant a sparse crowd and music at a tolerable level. A few women were scattered throughout the bar, some shooting pool in the back, some sitting at tables and talking over beers. Lisa spotted Frankie chatting with a woman at the bar.

"Hey, Lisa, how's it going?"

"Good, Frankie."

Before Lisa could even make it to the bar, Frankie had an open bottle of Michelob waiting for her.

"You always know how to make a girl feel wanted." Lisa sat down on one of the worn, wooden stools.

"I hope you know you're always welcome here." Frankie's dark brown eyes were warm. "Always."

Lisa tilted the bottle toward Frankie. "Thanks." She took a long drink. "God, that tastes good."

"Rough night?"

"No, not really. I put up with a jerk of a coach, but that's part of the job." She took another sip. "Just not the good part." Lisa studied Frankie a little closer. "You got a haircut."

Frankie's salt-and-pepper hair was definitely shorter than the last time Lisa had seen her over the weekend at Frankie's house.

Frankie touched her bangs. "A little shorter than I'd like it."

"It's very chic."

"Why thank you, Ms. Collins."

"You're quite welcome, Ms. Dunkin."

"Other than putting up with the coach, how are things at the paper?" Frankie poured a beer on tap into a frosted glass for another customer.

"Good. Jack has me hopping, but that's the way I like it. I'd rather be busy than waiting on a phone call from my editor every day." Lisa paused while Frankie poured another beer for a customer farther down the bar. When she returned, Lisa continued. "He's still trying to sign me on full-time, but I keep putting him off."

"Will the man ever give up?"

"He must enjoy hearing the word 'no.' I love working for Minor League.com too much. He blissfully ignores that each time I point it out to him."

"Still, that has to make you feel wanted," Frankie said. "He knows you're damn good at what you do."

"I guess."

"The most important thing is those baby editors at Minor League know it, too."

Frankie had picked up the term that Lisa used when referring to her editors in New York. Lisa was thirty-five. The editors were only a few years out of college and in their twenties.

"All I care about is that they stay happy with my coverage of the Indians."

Frankie looked at her like she'd stated the impossible. "You don't have a problem there."

"Thanks." Lisa felt the heat rise up her neck.

"Hey, didn't mean to embarrass you."

"I appreciate the compliments." Lisa noticed one of the pool tables was free. "I think I'll get in a game while I have a chance." She stepped down from the stool. "I have to stay sharp if I want to keep up with you." She downed her beer. "But then again, you have a freaking pool table in your den."

"Which you use frequently, so no excuses," Frankie said. She pointed at Lisa's empty bottle. "Another?"

"One more, and that'll be it." Lisa saw that Stacy, one of the part-time bartenders was throwing darts in the corner of the bar. "Since you're not busy, could Stacy take over for a few minutes while we shoot a game?"

"You're sure you want to do that? It gets kind of tedious for me to win all the time."

"You're pushing your luck, you know. And wipe that smirk off your face."

"What can I say? When you got it, you got it."

"Oh, now you're really pushing your luck."

Frankie ignored her. "Stacy!" she shouted. "Could you tend the bar for a few while I beat Lisa in a game of pool?"

"Sure, boss. I suck at darts anyway."

As Stacy approached, Lisa told her, "Ignore Frankie. She's delusional."

"Thanks, Stacy." Frankie stepped out from behind the bar. She reached up to put an arm around Lisa's shoulder. It was quite a stretch since she was four inches shorter than Lisa's lean five-eight frame. "Promise me you won't whine when I clear the table."

Lisa bumped her playfully. "You're a shit, you know that? Actually, you're a little shit."

"You realize that height's relative with you, don't you? I'm average for a woman. You, on the other hand, are pretty damn close to Amazon status."

"I'll let that one go," Lisa said while picking out a cue. First, she picked out the shortest one in the rack. "Here." She tossed it to Frankie who caught it deftly with one hand. "That one should suit you fine."

"Just for that, I'm breaking. March your sorry butt over to that stool, and see if you can learn anything."

Lisa sat down and watched while Frankie racked up the balls. They'd been shooting pool and trading fake insults almost since the first day that Lisa walked into Frankie's bar five years ago.

Two stripes dropped into the far side pockets.

"Rest up and enjoy your beer. This shouldn't take too long." Frankie drew her cue back.

"Yeah, yeah, yeah." Lisa tried to keep a straight face. The sad truth was she knew Frankie was only half joking.

In the next several minutes, Frankie knocked in all but one of the stripes.

Lisa sipped her beer in silence.

Frankie chalked her cue. "Hmm... decisions, decisions." She strutted around the table, peering at one angle and then another.

Lisa finally lost her patience "Oh, good Lord, knock the damn thing in, will you?"

Frankie prepared to strike the cue ball. "You can't hurry perfection, my friend."

Lisa wadded up the napkin that was under her beer bottle and threw it at Frankie. The napkin hit its target at the precise moment Frankie hit the cue ball. The cue ball skipped in the air for several inches, dropped with a loud "thunk" onto the table, and slowed to a stop directly in front of the four ball.

Frankie stared at Lisa. "You do realize that's cheating, don't you?"

"It's all in your perception. You see it as cheating. I see it as missing that trash can behind you."

Frankie turned around. The trash can was a good fifteen feet away. "You're so full of it."

Lisa hopped off the stool and checked out the various shots she had on the table. "That's what you get for being so cocky." Lisa could see that Frankie was trying to appear angry, but her half smile gave her away.

Frankie moved out of the way to allow Lisa to hit her first shot. "Just wait. Paybacks are hell."

Lisa didn't respond, but focused as she began her own run of the table. In less than five minutes, Lisa was down to the seven ball and the five ball.

"Only one more, and we're even." Lisa stuck her tongue slightly out the side of her mouth, concentrating on the shot. She struck the cue ball and knocked the seven ball into the right corner pocket. Now there was one more tricky shot before she could call the eight ball. She measured the angle with her cue and decided to bank the cue ball off the side.

"If you make that one, I'm buying you breakfast the next time we're out."

"You're on." After several seconds of getting the perfect angle, Lisa struck the cue ball. It careened off the side and hit the five ball perfectly to drop it into the middle pocket. Lisa thrust her fist in the air and did a little dance.

"Steak and eggs sound good to me, especially since you'll be buying." Lisa waited for Frankie's sarcastic comment, but it didn't come. She turned to find Frankie observing her with a bemused expression, her chin resting on the hand that held her cue. "What's that look for?"

"Nothing, except you were kind of cute there with your tongue sticking out of your mouth."

"Oh, for that…" Lisa called the shot for the eight ball and nailed it. She took a deep bow. "Thank you. Thank you," she said loud enough for others in the bar to hear her. "Hold your applause. It was nothing."

"Way to go, Lisa!" Stacy shouted.

Frankie sighed and placed her cue in the rack. Lisa came up beside her and set hers in the open slot. Frankie stuck out her hand. "Nice game."

Lisa took her hand. "Yes, it was, wasn't it?"

"You don't know when to quit, do you?"

Lisa patted her on the back on their way to the bar.

"I'm heading on home," Stacy said, picking up her jacket.

"Thanks for helping out."

"You're welcome, Frankie. I'll see you tomorrow night."

Lisa sat down on a stool while Frankie stepped behind the bar.

"Seriously, how does breakfast Thursday morning work for you?" Frankie asked while sipping her bottled water.

"Sounds perfect." Lisa scooted nearer to the bar. "Hey, I almost forgot. You'll like this one. There's a professional women's baseball team coming into town. They're playing an exhibition game Saturday night against some of the Indians who weren't called up to Cincinnati earlier this month."

Frankie's face lit up. "You're kidding."

"It gets better. They have this first baseman, Amy Perry, who's been hitting the hell out of the ball for seven years now. The buzz on Minor League.com is that a major league club might scout her to start in the Arizona instructional league."

"Wait. You're telling me there's a chance she can make it to the big leagues?" Frankie asked.

"Sounds like it. Of course, she'd need some work before she'd get the call. They scheduled the exhibition game so the Reds management can see her play in person. Some are thinking it might be a publicity stunt. I'm sure the Reds could use more bodies in the seats. But she's supposed to be that good. I only wish I'd had a chance to make it to a Bandits game. They played an exhibition against a men's team up in Chicago last year, but I couldn't make it because of work."

"I'd be thrilled if she's given the chance. I always told you a woman could play professional baseball."

"And I agreed with you one hundred percent."

Frankie seemed lost in thought. "I'd sure like to see this before I die."

"Oh, stop. You're only fifty."

Frankie's face clouded over. "You never know."

Lisa suspected Frankie was remembering her battle with breast cancer six years ago, the year before they'd met. When she first met Frankie, mutual friends had told her that Frankie had undergone a mastectomy and struggled through chemotherapy. The chemo had almost killed her.

Lisa put her hand on top of Frankie's. "I'm sorry, I didn't mean to…"

"It's okay, Leese." Frankie blinked and briefly turned her face away. "Well, I hope this Amy Perry can make it."

"I'll be there tomorrow night to see her team practice and write a feature on her. I'm hoping Jack will pick it up. If she gets a shot at this, I'll cover her story on Minor League.com. A feature for the paper would be a nice place to start." Lisa swallowed the last few sips of her beer. "I need to get home."

"Good luck with Jack, and good luck with your article. I'm sure you'll shine."

"You know you're my biggest cheerleader, don't you?" Lisa asked.

"That's because you deserve it."

Lisa patted Frankie's hand. "Thanks." She stepped down from the stool. "I'll see you on Thursday. Flapjacks?" It was their usual place for breakfast.

"Yep," Frankie said. "Why don't you drive on down to my house, say, around eight?"

"Will do. Have a good night." Lisa was almost to the door. "Oh, and, Frankie?"

"Yeah?"

"It was fun kicking your ass tonight."

"Get the hell out of here."

Chapter 2

The next morning, Lisa stumbled into the bathroom. She tried to focus on her reflection in the mirror, but her bleary, hazel eyes didn't seem to want to cooperate. Her hair was sticking out in different directions. She was pale, and deep, dark circles lay under her eyes. "Damn, you'd think I got drunk last night." She splashed cold water on her face in an effort to wake up.

The phone rang. Lisa checked the clock on the bathroom wall. Who could be calling at seven-fifteen?

"All right," she shouted as the ringing of the phone pierced her ears. She sprawled across the bed to pick up the portable from its cradle. "Hello," she snapped.

"Aren't we little Miss Merry Sunshine this morning?"

She heard the distinct, two-pack-a-day gravely voice of the editor at the *Gazette*. Lisa ignored the sarcasm. "What do you want, Jack?"

"You mentioned something about a player and an exhibition game on Saturday night."

She flipped onto her back. Lisa filled Jack in on the Kansas City Bandits' background. "They have a phenomenal first baseman. She's the one I want to feature," Lisa said. "The Reds have hustled up to scout her this last week of September so they can work with her in the Arizona Fall League starting next month. Then it might be on to their Double-A team in Chattanooga next spring. I know some people think it's a joke, but there are those who say she's really that good."

"How old is she?" His voice took on the skeptical tone he frequently used when his idea of a scoop didn't exactly mesh with Lisa's.

"She's twenty-seven."

He grunted. "She's got some age on her to be coming up in the minors. They're usually in their early twenties."

Lisa sighed heavily. It amazed her how players in their late twenties were thought of as "having age on them" when breaking into the majors. The old baseball adage said twenty-seven was the magical year a player finally hit his potential in his career.

Lisa hastened to seal the deal. "This is a legitimate story. I hope to do a feature on her for the paper before the exhibition game. I know I'll cover her story on the website."

"Quit trying so hard to convince me. If there's something there, I trust you'll make it work. When did you plan on writing the feature?"

"The Bandits are practicing over on the University of Indianapolis campus today. I want to be there around five."

"Can you get an article to me before deadline tonight for tomorrow's paper?"

"Not a problem."

"I look forward to seeing it," Jack said. "Good luck today."

"Thanks." Lisa hung up. She'd hoped he'd go for the story. If a feature appeared in the daily paper, more readers would be interested in following the story online.

Lisa stepped into the shower. She lathered up her hair with shampoo and thought about last night and Frankie. Frankie was right. A woman could play baseball. The Bandits proved it every time they took the field. But now it was time to see if a woman could break the gender barrier into the major leagues.

Lisa thought, too, about Frankie's comment of wanting to see a woman make it in the big leagues while Frankie was still on the planet to witness it. She hated to see the pain that passed over her friend's face. She wished she had known Frankie six years ago. She would have supported her any way she could. Instead, Frankie not only had to deal with the mastectomy, but also with her partner of eight years cheating on her and leaving her after the surgery.

Lisa stood under the water and rinsed her hair. Like Frankie, she hadn't had much luck with women, even though there had been plenty of them during the past ten years. One relationship had managed to last a year. But Lisa inevitably moved on. Because she had never known her father, and her mother had died when Lisa was twenty-five, her therapist attributed her reluctance to commit to her fear of abandonment. He was convinced Lisa was afraid that if she allowed someone to get too close, they'd leave her, too. Lisa snorted and soaped up her washcloth. Therapists. They served their purpose, but hers annoyed the hell out of her sometimes.

Lisa finished bathing. She cleared her mind of everything else and focused on her story. As she toweled off, she formed questions in her mind for her interviews. She had the day to jump on the Internet and do further research on the Bandits. She could do that at her apartment, but she decided to drive to the main library to research online without distraction. If she stayed home, she might fall into the temptation of crashing on the couch and vegging in front of the TV.

Lisa dressed in a pair of jeans and one of her nicer sweatshirts. She checked out her hair in the mirror one more time before leaving. Definitely a butch thing.

* * *

With statistics on the Bandits bouncing around in her brain, Lisa drove south to the University of Indianapolis. She parked the car in the lot nearest to the baseball field where she could see the Bandits warming up. With notebook in hand, she walked over to a woman she knew was the coach, because she'd seen her photo online. She had blonde hair that was graying at the temples, a deeply tanned and weathered face, and a voice that anyone within three miles could hear. Lisa wouldn't have needed to see the picture from the Internet. There was no doubt who was in charge.

"Dee, goddammit, I told you to keep your head down, didn't I?" The coach, who was all of five-two, strode over to the shortstop fielding grounders from another player. She snatched the shortstop's glove and yelled, "Suz, smack me some hard ones." The player obliged, and the coach demonstrated exactly what she wanted. "Like this, Dee. Do you see my fucking head bobbing up? No. I'm following the goddamn ball all the way into my glove." She handed the glove back to the shortstop. "Work on that for the next fifteen minutes."

"Yeah?" the coach barked at Lisa waiting nearby.

Intimidation didn't work on Lisa. She had once interviewed Coach Bob Knight in Bloomington when she worked for the student newspaper there. He had given her some grief for a few minutes. Then she asked him some informed questions about his team's defense. After that, he became almost polite… almost.

Lisa approached her. "Coach?"

The coach barely acknowledged her, raising her eyebrows slightly as if to ask why Lisa was interrupting her practice.

Lisa stuck out her hand. "My name's Lisa Collins. I'm writing for the *Indianapolis Gazette.* I've heard about your team and would like to feature one of your players in an article."

The coach's expression softened a little. She grabbed Lisa's hand with a firm grip. "Marge Tompkins. Good to meet you." The coach gestured at the bleachers to sit and talk. "Let me guess. My first baseman, Amy Perry, right?"

"Yes. I understand the Cincinnati Reds are thinking about sending her down to the fall instructional league and have her come up through their Double-A team as early as next year."

"It's about time. She's been knocking the hell out of the ball for almost seven years now, as long as our team's been around. She can hit a sharp breaking ball and a ninety-mile-an-hour fastball just as easily. One of our pitchers can pitch in the low eighties, but we had Amy face a kid from the University of Kansas once. She hit his second pitch over the left field fence. We clocked it at ninety-five. It's a shame it's taken this long for men to admit that a woman can be this good at the game of baseball. And you don't have to be built like a linebacker to play it either."

Lisa scribbled down notes, at the same time deftly maintaining eye contact with the coach as much as possible.

The coach continued. "But we know hitting that breaking ball is the trick in making it."

"Absolutely," Lisa said.

Coach Tompkins stepped down from the bleachers, and Lisa joined her. The coach motioned at one of the players stretching in the grass. "Amy, come over here."

Amy Perry stood up. Lisa shielded her eyes from the sun to get a better view. She appeared to be about six-feet tall. She was a big woman, but Lisa could tell it was all muscle underneath her maroon Bandits long-sleeved T-shirt and sweat pants. She drew nearer, and Lisa could see she had short, light brown wavy hair. Even closer, Lisa could make out her features. Her face was round with a well-defined nose. There was a cleft in her chin, and she had a dark tan.

Amy stood in front of the two women, and Lisa got a better look at her eyes. They were a pale green, the kind that probably changed in different light. They were bright and sparkling in the autumn sun.

"Amy, this is Lisa Collins," Coach Tompkins said, gesturing to Lisa. "She's a reporter with the *Indianapolis Gazette* and wants to do a feature on you."

Lisa held out her hand for Amy to grasp.

"Hey," Amy said in a soft voice.

"Amy hails from a town outside of Lawrence, Kansas," the coach said. "And believe me, you'll know once you start talking to her. She's all country."

Amy laughed, and her white teeth contrasted against her bronzed skin. Her eyes reflected her amusement. That decided it for Lisa; she wanted to know this woman. Amy's eyes came alive as they held Lisa's for a brief second.

"Coach Tompkins is always giving me a rough way to go." She stared down at the ground while she spoke.

"I'll leave you two alone. I see that Dee is back to her bad habit of raising her head." The coach stomped over to the shortstop. Again, Lisa could hear her bellowing, "Goddammit! What'd I tell you, Dee?"

"Would you mind if we sit over there while I interview you, Amy?" Lisa pointed to the bleachers.

"No, not at all." They sat down onto the cool metal.

"So, what's your hometown in Kansas?"

"Lecompton. It's to the northwest of Lawrence."

"How long have you been playing baseball?"

"About twelve years."

Apparently, Amy's answers wouldn't be very expansive and wouldn't allow Lisa to develop an article. She needed to coax her to go beyond that.

"That means you started when you were about fifteen."

Amy nodded.

"That puts you in high school. You played fast-pitch softball before that?"

Amy nodded again.

Let's try this. "You tried out for the high school baseball team?" Lisa received yet another head nod. "What was that like?" *That's not a yes/no question, Amy. Let me know how you felt.*

Amy's face brightened. "It was a good experience."

Lisa feared that was the extent of her answer. But, after a few seconds of contemplation, Amy started opening up.

"At first, the coach fought it. The principal backed him and tried to fight it, too. But I was allowed to go in front of the school board and explain why playing baseball meant so much to me."

"And why does it mean so much to you?" Lisa wasn't asking it for the article. She really wanted to know.

"Because I knew if I'd ever achieve my dream of playing for a professional men's team, it'd have to start at the high school level. And I knew the coach at my high school was one of the best in the area. He had a couple of players go on to make it in the minors. When I came in front of the school board, I was able to explain all that."

"Was that a problem for you? You seem to be shy."

"Yeah, but it was one of the most important moments of my life. And I knew it. I knew I needed to tell my side of things. Do you know what I mean?"

"Yes," Lisa murmured, captivated by Amy's words.

They sat there for another twenty minutes or so, while Lisa took notes.

"Is it okay if I stick around while you take batting practice and field some?" It was part of Lisa's job to stay for the practice, but asking Amy's permission changed the feel of it.

"Sure."

"Good. I've enjoyed talking to you." Lisa offered her hand.

"Thanks. I've enjoyed it, too." Amy shook her hand again. It felt to Lisa like Amy held on a little longer than she had before.

"The article should be in the morning paper, if you're interested in seeing it."

"I'll look for it," Amy said before jogging over to the diamond.

Wow. Lisa was lost in thought until she saw Jenny, the sports photographer from the paper, crossing the parking lot next to the field. Lisa pointed out Amy.

"Some action shots of her batting and fielding, and Jack will probably want a few casual ones of her standing around with the other players."

Jenny slung her camera bag high up on her shoulder and made her way over to the diamond.

"Hell of a nice girl, isn't she?" Coach Tompkins said, approaching Lisa.

"Yes, she is."

"Hell of a ballplayer, too. Watch."

A tall, lanky player took the mound and fired a fastball toward the plate. In one smooth motion, Amy, who batted right handed, hit a frozen rope into left field. The next pitch was on the outside corner. She went with it and lined one over the second baseman's head.

"All parts of the field," Coach Tompkins said in a confident voice.

The next pitch was a fat, batting practice fastball down the heart of the plate. Amy connected, and the ball arced into the clear blue sky. Lisa cupped her hand over her eyes, following the flight of the ball as it traveled over 300 feet.

"Damn," she said under her breath.

After about fifteen minutes of hitting, Amy took her position at first and fielded hot shot after hot shot, diving to her right and snagging one line drive out of the air. One of the other players came up for her batting practice, and Amy took the throws to first. The shortstop fielded one tricky hop cleanly.

"Finally listening to your old coach, huh, Dee?" Coach Tompkins yelled. Dee fired the ball over to Amy. The throw was a little off, and Amy stretched to stay on the bag. "Way to hang in there, Amy," the coach shouted. She turned to Lisa. "I think you have your story, don't you?"

Lisa didn't answer, but observed Amy make play after play while cutting up with her teammates. It seemed she only reserved her shyness for first-time encounters.

"Thanks, Coach Tompkins." Lisa flipped her notebook shut and shook her hand again.

"Glad we could talk," Tompkins said. She joined the team. "Time for diving drills, ladies." They moaned as they formed a line. Another coach handed Tompkins a bat, and she started smacking balls to the right or left of each player. Each woman sacrificed her body with a headfirst dive to retrieve the ball. After Amy made her play, she took her place at the back of the line and began talking with one of the other players.

Yeah, I'd definitely like to know her better.

"I got some pretty good shots," Jenny said. "I'll take these back to the paper now."

Lisa didn't answer her right away.

"Lisa?"

"Sorry. Thanks, Jen." She watched the team a few more minutes and then walked to her car, wondering about how she had felt while she was talking to Amy. It was probably nothing.

But it was a good feeling.

Chapter 3

After finishing her article, Lisa entered the Watering Hole around nine. She hadn't planned on stopping in, but she couldn't wait until breakfast the next morning to see Frankie.

"Didn't expect to see you here tonight," Frankie said.

"I couldn't wait to tell you about Amy Perry." Lisa slid onto a stool. "I'll take a Coke."

"How'd she look?" Frankie poured the Coke over a glassful of ice.

"Impressive. You should see her hit. If she were a guy, she would've been playing for a major league team these past five years."

Frankie gave a sarcastic laugh. "Men aren't too hip on a woman outperforming them in anything, let alone at a sport they think is their own. You, of all people, should know that."

"They won't be able to ignore her if she plays like she did this afternoon. Like I said, you should see her."

Frankie's attention was on something behind Lisa. "Maybe I have. I've never seen these women before, and they're definitely athletes."

Lisa swiveled on her stool to take a quick look. Five Bandits players, including Amy Perry, wearing jeans and a University of Kansas sweatshirt, had entered the bar. Lisa faced Frankie again. "The one in the Jayhawks sweatshirt," she said in a low voice.

Frankie assessed the newcomers. "Amy's kind of cute."

Dee came to the bar and ordered five Budweisers. Because of the hat she'd worn at practice, Lisa hadn't noticed that her hair was spiky and bleached out. She was stocky and about an inch shorter than Lisa.

"Hey, you're the reporter, right? How ya doin'?" Dee asked in a strong New York accent.

"All right. And you?"

"I'll be better after this," Dee said and held up one of the Buds, "and a game of pool." She yelled over at the group of players gathered around two of the pool tables. "Yo, Ginger, get over here. How am I supposed to carry all of this?"

Ginger hustled over. She was young, maybe in her early twenties. Dee and Amy were the only two who appeared to be approaching thirty.

Ginger picked up two of the bottles while Dee carried the other three. Dee started back with the beer, but stopped and addressed Lisa. "Do you play pool? There are three pool tables, and with you, it'd make six of us. We could have a mini-tournament."

"Oh, no. I'll probably go home after I finish this." Lisa eyed her Coke. *Gee, ain't I tough?*

"Ah, come on. It'll be fun. I'll buy you a beer. What do you drink?"

Lisa could see she wasn't getting out of this.

"I guess I could play for a while. And it's Michelob."

Before Dee even asked, Frankie plopped the beer in front of Lisa.

Lisa followed Dee over to the tables, put her beer on the ledge, and pulled off her sweatshirt. The rest of the ball players had done the same. Amy stayed true to her team with a blue Jayhawks T-shirt.

"Suz, you take on Ginger. Amy, you take on Joely, and you," Dee said and pointed at Lisa, "can try and beat me."

Lisa racked up the balls, ignoring Dee's bluster. About twenty minutes into their game, Lisa had two solids to knock in, Dee one stripe. It was Dee's shot, and she had a perfect opportunity to tap it into one of the side pockets. She hit the cue ball, and it stopped barely short of its target.

Dee briefly leaned her head down onto her forearm. "Damn it. I knew I should've hit it harder."

Lisa chalked her cue while checking out her shot. The other two games had concluded, and the four women sat on nearby stools. If she hit this right, she should be able to knock them both in, one to each corner pocket. She lined the shot up and struck the cue ball. The two solids went into opposite directions and smacked into the pockets.

"I dunno, Dee, I think you've got yourself a hustler here," Ginger said with a giggle.

Dee was definitely pouting. Lisa lined up the shot for the eight ball and called it. It rattled in, and the other players clapped.

Dee walked over and patted her on the back. "That's the first time I got beat in about twenty games. You know, I didn't catch your name earlier today."

A familiar voice spoke up behind Lisa. "It's Lisa Collins."

Lisa turned to find Amy staring at her.

"All right, Lisa, you take on Ginger next. Amy, I know you won, but you sit this one out. Since you're oh-so-special-and-all and about to have a big spread on you in the morning paper, we'll let you play in the championship."

Lisa cleared the table and beat Ginger handily.

Before she and Amy started their game, Amy said, "I'm pretty good at this, too."

Watching Amy lean down for her shot, Lisa thought of other questions she had for her, but not as a reporter. She wanted to know more about her besides her love of baseball.

Lisa had trouble concentrating on the game. She didn't mind when she lost and walked around the table to shake Amy's hand. This time, Lisa was the one who held on a little longer.

Dee stepped between them. "Loser buys the next round."

Lisa didn't hear her. She was staring at Amy.

"Yo, Leesey, we're dry here." Dee held up her empty bottle.

"Oh, sorry." Before she even made it to the bar, Frankie already had the lids popped on the Buds.

"They seem like good people." Lisa didn't hear Frankie at first. Frankie finally caught her attention. "You enjoying yourself?"

"Yeah, I am."

"Good. I like seeing you happy." Frankie left Lisa when another customer shouted for a drink.

Dee met her halfway to grab the tray of beers and pass them out to the others. Lisa was suddenly at a loss for words in front of the five women, especially Amy.

"You know what?" Dee said. "Why don't you and Amy get a table, and Amy can fill you in on anything else you need for your next article. 'Cause we all know there'll be a next article. Right, Lisa?"

Lisa's face flushed.

"There's no need to get flustered." Dee grabbed her and Amy by their elbows and led them to a table. "Amy here won't bite." She left them alone.

"Sometimes you have to excuse Dee," Amy said while they sat down. "She gets a bit pushy. It's the New Yorker in her."

"You two make quite a pair as friends. Do you ever have

trouble understanding her accent?"

"Nah."

Lisa grew quiet.

"You know, I could say the same about you being shy," Amy said.

Lisa stared down at the worn table. Someone had carved, "Girls Kick Ass!" into the wood. She ran her fingers in and out of the grooved letters. "Sometimes," Lisa said and then cleared her throat. "Depends on the situation."

"Hey."

Lisa shivered. She loved the way Amy said that simple word.

"Tell me some things about you," Amy said. "You know some about me."

"What do you want to know?"

"How about how you got started in sports writing?"

Lisa sat back in her chair. "After graduating from IU, I got hired by a newspaper in Ohio. I worked there for a few years and moved on to a bigger paper in Pittsburgh. About five years ago, the job at Minor League.com opened up here in Indy. I jumped at the chance to come home. Then a correspondent position came up at the *Gazette*. I took it because I could cover high school sports like I'd been doing in Ohio and Pittsburgh. But I loved that it was on a part-time basis. That way I could still concentrate on covering the Indians for the website."

"That's a busy schedule."

Lisa took a long drink of her beer. "It is, but I love it."

"How about your family?"

Lisa's stomach did a quick drop, and a lump came to her throat. She knew her face betrayed her discomfort.

Amy leaned over the table and took Lisa's hand. "Hey, I'm sorry if I upset you. I didn't know."

"It's all right. It just sneaks up on me sometimes when someone asks." Lisa hesitated, but went on. "I never knew my dad. My mom died from ovarian cancer ten years ago." She glanced away for a brief moment, but turned to find Amy looking at her with compassion. Amy gently squeezed her hand. "I don't have any brothers or sisters, so I get lonely sometimes."

"I know that's rough. I lost my dad two years ago to a heart attack."

A quick flicker of sadness rushed over Amy's face and then vanished. Lisa glanced down at her hand that Amy still held. It felt good, but Amy let go.

"I'm sorry for your loss, too." Lisa wasn't thinking before asking her next question. "What are you doing Friday night?"

"We have practice. After that, I'm free."

"I'm working, but would you like to join me in covering a high school football game? We could share some sloppy hot dogs."

"I'd like that very much."

A loud voice interrupted their conversation.

"Yo, Aims, gotta get back to the hotel." Dee was already at the door with the other players. "You know the boss lady will want to know where we are."

"Where are you guys staying? I can pick you up."

Amy yelled over to the shortstop. "Where are we staying?"

"The Hyatt," Dee answered.

"How about six?" Lisa asked. "I should be at the field before seven."

"Make it six-thirty. That'll give me time to shower and cool down from our afternoon workout."

"I'll see you then."

Amy joined her teammates.

"Leesey, been fun hangin' with ya," Dee boomed.

"You, too." Lisa picked up her beer and carried it over to the bar to sit in front of Frankie.

"So?" Frankie asked.

"What?" Lisa tried to play coy, but couldn't keep the corners of her mouth from twitching upward.

"You know what."

Lisa stalled briefly before answering. "She's going with me to the high school football game I'm covering Friday night."

"Good for you."

"Yeah?"

"Yes."

"Guess so, huh?" Lisa was nervous. She hadn't been out with anyone for a while. She enjoyed her weekend visits to Frankie's house, but that was different.

"What else do I need to say? You don't get out that much, and this is what you need."

"You're a good friend. You know that, right?"

Frankie swiped at the bar with her towel. "So are you. Why don't you get out of here before we break into a chorus of 'You've Got a Friend'?"

Lisa laughed and Frankie joined her. "That song has great lyrics, by the way," Lisa said while tugging on her sweatshirt.

"I know. But let's not drive everyone out of here with our caterwauling."

Lisa backed up toward the door and pointed at Frankie. "You got it."

"See you tomorrow morning at my place."

Chapter 4

Lisa got up even earlier than usual the next morning. She wanted to see the paper. She could go to the *Gazette*'s Internet site for the article and the photos, but it meant something to her to hold the newspaper in her hands and actually feel what she had written.

She opened to the sports page. Jack had placed the article in the top fold. The headline read, "Is She Ready for the Show?" He had chosen two photos to accompany the piece. One was Amy with a determined expression as she connected with the baseball. The other was of her sitting on the ground and leaning over to stretch her legs while sharing a laugh with a teammate standing nearby. Both captured the player perfectly.

Lisa read the article, even though she knew exactly what she had written. It was good. She was the first to admit it if her work was crap.

The phone rang.

"Hey, you," Frankie said. "Wanted to catch you before you left. I couldn't wait to tell you that I love the article. I figured you'd be up early to read it. I'm sorry Saturdays are so busy at the Watering Hole, or I'd be at the game."

"Wish you could see her play." Lisa stared at the two photos of Amy. "I need to hit the shower, and then I'll be down there."

"See you in a few."

* * *

Lisa stepped up to Frankie's door and knocked. She heard Frankie stomp through the house.

"Come on in for a few minutes. Gotta get my shoes on."

Lisa sank down on the worn leather recliner in the living room. It faced Frankie's wall of family pictures. One large one of her parents and several smaller ones of her brothers, sisters, nieces, and nephews hung there. The photo of her mother showed the striking resemblance between the two women. They shared the same thick hair, dark brown eyes, and round face.

Lisa resisted the urge to sigh. She missed her mom. Sometimes, the ache was almost unbearable. She missed picking up the phone and knowing she could talk to her about anything. She became aware of Frankie standing in the entryway to the hall.

"Everything okay?" Frankie asked.

"Yeah." Lisa shook free from her memories. "Almost ready?"

Frankie came in and sat on the couch to put on her clodhoppers, as she liked to call them. She was wearing the soft plush dark green sweatshirt that Lisa had bought her. And of course jeans. Lisa couldn't remember the last time she saw Frankie dressed in anything other than jeans.

"Damn, woman, don't you have any sweatshirts other than IU?" Frankie asked while tying her boots.

"You only have a problem with it because you're a die-hard Kentucky Wildcats fan. Remember, I got my degree from this school."

"No comment."

Lisa stood up and held out her hand to pull Frankie to her feet. "How about we go clog our arteries?"

"Isn't that why we go to Flapjacks?"

* * *

They walked to their favorite table by the window and sat down.

The waitress, Wanda, approached them. "The usual for both of you?"

"Are we that predictable?" Frankie asked.

"You are after five years of coming here, hon," Wanda answered.

Frankie replaced her menu in the slot on the table. "You're right. The usual."

"I'm having something different today," Lisa said with a smug grin. "Steak and eggs with the steak medium well and eggs over medium, please." She pointed at Frankie. "She's treating me this morning because I made a really tricky pool shot."

"Which I'm sure I'll be reminded of quite frequently," Frankie said.

Wanda laughed and then shouted out the order to the cook. She brought over a glass of orange juice for Lisa and poured Frankie a cup of coffee.

After she left, Frankie asked, "Ready for your date tomorrow night?"

Lisa almost spit out her orange juice. She put the glass down with a little more emphasis than she'd intended. "It's not a date." She used her napkin to wipe up the juice that had spilled over the lip of the glass. "Amy's only coming along while I work. That's all."

"Whatever you say."

Lisa let the remark go by.

"In the amount of time you've talked to her, what do you think?" Frankie asked. "And I'm not talking about her playing skills."

Lisa remembered her conversation with Amy the night before. "I love the confidence she has in her abilities. She needs to hold onto that if she wants to make it, but…"

Frankie was about to take a sip of her coffee and stopped. "But what?"

"I think it's safe to assume she's gay, but I wonder if she's as open as I am about her sexuality. If I'm right, I can see her going farther into the closet if she does make it in baseball. I can totally understand that, but I don't know how I'll handle it if we were to, well, you know, were to…" Lisa squirmed in her seat.

"Were to get involved." Frankie finished the sentence for her.

"Yeah."

Frankie furrowed her brow. "You've got to realize some people might not be able to be as open as we are. You're a sportswriter. I'm sure you know what this'll be like for Amy. It'll be hard enough that she's a woman trying to make it in a man's game. If she could be out, she'd be an inspiration to a lot of others. But maybe you need to see it from her perspective."

"Really?"

"You're surprised at what I said?"

"Yeah, because you're one of the most out lesbians I know."

"That doesn't mean that every lesbian can do the same. Some situations and jobs unfortunately force some of us into the closet. This might be one of them." Wanda set their food down.

Lisa picked up her knife to cut her steak. "I'll wait and see how things go tomorrow night and try not to worry about it."

"Cuz tomorrow's anotha day?"

"Very funny, Scarlett."

"What? Not a fan of *Gone with the Wind?*"

"You're too much, you know that?" Lisa took a bite of her steak and tried to banish the worries from her mind.

Chapter 5

Lisa pulled on her IU jacket over her gray sweatshirt. She paused at the mirror by the door and did a quick comb-through. She noticed the time. Damn. It was six-thirty. She hated being late, even though the Hyatt was only a few blocks away from her downtown apartment.

She pulled into the roundabout at the hotel. Amy, wearing a bright blue Jayhawks jacket, was there with her back against the brick wall of the hotel.

"Hey," she said, getting into the car.

"Hey. Sorry I'm late."

"You really aren't that late. Where's this game of yours?"

"It's on the west side. Two of the city's biggest rivals are hooking up." Lisa glanced over at Amy. "Kind of late to be asking, but do you like football?"

"I like the Kansas City Chiefs."

"Ah. Well, around here, the Colts and Peyton Manning are all people talk about."

"Somehow, that doesn't surprise me."

They arrived at the football field. Lisa picked up her laptop case from the backseat and hung the strap over her shoulder. She led Amy up the bleachers to her seat before leaving to interview both coaches.

She wrote down the typical quotes about the importance of the game and that their opponent was "so talented." They hoped they could "pull this one out." Coach Billups was civil to her, which she assumed meant he liked her article. She finished and took her seat next to Amy.

Lisa gathered her notes together before asking, "How about those horrible hot dogs I promised you?"

"I'm always up for a hot dog, especially at games."

"My treat." They stomped down the bleacher stairs to the refreshment stand. "To make these taste semi-decent, you've got to slap as much junk on them as you can," Lisa said while piling on relish, mustard, and ketchup. Amy did the same, and they tried to eat the hot dogs without getting too messy in the process.

There was a spot of ketchup on Amy's chin. Lisa reached out to wipe it away with her napkin. Amy quickly jumped back and shot furtive glances at the people around them. The sounds of the band warming up helped diffuse the awkward situation. They went back out to the bleachers and sat higher to allow Lisa a better view of the field. Amy stretched her long legs out in front of her. Lisa took out her laptop to keep stats.

They didn't talk much during the game. Amy tried to help a couple of times by providing a description of the plays on the field while Lisa typed. At halftime, Lisa added stats and selected pertinent quotes for the article, continuing to chat with Amy.

"Do you want to get a beer after the game at that bar we were at last night?" Amy asked. "I know you need to get your article in, but maybe you can come by later?"

"Sure, I'll finish it up at the *Gazette* offices. Then I'll be at Frankie's place."

Lisa excused herself from Amy one more time after the game to interview the coaches and players. She found Amy waiting for her at the bottom of the bleachers.

"I'd better take you back."

Lisa pulled into the Hyatt and once again promised she'd stop at the Watering Hole later.

"You'll really be there, right? I won't get stood up?" Amy asked, leaning into the car through the open door.

"Why would I do that? I had fun tonight."

"It's that… that I don't want to feel stupid sitting there."

"When I say I'll be somewhere to meet a friend, I'll be there."

A couple passed by on their way into the hotel. Amy's expression changed, and she hurriedly shut the door. She started walking away. Lisa buzzed down the passenger-side window.

"Hey. I'll see you later."

Amy continued her quick escape through the revolving doors.

Lisa sat there a while before pulling away. What the hell was that all about?

The scene replayed in her mind while she waited for the stoplight to change at the next intersection. A horn blared behind her when the light turned green.

"Jeez! Get a grip!" Lisa yelled.

She parked her car in the lot at the *Gazette* and went into the sports office. She sat down at an empty computer and took out her laptop to pull up the stats and quotes. The cursor blinked at her from the blank screen, but her mind wasn't on writing the article.

"Collins, the story won't write itself." Jack stood beside her desk. He was tall and thin with a receding hairline.

"You know, sometimes you're a real pain in the ass."

"Love you too, babe."

"And do you always have to smell like an overflowing ashtray?" Lisa asked loudly as he walked away.

Jack stopped at the entrance to his office. "Article. Soon. Write."

Lisa bought a Coke at the soda machine in the break room. She took her seat again in front of her computer and started writing, using the quotes she had jotted down. She checked her notes and stats and inputted them. She read it over one last time. It was a decent article. She saved it and got up to leave. She daintily waved her hand at Jack on her way out.

"You're lucky you're such a good correspondent, or I would've gotten someone else to cover these games a long time ago," he yelled at her.

Lisa walked back to his office door and poked her head in. "You know you love me."

"Sure I do, but give me your best work tomorrow night. This is a big story. I'm sure I don't need to tell you that. There'll be quite a few reporters from other cities at the game."

It would probably be the last article about Amy she'd be writing for the *Gazette*. After tomorrow night's exhibition, she'd write for the website.

"I'm anxious to see her play against these guys." She hoisted her laptop strap higher up on her shoulder. "Have a good night."

"You, too."

Lisa zipped up her jacket when she stepped outside. It had cooled considerably in the last few nights. It was after ten-thirty when she started for Frankie's.

* * *

Lisa squinted, trying to peer through the smoky haze. The music pounded her ears and the floor under her feet. Melissa, of course. She was walking across that fire.

It was a typical Friday night, and the place was packed with women. Lisa got a few lingering looks, but ignored them.

"Frankie," she yelled. Frankie was at the other end of the bar talking with a friend. "Hey, Frankie."

The other women sitting at the bar helped her. "Hey, Frankie," they mimicked. One of the women tapped Frankie on the arm and pointed at Lisa. Frankie stepped down to her.

"How was the game?" Frankie yelled.

"It was a tight one, like I expected it'd be. Have you seen any of the players tonight?"

"You mean Amy, right?" Frankie asked with a cocked eyebrow.

"Yeah."

Frankie jabbed her thumb toward a table in the corner where Amy sat with Dee across from her. Dee was busy talking to a blonde. Lisa could see Amy's sneaker-clad foot tapping under the table to the beat of the music.

Before Lisa could ask, Frankie slid a Michelob down to her without a word. She walked to Amy's table, but Amy's attention stayed on the dance floor.

"Hi, Amy," Lisa shouted to compete with the music. She was pleased Amy seemed excited to see her.

"Glad you could make it. I was starting to get worried."

"Like I told you earlier, if I say I'll be somewhere, I'll be there." Lisa motioned to the dance floor. "Do you dance?"

"I'm not very good, but I'll get out there."

The next song was an upbeat Cher song—the 2000 version of Cher. Lisa set her beer down and led Amy to the dance floor.

Lisa watched Amy as they moved to the music. Not very good, my ass. Lisa wasn't a good dancer, and she was the first to admit it. The more she watched Amy dance, the more Lisa got lost in the music. The song ended, and a slow one started.

They stood there awkwardly at first, but eventually Lisa made the move toward Amy. She silently asked the question by holding out her hand. Amy answered by stepping into Lisa's arms. Amy pulled her even closer. Lisa got lost in the music again, this time while pressing up against Amy's muscular body.

The song slowed to a stop. On their way back to their table, Lisa made a quick decision. "Do you want to maybe get out of here and go someplace where it's a little quieter?" she asked.

"Let me tell Dee." After Amy told Dee they were leaving, they walked to Lisa's car.

Lisa studied her shoes for a long moment before meeting Amy's eyes. "Would you like to go to my apartment?"

Amy's answer came fast and simple. "Yes."

* * *

They rode the elevator without speaking. Lisa opened her door and flipped on the light.

"Want another beer?" she asked. Her voice came out in that octave that was higher than her regular one, which happened when she was nervous. Damn.

"No, thanks." Amy sat down on the couch. She smiled and patted the cushion.

Lisa took the gesture as an invitation to sit next to her. She joined Amy, but sat on the edge of the couch, staring straight ahead.

Amy squeezed Lisa's thigh. "Why don't you sit back?"

Lisa sank into the cushions. "I invited you here, and now I'm nervous as hell. Can you tell it's been a while since I've dated?"

Amy squeezed her leg again. "You're not the only one."

Lisa looked into Amy's eyes and held her breath. "But I've wanted to do this," Lisa whispered. She brushed a curl off Amy's forehead. "And I've wanted to do this." She brought her mouth to Amy's. Their lips parted and tongues melded together in a long, sweet kiss. When it ended, Lisa ran her thumb along Amy's jaw. "Now that was a kiss."

Amy ducked her head, but Lisa gently tilted her chin up. "That's definitely a compliment, and it's most definitely nothing to be shy about."

"Sorry. I can't help it sometimes. I…"

Lisa put her finger to Amy's lips. "I understand." They situated themselves sideways on the couch to face each other. Lisa lightly stroked Amy's forearm with her fingertips. "I get the sense that maybe you've had some heartache before." The muscles under Lisa's fingers instantly tensed.

"There was someone back in Lecompton a few years ago." The emotion played across Amy's face while her words came out haltingly. "First of all, you have to understand what it's like being gay in a small town."

"How were your parents about everything?"

"Oh, they were very accepting. My mom had some trouble at

first, but we're really close now, especially since my dad died. But I wasn't out. For one thing, there wasn't that much of a community. There are a couple of gay bars in Lawrence. I met Carly at one of them during a break in the Bandits schedule. She was something else. She was a grad student at the university, studying for her master's in history…" Amy's voice trailed off. Lisa could tell she was reliving the memory.

"She sounds special."

Amy forged ahead as if Lisa hadn't spoken. "It's the only time I've been in love. When the Bandits' season started up again, we kept in touch. She made it to a few games, but she wanted something more. She was out and proud of it, and she didn't understand why I couldn't be." Amy lowered her eyes. "She came to the games, but I barely acknowledged her. And when we were out together, I was always careful about being physical. I never wanted us to be too close or to touch in public."

Silently, Lisa guessed how this story would end.

"Finally, after two years of this, she'd had enough. We argued. It was a terrible fight. We said stuff that shouldn't have been said. And she left. Left me, left Lawrence. She had planned to get her doctorate there at U of K, but our break-up made her pack up and move out of state."

Amy's voice caught. She brushed away a lone tear that rolled down her cheek.

"I tried to explain to her how it was for me at home and especially how it was playing baseball. She knew my dream was to play in the majors. She'd try to tell me I could make a statement for all young lesbians, but I told her I couldn't do it." Amy took a deep breath and let it out slowly as if to release all the memories of the past.

Lisa wanted to ask Amy if she felt she'd made the right choice. Instead, she talked about herself.

"I'm out, but I can understand what you're saying. I especially understand because I'm a reporter. I know how the sports world is. It's that…"

"It's that you understand more where Carly was coming from," Amy said evenly.

"But I haven't exactly been the best at relationships. I've dated off and on all my life. I had only one relationship that lasted a year. I guess the closest and longest-lasting relationship I've had has been with Frankie, the owner of the bar we were at. We've been best friends for five years now." Lisa touched Amy's arm. "It's not like you're talking to Dr. Phil here. I'm not the best person to be offering advice." She hesitated. "But I know I can't... can't..."

"Stay in the closet."

"Right. It's not who I am."

They didn't speak for several seconds.

"How'd we go from kissing to talking about this serious stuff?" Amy asked with a smile.

"I don't know. The reporter in me took over, and I kept asking questions." Lisa scooted closer. "Let's at least end the evening with something more pleasant." She brushed Amy's lips with hers. Amy opened her mouth and their tongues touched briefly for another kiss.

They drew away from each other, and Lisa noticed the time.

"I imagine I need to take you back to the hotel now, huh?"

"Oh, wow, it's almost eleven-thirty. But I'm okay if you can get me there in ten minutes. Coach gave us an extra half hour out tonight because she worked us like dogs this afternoon."

They rose from the couch and moved toward the door.

"You have a big day tomorrow," Lisa said as she held the door for Amy. "Are you nervous?"

"I'm nervous now, but it's kind of weird. Once I hit the field, it all clicks for me, and I focus on the game. Tomorrow might be different, though. I've never played in a game like this."

"You'll do fine." Lisa patted Amy on the back.

On the drive to the hotel, Lisa told Amy about the Indians pitcher who'd be on the hill Saturday night.

"He's got a fastball in the low nineties, but his big pitch is the splitter. Be prepared to hold your swing."

They drove up to the Hyatt, and Amy opened the door. "Thanks."

"You're welcome. I wanted to give you a heads-up on the pitching."

"No, I mean thanks for the evening. I'd like to see you again."

"I'd like to get to know you better, however we can do that. We'll talk again before you leave. I'll definitely see you tomorrow night. Try to get some rest."

"I will."

After Amy shut the door, Lisa waved from behind the closed window. There was no one around when Amy made it to the revolving doors, so it didn't surprise Lisa that Amy returned the gesture. Once Lisa could no longer see her tall figure walking through the lobby, she pulled out of the roundabout.

Chapter 6

Victory Field was filled to near-capacity for the game.

Although Lisa anticipated the extra interest, the size of the crowd still exceeded her expectations. The Bandits were warming up, but the Indians had yet to make their appearance. Lisa showed her press pass to security before entering the gate to the field.

"Nervous?" Lisa asked, approaching Coach Tompkins from behind.

The coach spun around. "Ah, hell no. It sure as shit isn't me they've come to see."

Amy was a few feet away, stretching on the grass and talking to Dee who stood nearby. If Amy was nervous, it didn't show, just like she'd told Lisa the night before.

"Any wise quotes you want to give me before the game?" Lisa deadpanned.

Coach Tompkins laughed. "That's the first time a reporter's been totally honest with me with a question. Not that you weren't honest the other day, but you hear the same crap over and over."

"We can't be serious all the time. It's not in our union contract."

Coach Tompkins rubbed her hand over her face. "I have to admit, I lied. I'm nervous for Amy. She's such an outstanding athlete, but I'm afraid this crowd will cause her to tense up so much, she might fall short of what you and I know she's capable of doing."

"She should be okay, Coach."

"You don't think it's hype, do you?" Lisa heard a hint of apprehension in Coach Tompkins's voice, which told her how protective the coach was of her star first baseman.

"I could be wrong, but I think with the number of scouts here from the Reds, they're serious about this. Do they only want to bring in a bigger draw to Cincinnati? That's another matter. Because of their record, they've had low attendance the past couple of years, and I don't know if next year will be any better. But I believe, if given the chance, Amy will tear through Double-A on her way to the majors."

The coach seemed to relax with Lisa's reassurance. "That makes me feel better. I think she'll make it, but it's nice to hear it from someone else who knows baseball."

"It's time to go over and talk to the all-star," Lisa said. "I'll catch up with you again after the game."

Coach Tompkins barely acknowledged Lisa's last comment before yelling at the second baseman. "Hey, you can make the fucking pivot better than that, goddammit!"

Lisa cringed at the coach's words when she saw the glares from the parents in the first few rows. She wouldn't blame them if they covered their kids' ears in case there was another outburst.

Lisa walked over to Amy who loosened up by swinging a few bats before stepping into the batting cage.

"Ready to wow 'em?"

"I hope so." Amy's face was impassive, and the words were spoken without any warmth.

Okay, I get it. We're in public. Lisa glanced around at the crowd. *No, make that really in public.*

Lisa took on her sportswriter persona. "What are you hoping to do tonight?"

"I don't know. I'd be happy getting a couple of hits, I guess, and have a good defensive game at first." Amy went back to swinging her bats, but kept her distant expression.

"What about the young girls in the crowd? Is there something you hope to pass on to them in the way of inspiration?"

Amy's face softened. Lisa caught a glimpse of the woman she'd seen in private.

"That because you're female doesn't mean that you can't dream a dream that even most men think is impossible for them. And believing in yourself is the most important thing to remember, because there'll be times when you're the only one who does."

Lisa scribbled down the quotes.

"Any fear in facing a male pitcher?"

"You know, I've faced some tough, tough women with wicked fastballs, cutting breaking balls, and every other pitch you can think of, including a spitter. To me, the only difference between a male pitcher and a female pitcher is a question of anatomy. It's the same distance from home plate to the pitcher's mound." In an instant, Amy's cool demeanor returned. "I need to get some hitting in."

Lisa shut her notebook and tried to shake off the impersonal treatment. "Good luck."

Amy strode to the batting cage as flashbulbs went off around the home plate area. Some of the Indians players had straggled into their dugout. They leaned their elbows on the cushioned railing, watching Amy.

The Bandits pitcher fired in some pitches, but they weren't to Amy's liking. Then one came in on the outside part of the plate. She went with it like she had in practice and slapped a drive down the right field line. She hit a few more liners into various parts of the outfield. Then the pitcher threw one of those fat fastballs. In one smooth motion, Amy got every piece of the ball. Highlighted by the stadium lights, it arced in the dark sky and bounced against the left field fence. A few of the Indians players were talking to each other now and shaking their heads.

Yeah, boys, she's the real deal.

Lisa carefully stepped behind the batting cage and approached the Indians dugout to interview the manager standing on the top step.

"How ya doin', Lisa?" Max Murphy had won two Triple-A International League championships in the three years he'd been with the Indians. He was about five-ten with light blond hair, thick forearms and bowlegs, and a round face that lit up when he talked about his players.

"Hi, Max. Pretty good. You?"

Amy had finished her batting practice after hitting a few more to the left-center gap.

"I'm good," Max said, nodding toward Amy. "She's something else."

"Can she make it in Double-A? Maybe even on to the majors?" Lisa asked.

"We'll have a better idea after Jerry pitches against her. It'll be a good test for her to see if she can handle his forkball."

Amy trotted to first to start taking throws.

"It's a shame that someone with talent like that had to wait until they were her age to have this chance, just because she's a woman," Max said. He watched Amy as he said this, but turned back to Lisa to meet her gaze. "What? Because I'm a man, I wouldn't feel that way?"

"No, but it's good to hear you say that, Murph."

"If she's as good as what I've heard, she should fucking get a shot." Max didn't say "fuck" that much. That one word revealed the depth of his passion about the subject. "But if she's given the chance, she's got a hard road ahead of her. Men aren't the best at believing a woman can do a job, let alone a woman taking one of their places in the majors."

"You won't get any argument from me."

The Bandits finished, and the Indians took the field. Lisa interviewed a couple of the players to get their reactions. Most of their answers amounted to, "We'll see."

Lisa made it up to the press box and plugged in her laptop before the first pitch. After the first two Bandits grounded out, Amy stepped to the plate to a thunderous ovation. Lisa glanced at the TV monitor in the press box. Amy settled into the batter's box, but then asked for time from the umpire. She took some deep breaths.

She took the first pitch, a fastball, on the outside corner for a strike. The next pitch was high for a ball. Then Jerry's first forkball dipped across the plate. It appeared that Amy held back, but after the catcher appealed, the first base umpire ruled she had swung through it. The catcher shifted to the outside part of the plate for the next pitch. Amy stood there and took another fastball for the third strike. The crowd moaned, but then applauded when she walked back to the dugout.

In the bottom half of the first, the Bandits pitcher fooled a couple of the Indians batters with her sharp curve. Heading into the top of the fourth, both pitchers were hurling shutouts. The Indians had a couple of singles, but the Bandits had yet to get a hit.

Again, Amy was up third. Again, she walked to the plate to thunderous applause.

The first pitch was another wicked forkball. Amy swung through it. Lisa lowered her head. *Come on, Amy, I know you can hold back.*

Jerry tried another one. This time, Amy checked her swing and came out of the batter's box. She adjusted her batting gloves and stepped back in.

Jerry tried to sneak a fastball on the outside part of the plate one time too many. Amy lined it just past the diving first baseman's outstretched glove. Flashbulbs went off everywhere. The right fielder hustled over and got the ball to second, but not before Amy made it there with a headfirst slide.

The crowd erupted. Jerry picked up the rosin bag and tossed it down after catching the ball thrown to him. Lisa watched his reaction closely on the television monitor. He faced Amy on second base and gave her a slight nod.

The next innings went by quickly with the Indians picking up a couple of runs in the sixth. In the top of the seventh, Amy came to the plate with two on. A new pitcher, Bob Jenkins, had taken the mound. He was a notorious junk-ball reliever. It was again a test to see how Amy would react to breaking pitches.

The first pitch painted the inside of the plate for a strike. The next one was in the dirt, but she held her swing. Then Jenkins threw her his curve ball. It was a beautiful pitch. Lisa had seen Jenkins get so many out on it, with the batter frozen in the box, knees buckling, taking the pitch for a called third strike.

Before it dipped down, Amy brought her bat through the strike zone and slammed the ball into deep left field. The crowd cheered even louder as the ball cut through the air. The left fielder tried to catch up with it, but it bounced once and hit the wall.

Amy was on second again, this time with a stand-up double.

Lisa noticed that the Reds scouts in the box seats were talking animatedly. Amy bent over with her hands on her knees and then tilted her head up to the night sky, as if to say "thank you." She glanced up at the press box. It was quick, but Lisa caught it.

The game ended with the Indians on top 4-2. But the real story was Amy, surrounded by photographers and reporters on the field. Amy pushed her way down into the dugout, following the rest of the Bandits into the clubhouse.

Lisa didn't step onto the field but left for the makeshift pressroom where a table had been set up with microphones. Lisa recognized a couple of reporters from ESPN, along with CBS and Fox Sports, but a lot of the others were unfamiliar. She took her seat near the front.

Shortly, the Reds management entered. One was the GM, Dan Taylor. The other was one of their lead scouts, Abe Sanders. Lisa liked Abe, who, in his twentieth year of scouting, was one of the best in the game. He saw her and winked. The wink didn't bother her. She'd known him long enough to know that it meant nothing. The entire pressroom had filled, and those who were fortunate enough to grab a seat sat down. The rest stood against the wall in the back.

ESPN asked the first question.

"What about it, Dan? Will you take a chance?"

Taylor raised his hands as if to offer the question back to the reporter. "What do you think, Patrick? What about all of you? Are we really taking a chance here?" The room broke out in laughter. "I don't think so. And yes, she's getting a shot."

With those words, a chill rushed through Lisa.

"She'll go down to Arizona for a week of workouts with the other players in preparation for the Fall League that starts October seventh. Most of you know that each club can opt to send one player we consider Single-A. That would be Amy this year. She'll be one of our seven prospects with the Mesa Solar Sox. We'll carefully monitor her progress in the six-week season and then go from there."

A reporter for the *Cincinnati Enquirer* yelled out, "This isn't a publicity stunt?"

"Hell no, George. Did you see her hit? Did you see her play defense? She's legitimate. She just happens to be a woman."

At that moment, Amy entered the room. She was still in her dirt-stained uniform. She appeared to be extremely nervous.

"Amy, would you mind taking some questions?" Taylor asked her.

"No, sir." She took her seat next to the general manager.

"Amy, Dan Taylor here told us you're getting a shot with the Mesa Solar Sox this fall. How do you feel about that?"

Her face reddened under her dark tan. She briefly turned to the GM. "Thank you, Mr. Taylor." She addressed the reporter. "I'm honored. I hope I can do well for them."

Lisa got a question in. "You won't have a break between your season with the Bandits, which started in April, and your season with the Solar Sox, which lasts six weeks. A lot of games are jammed into that time period. How will you handle the extra work?"

Amy's distant expression instantly reappeared.

Damn, how in the hell does she do that? Just turn it on and off in an instant.

"I've handled pressure all my life. I guess I'll try to take this in stride." She pointed to another reporter for the next question.

Lisa felt like she had been slapped in the face. It wasn't that Amy treated her like the other reporters. It was the cold look and the tone to Amy's voice. Lisa swallowed. *Am I going to be able to do this?*

Lisa sat there quietly while Amy handled some more questions. After about fifteen minutes, Taylor interrupted. "Amy's had enough now. Thank you all for your time."

Lisa stood. Amy got up from the table, glancing Lisa's way again. Lisa stared at her before turning to talk to some of the other reporters. Maybe she was being too sensitive about the whole thing, but it hurt.

Lisa said her goodbyes to the others and walked out to her car. She needed to get her article in before deadline. She'd written most of it in the press box, but she wanted to polish it off with some of the press conference quotes. While unlocking the door, she heard someone behind her.

"Lisa." Amy, a little out of breath, was approaching the car. "Do you want to get together again before I leave for Mesa? I found out I'm supposed to fly out on Monday morning. That means we have tomorrow to maybe have dinner."

Lisa leaned her back against the driver's door. "Now we're friends again, huh?" She hated being angry about this, but she was.

"I'm sorry about all of that. It's that..." Amy stopped and stared at her cleats.

"It's that you don't even want there to be a chance that someone thinks you're gay. You're treating me like you treated Carly, right?"

Amy's head snapped up. "I thought we'd already been over this. I'm not like you, and I can't help it."

Lisa didn't respond.

"I want to get to know you. Can we at least try that?" Amy asked.

"I have to finish my article." Lisa started to get into her car. Amy gently grabbed Lisa's arm.

"Hey," Amy said.

Damn it, quit saying that word like that.

"I want to see you again before I leave. Can we at least have lunch or dinner tomorrow and talk about it? Don't you think something's happening between us, Lisa?"

"Yeah," Lisa said quietly. "Yeah, I do, especially after last night." She stared at her keys as though they had all the answers to the mixture of emotions pulsing through her. She turned to Amy. "I'll pick you up tomorrow about six. Is that good for you? We'll have dinner at The Ruby Slippers. You'll like it. It's an old haunt of mine." She climbed into the car.

"Please don't be mad. We can figure out all this other stuff later."

"I'll see you tomorrow." Lisa pulled away. In the rearview

mirror, she saw Amy walk back to the clubhouse.

Lisa drove on. She didn't realize how much she was clenching her teeth until she felt the strain in her jaw.

Chapter 7

After finishing her article, Lisa drove to the Watering Hole to have a beer. The pounding bass of another Melissa song greeted her when she entered the bar. She took a seat.

"Hey, you," Frankie said loudly. "Amy looked good out there tonight. I had the game on and caught some innings."

"I guess she did well." Lisa said it without much enthusiasm.

"What's wrong? She's getting a chance."

"That part's great. It's the other that's iffy."

"Stacy, I need you to take over for a minute." Frankie came out from behind the bar and pointed at an open table in the corner.

"So, what's the problem?" Frankie asked after they sat down.

Lisa thought about it before answering. "I've never been with anyone this closeted. You know how I am. I don't know if I can do this. It's not like I want to run up and down Meridian Street waving a huge rainbow flag. But I don't want to be careful what I say or how I look at a gay woman because she's worried about being outed. I'm trying to understand Amy's point of view, but what'll I do when she has to ignore me or pretend I'm just another reporter like she did tonight? That's what she'll have to do, by the way, especially now, while she's trying to make it."

"You're already feeling all of this?"

"Yeah, and I only see it getting worse the more publicity she receives, which she will be getting." One of the servers passed by. "Hey, Val, I'll take a Long Island when you have a chance." A beer didn't seem strong enough.

"Now, Ms. Collins, nobody's worth getting drunk over," Frankie said.

"You're right, but I want to take the edge off these emotions." Val brought the drink. Lisa took a five out of her wallet and held it up for Val.

"You know better than that," Frankie said. "It's on me, Val."

Lisa grabbed her glass and swallowed a big gulp. It only took a few seconds for the alcohol to burn into her stomach. Damn. Stacy sure knew how to make potent Long Islands.

"Have you already fallen for her?" Frankie searched Lisa's face.

"I don't... I mean, we..." Lisa stopped. "I don't know how to describe it." Lisa thought for a moment. "It's kind of like how when I'm with you."

"Except with Amy you'll be uncomfortable to be yourself in public where others can see the two of you together, right?"

Lisa sighed, but didn't answer. She noticed the look on Frankie's face.

"Don't get on me for seeing a closeted woman, Frankie. Sometimes we can't help who our heart goes after. She captured me with her eyes. She has these beautiful eyes that change color in different light." Lisa shook her head. "Oh, the hell with it. I'll shut up now."

"Maybe we need to put Amy in the heartbreaker category."

"Sometimes I can't help it," Lisa snapped. "Sometimes my heart leads me, and I have to follow it. Maybe that sounds stupid, and maybe it is. It's pissing me off because I don't know what to do about it."

The heat rose in her cheeks, and she took a deep breath. Frankie gave Lisa a steady gaze. Lisa put her hand on top of Frankie's.

"I'm sorry. I shouldn't take it out on you, and I am. What's that they say about taking things out on the person we trust the most?"

"Oh, that's what they call it? I'd call it taking a big bite out of my ass."

Lisa couldn't help but laugh. "Now that you mention it, I guess you could call it that, too."

"You know I'm always here for you, right?" Frankie asked gently.

"I know. Thanks."

Frankie stood up. "I need to get back to work. You"—she pointed her finger at Lisa—"are going home right now. No more drinking."

"Yes, Mother."

Lisa got up, impulsively gave Frankie a hug, and slapped her on the back before leaving.

* * *

Lisa dressed up for her date with Amy. She picked out a pair of black dress slacks and a dark gray pullover V-neck sweater. She ran her fingers through her gelled hair one last time.

When she arrived at the Hyatt, Amy was there, but wasn't alone. Five little girls with paper and pens surrounded her. She seemed to be enjoying the attention.

As Amy walked toward Lisa's car, the girls screamed, "Thank you, Amy!" She waved at them and climbed in the passenger side.

"Well, well, well, Ms. Perry, I see you've already gotten some fans."

"Thanks to you and ESPN."

"You look nice," Lisa said, pulling out into traffic. Amy was wearing a long-sleeved blue denim shirt tucked into a pair of khakis.

"Thanks. I figured this was more of a date. You do, too, by the way."

"Thanks."

"Where's this place we're headed to?" Amy asked.

"It's a few streets over." They drove for a few moments and then turned into the parking lot at The Ruby Slippers.

"Heya, Lisa," one of the servers shouted at them when they entered. "You eating tonight or just shooting some pool?"

"We're having dinner, Tom."

"Take a seat wherever."

The dining area was empty. The patrons who were there sat at the bar.

The Wizard of Oz theme was readily apparent. Collectibles were scattered throughout, including a pair of ruby slippers behind the bar. A neon rainbow adorned the window.

"Kind of a cool place, huh?" Lisa asked. They sat down at a booth.

"It is."

Here we go. "I want to talk to you about being closeted."

Amy sat back in the booth and folded her arms across her chest. Her chin jutted out defiantly.

She thinks I'm about to lecture her on needing to be out. "I've been thinking about it. I'm a sportswriter. I know how this works. I've covered some gay professional athletes over the years. It's been a constant struggle for them. They love the sport they excel in, but at the same time, they're torn."

Amy uncrossed her arms.

"They hate the fact that they may be betraying their gay family. But they also know the ridicule they'd face if they were to come out while they still played ball. It's not fair. And I especially know that, being a woman, it'll be rough for you. You'll have a tough enough time as it is." Lisa took Amy's hands in hers. "I want you to know that I do understand, but because I'm so out, I can't help but wonder how this might go."

They were interrupted by Tom. "What'll you be having to drink?"

"I'll have a Mich. What do you want, Amy?"

"Foster's with a glass, please."

After Tom left, Amy said, "I know all of this seems like what happened to me and Carly. But I'm scared of…"

"It's okay. Let's try to take it one step at a time."

Amy seemed relieved.

Tom came back to their table with their beers. "Have you decided what you'd like?"

"We haven't even opened our menus," Lisa said.

"Do you need me to give you some more time?"

"I'll have a burger with Swiss and fries," Amy said.

"Me, too."

He took their menus.

Lisa changed the subject. "Let's talk about you and your baseball. You're flying to Arizona tomorrow? Are you going to be all right?"

Amy drew in a breath. "I leave first flight out tomorrow to make it for afternoon workouts, and I don't know. It'll be lonely."

Lisa made a quick decision. "I'd like to keep covering your story for the website. Maybe I can try to come to Arizona while you're there."

Amy's mood instantly lightened. "Oh, that'd be fantastic."

They chatted until their food arrived. After they finished dinner, they shot some pool before Lisa drove Amy back to the Hyatt. A lot of people milled around out front, which Lisa knew meant a casual drop-off.

Before she got out of the car, Amy said, "I think this might work between us, Lisa."

"I know I'm attracted to you, Amy, and would like to see where this goes."

Amy smiled. "Good."

"Oh, hold on." Lisa reached above her visor and pulled out a

Minor League.com card with her cell number. "Give me a call when you get there."

"I will." Amy took the card and patted Lisa on the leg. Lisa grabbed her hand and held it there. Amy tensed up.

"Take care, Amy, and have a good flight."

Amy got out of the car and made her way quickly through the group of people in front of the hotel.

I'm in way over my head here. Lisa drove to her refuge—Frankie's.

Chapter 8

Lisa smacked the softball in front of the onrushing left fielder and hustled down to first, taking a wide turn. She trotted back to the bag. Frankie, the first base coach, patted Lisa on the butt.

"Good hit." It was the Wednesday after Amy had left for Arizona. Frankie had asked Lisa to fill in for the second baseman on her team. It was one of the rare occasions Frankie took time away from the bar.

Lisa put her hands on her knees, waiting for the pitcher to start her motion toward the plate. The next batter pulled the ball down the right field line in front of the first base bag. Lisa hopped over the ball and hustled around to third. She took another wide turn and returned to the bag.

Lisa tagged up and scored on a deep fly ball. She stepped on home plate and picked up the bat. The game ended with Frankie's team on top, 10-1.

"How about dinner at Sam's?" Frankie asked while helping Lisa gather the bats.

"You read my mind. I'm freaking starving." They drove to a nearby pub that, in their opinion, had the best burgers in town.

They settled in the booth. Lisa hesitated starting the conversation, but knew it would be better to tell Frankie about her plans. "There's a good chance I'll be flying down to Phoenix to cover Amy's story for Minor League.com."

Frankie set her menu aside, and her dark brown eyes met Lisa's. "You will?"

"I need to talk it over with my editors, but I'm pretty sure they'll go for it."

The server, a young woman with a pierced nose and a bored expression, showed up at the table with their water. "Do you know what you want?" she asked in a monotone, popping her gum.

"I really don't know why I even get a menu," Lisa said, handing it back to her. "I'll have a Sam's burger, medium well, with everything, and loaded fries."

"To drink?" Pierced Nose popped her gum again.

"A Coke."

The server waited for Frankie.

"Hmm… what to order…" Frankie tapped her finger on her chin. Lisa had witnessed this playful side of her friend many times and struggled to hold in her laughter.

The server sighed.

"Guess I'll have the same." Frankie handed the menu back to Pierced Nose.

She practically snatched the menu from Frankie and huffed away.

Lisa chuckled. "You're too much."

"I'm telling you, once you hit fifty, you don't put up with shit anymore. Now, what were you saying about Arizona?"

"I'm hoping to fly down there this week and stay for the season, but I need my editors' approval."

"How long's their season again?"

"Six weeks."

Frankie played with the napkin under her glass of water. They were interrupted when the server brought their drinks. She practically slammed Frankie's glass down on the table in front of her.

"Thank you so much." Frankie glowered at her.

The young woman did a quick about-face and stomped off.

"Remind me not to leave a big tip." Frankie took a drink of her Coke. "Six weeks. That'd cover the second weekend of October, wouldn't it?"

"I guess so." Then it hit Lisa. "Oh, Frankie, I didn't even think of it. I won't be here for the race." Every year, she walked with Frankie in the Susan G. Komen Race for a Cure.

A flicker of hurt passed over Frankie's face.

"I'll see if I can make it back that weekend," Lisa said.

"No, that'd cost too much, and you wouldn't be doing your job."

Lisa heard the disappointment in Frankie's voice. "But I can try."

Frankie reached over and squeezed Lisa's hand. "Don't worry about it."

The server brought their food.

"God, I love the hamburgers here," Frankie said. She poured

ketchup and mustard on top of all her fixings and took a big bite out of her burger.

Lisa pushed her food around on her plate.

"Don't tell me you're not hungry now," Frankie said between bites.

"No. I'm still starving." Lisa picked up the ketchup and doused her burger.

After they finished, as Lisa drove Frankie home, she turned to Frankie a few times to find her staring out the window. She pulled into Frankie's drive.

"If I leave for Phoenix in the morning, do you think you can take me to the airport?"

"Sure. Give me a call after you talk to your editors."

Frankie stepped out of the car. Lisa leaned over into the passenger seat to maintain eye contact.

"I really appreciate it, Frankie, and I enjoyed tonight."

"I did, too. I'll talk to you later."

* * *

Lisa entered her apartment at eight-thirty, but knew she might be able to catch her editors in the office. She dialed the number.

"Sean, I'm glad I caught you."

"Lisa, how's it going? Sorry if you tried to get me earlier. We had a mini-crisis with our correspondent in Des Moines. He quit without even giving a two-week notice."

Lisa nodded, as if Sean could see through the phone line.

"What can I do for you?" Sean asked.

"I have a proposition for you. You know Amy Perry, right?"

"Pretty much everyone in the sports world knows about her now. That was a helluva jump on the story, by the way. We won't forget it either. You'll see a nice increase in your check next month."

Wow. That was unexpected, but she hoped to cash in on this in more ways than one.

"I want to cover her story, but I want to do it full time or as full time as I can. I'd like to be down in Arizona for the entire season."

"Remind me. How long does that last?"

"Six weeks."

"Hmm." There was a pause. "Yeah, we can do that. This is a big story, and she deserves the coverage. We can give you a special column for the website."

Lisa took a deep breath before continuing. "I don't want to stop there. I'd like to follow her through the whole process. I know that might be asking—"

"Wait. You're talking into spring training and then next summer wherever the Reds send her?"

"Yeah." It was again quiet on the other end of the line.

"What about your job there with the Indians?" He took on the clipped-New-York-style of speech, standard for when he talked business.

"I know someone at the paper where I freelance who might be interested in taking over for the summer." She was stretching the truth. Fred Garrett, who also freelanced covering high school sports, had mentioned he'd love to do her job for one summer. But she hadn't approached him about it. If Sean approved, she'd need to get in contact with Fred soon to make sure he could do the job.

Again, there was a beat-and-a-half of silence on the other end.

"Shit, let's do it, Lisa."

Lisa breathed a sigh of relief.

"This is big, which I'm sure you know. You're our best reporter, and I'm talking for all of Minor League.com."

Lisa's felt her face flush with the compliment.

"And don't disagree with me on that, Collins. You know you're good."

"Thanks, Sean." She was glad she didn't have to argue with him about covering the story. She needed to contact Jack at the *Gazette* to inform him she'd be out of commission for the next six weeks and in the early spring.

"Their season starts when?" Sean asked.

"Monday. Their workouts end this week."

"That means you need to get down there ASAP. Get online and get a flight. Give me the information, and I'll get purchasing to get the ticket. Your regular pay will be in place. Guess you'll start earning that increase a lot sooner than we thought."

"I'll do a good job for you."

"Oh, I know that. Do you think we'd let anyone else cover this story?"

She didn't answer. It was a hell of a compliment.

"You're right. We wouldn't," Sean said in answer to her silence.

"Thanks. I'll get online and call back with the flight

information."

"Good call on this one. Can't wait to see your articles."

"I'll keep 'em coming."

Lisa connected to the Internet. There were plenty of flights for the next morning. She punched in her travel dates and thought about Amy. She probably had anticipated Lisa only being in Mesa for the first week of games. Now, Lisa could let her know she'd be following her story through the minors, too.

Lisa was picturing Amy's reaction, but thoughts of Frankie interrupted. She really hated to miss the Komen Race. Suddenly, a sharp pang shot through her chest. What the hell? She picked a departure and arrival date and time, still rubbing the spot, trying to ease the ache.

It wasn't working.

She called Frankie to tell her when to pick her up in the morning, but decided not to tell her that, in the not-too-distant future, she'd be gone a lot longer than six weeks. She also gave Jack a call at the paper. She'd predicted his reaction accurately. He wasn't happy with what she told him, but was appeased that she'd pick up writing for the paper upon her return in the middle of November.

She also set up hotel arrangements in Phoenix. She'd traveled there a few times and knew the area. She chose one with suites located near the park where Amy would be playing.

The next morning, Lisa packed. She didn't realize the time until she shot a quick glance at her bedside clock. Shit. It was almost time to meet Frankie in front of the apartment building.

When she'd spoken to Amy the night before, Amy had told her it was unseasonably warm there for the first week of October. Lisa dressed in a pair of lightweight khakis and a button-down short-sleeved cotton shirt for the flight.

She slung her carry-on bag and laptop on one shoulder and pulled the suitcase behind her toward the door. She double-checked she hadn't done something stupid like forgetting to turn off the stove. "Like I ever cook," she muttered while struggling with her luggage.

On the way to meet Frankie, she mulled how to break the news. Telling her she'd be out of town for six weeks was one thing. Telling Frankie she'd be gone all of next summer was another.

Frankie was waiting in her big Dodge Ram in front of the apartment building. Lisa wheeled her luggage through the lobby while balancing her laptop case and carry-on bag on her shoulder. Frankie helped Lisa put the luggage behind the driver's seat.

"Thanks again for taking me to the airport," Lisa said, climbing up into the cab of the truck. "This saves me a lot of money."

"I'm glad I could help." Frankie drove a few blocks and took the turn to merge onto the interstate.

Lisa studied her friend's face.

Frankie kept her eyes on the road, but must have felt Lisa's stare. "Something wrong?"

Lisa hesitated.

"Lisa?"

"This trip to Arizona..."

"Yeah?"

"I'll be covering Amy all next summer," Lisa blurted out. She waited for Frankie's reaction. Over the years that she'd known her, Lisa had always been able to read Frankie by the expression on her face, but not this time. Frankie's face was blank, and she didn't look at Lisa.

"Writing for the website?"

"Yes."

"Did they ask you?"

"No. I brought it up with them."

Frankie turned to her briefly, but Lisa still was unable to read her.

"So, you'll be out of town all of next summer." Frankie wasn't asking a question. She said it slowly, as if to will the words to sink into her brain.

"Yeah," Lisa said quietly. She tried to lighten the mood. "I'll be back a couple of times, depending on what team Amy's assigned to and where we travel. Maybe there'll be a field close to Indiana where they'll be playing, and I can make a trip into town." If Amy played at the Double-A level in the Southern League, this would be impossible, but she wanted to say something positive.

"You'll be missed around here, especially by everybody at the bar."

"I'll miss you, too." Lisa didn't feel inclined to include the others in her statement.

They pulled up to passenger drop-off. Lisa jumped out of the truck and hefted her luggage out of the back.

"Thanks for bringing me. I'll call you when I get there. I know you worry sometimes."

"You're right. I do worry about you." Frankie stared straight ahead. "Take care. If I don't answer my cell, leave a message."

"Sure," Lisa murmured. Frankie put the truck in gear. Lisa shut the door, and Frankie merged into traffic. Lisa didn't realize it until the truck was out of sight that she had tears in her eyes. She quickly blinked them away before entering the terminal.

She checked her luggage at the counter and picked up her boarding pass, then found her departure gate. She set her laptop case and carry-on bag down beside her, plopped into a vinyl seat, and laid her head back on the cushion. The same ache she had felt the previous night returned to her chest. She'd miss Frankie. But she hadn't anticipated this sudden sense of loss.

Chapter 9

The hum of the jet engines lulled Lisa to sleep for the four-hour flight. It seemed like only five minutes had passed when the flight attendant's voice cut into Lisa's subconscious and dragged her back into reality.

"Ladies and gentlemen, we're beginning our descent into Phoenix. Please return your tray tables and seats to the upright and locked position."

Waves of heat radiated off the tarmac. It felt like they were descending into hell. They rolled to the gate, and the flight attendant cheerfully chirped, "The downtown temperature is now ninety-five degrees."

Holy crap, Amy was right.

Lisa tugged her laptop out from under the seat in front of her and stood to get her carry-on from the overhead compartment. She followed the other passengers off the plane.

At the luggage carousel, she unsnapped her cell phone from her belt. She first called Frankie. When it clicked over to voice mail, she left a message that she'd arrived safely and that she'd call often.

Lisa checked her watch. Because of the time difference, it was only eight-thirty in the morning in Phoenix. Maybe Amy could take a call before she hit the field for practice. Lisa found Amy's number on her cell phone contact list and punched the button. After a couple of rings, she heard Amy's soft Kansas accent.

"Hello."

"Hey, Amy. It's Lisa."

"Please tell me you're on your way down here," Amy said plaintively.

"I can do better than that. I'm standing at the luggage carousel in Phoenix making myself dizzy waiting for my bag."

"Oh, this is perfect timing. We haven't left for the park yet, but we'll be starting practice at ten. Can you make it?"

"I should be able to swing that. I need to get my rental car and check into the hotel. Then I'll be at HoHoKam." Lisa would wait until she saw Amy in person to tell her how long she'd be there.

"Then I'll see you soon?"

"I'll be there."

"You'll never know how much this means to me."

"It's good to be here," Lisa said softly. She flipped the phone shut and picked up her bag that had landed with a thud onto the metal carousel. She followed the signs to the rental car area.

Lisa checked her directions to the hotel at a stoplight before she merged onto the interstate. Phoenix traffic was crazy.

She found her hotel, checked into her room, and changed into shorts and a T-shirt before leaving for the ballpark.

* * *

Lisa drove into the lot at HoHoKam Park at ten-thirty. She walked across the searing asphalt, feeling the heat steam up through the soles of her sneakers. No one stopped her when she went through the gate. Fall League games weren't exactly big draws, so security was light.

The players were going through their stretches. She had no trouble spotting Amy. Lisa took a seat in the stands, put her feet up on the chair in front of her, and raised her face to the sun. She welcomed the warmth after enduring the damp cold of Indianapolis.

The team finished their stretches and moved into the outfield grass for their wind sprints. Amy worked out by herself, but the guys on the team paired off in twos or threes, talking and joking together. Lisa frowned. She hoped this wasn't the start of trouble for Amy. Lisa headed down the steps to talk to the manager and the coaching staff who had made it out onto the field. They were huddled in front of one the dugouts watching Amy.

Lisa opened the gate and approached them.

"Hi. My name's Lisa Collins. I'm a reporter from Minor League.com. I'm here covering Amy Perry."

The man she assumed was the manager stared at her. He was tall and lanky. Lisa thought he resembled a poor-man's Sam Elliott. Nicotine from the tobacco wad jammed into his left cheek stained his graying mustache. He spat off to the side before speaking.

"Gee, that's a shock." The other coaches snickered.

Lisa shook off the comment. He probably hadn't had the chance yet to see Amy play, except for maybe batting practice. She didn't remember seeing him with the Reds contingent at Victory Field.

"I'm pretty sure they're all here for the same reason," he said in a distinct southern drawl. He gestured to a group of cameramen and reporters from ESPN, Fox Sports, and other media outlets.

"Could I interview you, Coach..." Lisa let her voice trail off while waiting for him to tell her his name. Normally, she'd have all the information she needed before writing an article. But with the Fall League, the managers changed every year.

He stuck out his hand and gripped hers tightly. "It's Curt Reed from the Reds." He introduced the other coaches who were from other teams.

Lisa had to give the Reds management credit. They were handling this right. No chance a manager from another major league team might hold Amy back.

She and Curt went over to the dugout and sat down. They talked for a few minutes about the team and the top prospects from around the minors who were trying to impress their way into the majors. She asked him if he had a chance to see Amy play yet or maybe had attended one of the Bandits games, already knowing the answer.

"Nope."

"Do you have any thoughts about a woman playing professional men's baseball?"

"Nope." He spat out another stream of tobacco, barely missing Lisa's right shoe.

She stood and thanked him for his time.

"Since I'll be here for the entire six-week season, we'll be seeing a lot of each other."

Curt Reed merely nodded and rejoined his coaches.

Lisa walked over to stand with the other reporters and said hello to a few of them. Sarah Swift, her friend who was a reporter for *National Baseball Weekly,* ended her conversation with someone from Fox Sports.

"Hey, Sarah, how's it going?"

Sarah was short and stocky with short dark hair that was graying at the temples. Lisa suspected Sarah might be gay, but she was difficult to peg. She was divorced and hadn't remarried, which of course meant nothing.

"Hey, Lisa. Fancy seeing you here." Sarah nodded in Reed's direction. "You had the pleasure of talking to Mr. Warmth, huh?"

"I can't blame him. I'm sure the Reds have told him about her skills, but from his point of view, he probably thinks Amy's taking the place of some other player who's more deserving."

"Which is a polite way of saying he's an ass," Sarah said under her breath.

Lisa laughed. Amy must have noticed her. After she finished one of her wind sprints, she lifted her chin in Lisa's general direction. The silent lesbian salute.

Lisa returned the gesture, but Amy turned her back on her and started another sprint. Lisa sighed.

The players' workout lasted a couple of hours. The sun was now reaching its zenith, and the temperature had to be over 100 degrees. The players ambled off the field. Lisa was disappointed to see that Amy was still alone.

"Amy! Amy! Over here!" the reporters and cameramen shouted. They descended on her. Lisa joined them.

"How does it feel knowing you'll be debuting next week with the Solar Sox?"

"I'm anxious to face some live pitching," Amy answered. "We've been working out this week and have had batting practice and stuff, but it's not the same."

Lisa listened while Amy fielded the other questions, but had none of her own. After they finished with her, Amy gave Lisa a quick glance before she jogged off to the clubhouse.

She might not see Amy until later in the evening. Because she didn't want to call attention to herself by waiting for her to emerge from the clubhouse, Lisa started for her car.

"Hey, you."

Sarah approached her from the field. "Want to get a beer?" she asked.

Lisa felt the sweat trickling down the small of her back. "Sure, but let me take a shower and get changed before we go."

"Where are you staying?"

"The Comfort Inn Suites about a mile from here."

"I know where that's at. I'm at the Holiday Inn, not too far from you. I could use a shower, too. How about I swing by and pick you up around one-thirty?"

"One-thirty's good."

They split up and walked to their rentals. Lisa got into the car and flipped the air conditioning on high. "A lot of good this'll do," she said when the hot desert air blasted her in the face. Her cell phone chirped as she started out of the parking lot. "Amy Perry" popped up on the display.

"Hey, Amy. You've already showered?"

"No. I have to wait for the guys to finish. Do you want to get together later? Like for dinner or something?"

"Let's do dinner. I can pick you up at the—"

Amy cut her off. "No. How about I meet you at this convenience store by my apartment?"

Lisa tried to take it in stride. "Not a problem. Where's your apartment?"

"It's a few blocks down from the park." Amy named the complex.

"I've seen it. Which store?"

"It's the one connected to the Shell station there on the corner."

"Okay. What's a good time for you?"

"Seven?"

"Perfect."

There was silence on the other end and then Amy said, "Thanks for understanding."

"It's all right. I'll see you at seven."

On the drive to her hotel, Lisa thought about how open she and Frankie were in their lives and mentally contrasted it to Amy and her struggle. There was a big difference between being an out sportswriter or a lesbian bar owner and Amy's situation of playing on an all-male baseball team. The scrutiny she was under was overwhelming. Hell, Lisa was part of the pack of wolves covering the story. But knowing all this wasn't making her feel any better.

In fact, she got a headache from thinking about it.

Chapter 10

Lisa heard the toot of the car horn before she saw the car. Sarah's red Chrysler Sebring zipped into the roundabout at the hotel. Sarah's mouth quivered with amusement as Lisa got into the car and buckled her seatbelt.

"I know what you want to say, Collins. Go right ahead and lay it on me."

"Must be nice renting a car like this, Swift."

Sarah's raucous laughter filled the car, and she smacked Lisa on the thigh. "Thank you for not disappointing me." She punched the car into gear and merged into traffic.

"Glad I could be of service," Lisa said while Mesa flashed by outside her window. "Where are we going? Tucson?"

"Very funny. No, it's a bar about ten miles from here, Ms. Impatient. What? Do you have a hot date you need to get back to?"

Lisa's face flushed.

Sarah glanced at her. "Oh, my God. I was only joking! Okay, spill. Who is she?"

"It's not like that."

"Sure it isn't."

Lisa didn't respond.

"Hey, I didn't mean anything by it. I know it's none of my business."

"It's okay."

Sarah changed the subject, and they talked about work the rest of the way to the bar. They arrived at a place called Jerry's Benchwarmers. The pub wasn't crowded, probably because it was a Thursday afternoon. The server seated them at a booth by a window. She handed them menus and gave the obligatory rundown of the specials before breezing away.

"Like we'll remember all that shit," Sarah said after the server was out of earshot.

They ordered an appetizer. Beer sounded much better than

food. The server brought their potato skins, along with their iced cold bottles of beer with frosted mugs.

Lisa was pouring her beer into her mug when Sarah's next words almost made her drop the bottle.

"I know I said I'd leave it alone, but let's get back to this chick you're dating." Sarah brought a sour-cream-covered potato skin up to her mouth and took an exaggerated bite.

"Okay, Barbara Walters."

"Hey, at least I'm not asking you, 'If you were a tree, what kind of tree would you be?'" Sarah did a passable imitation of Barbara Walters's voice.

"Lucky me." Lisa took a sip of her beer before answering. "Yes, I'm dating. It's in the beginning stages, and no, I'd rather not talk about it."

"What? Don't want to jinx it?"

"Something like that." Lisa grabbed a potato skin and spread some sour cream on it.

"In answer to the question you've never asked me, yes, I'm gay," Sarah said, meeting Lisa's gaze.

"Dating anyone?"

"Oh, no-no-no. This conversation isn't about me."

"Ahh, but we could make it about you very easily."

Sarah watched Lisa over her beer mug before speaking again. "What do you think about Ms. Perry?"

Lisa went back to her food. "She's a hell of a ball player, and it doesn't mean jack that she's a woman. She'll have to put up with a bunch of bullsh—"

"No, I'm asking if you think she's family."

Lisa paused in her eating, but then shoved more of the potato skin into her mouth. She picked up her beer and took a big swig. "I don't know. Does it matter?"

"Oh, shit, Collins. You know I don't care. I'm only asking if your gaydar has gone off around her."

Lisa shrugged her shoulders and avoided eye contact.

"Oh, my God. Is it Amy?"

Lisa jerked her head up. "Wh-what?" She felt the heat of her skin, and the full blush worked its way up from her neck to her face.

"Why, you ol' stud, you."

"Shut up. It's not like that."

"Really? How is it?"

"I don't want to talk about this."

"Come on. You should know I won't report on it. It's nobody's goddamn business. I can tell she's a private person, too. She'll have a tough enough time, you know, with this, with the good old boys like Curt Reed. It's going to be hell."

"She's such a nice person, too. Have you had a chance to interview her?"

Sarah held up the last potato skin. "Want this?"

"Nah. You can have it."

"No, I haven't interviewed her yet. I'd like to do that before their first game on Monday. I want to do a nice feature on her for *National Baseball Weekly.*" Sarah bit down on the potato skin. She lifted her napkin out of her lap and wiped the sour cream from the edges of her mouth. "Again, I sure as hell will never ask her anything like who she's sleeping with. I haven't asked that of any of the players I've interviewed, and that includes the superstars. I never will."

"That's because you're a good reporter with ethics."

The waitress interrupted them. "Another for both of you?"

"What about it? One more?" Sarah asked Lisa.

"Just one. I need to get back soon."

"Guess it'll be two then," Sarah said to the waitress. After she left, Sarah said, "What? You really do have a hot date tonight?"

"You're hopeless, you know."

Sarah ignored her comment. "Back to what you were saying. Unfortunately not everyone's like us, Lisa. There are tons of sports rags out there that belong on the racks beside *The Enquirer* in the checkout lanes. I can understand if she needs to stay so deep in the closet that they'll never find out."

"It sucks."

"You're right. It does. But we know how this works."

The waitress brought their beers to the table.

"Give me the check," Sarah said.

Lisa protested, but Sarah shot down her objections. She poured her beer into her mug and said, "Let's talk about Perry's chances of getting in the Show."

They launched into a spirited discussion about Amy's prospects that lasted until they finished their beer.

Sarah dropped Lisa off at the hotel at four. Lisa started her article for the website. She lost track of time, and before she knew it, it was six-thirty. She changed into a pair of cargo pants and a short-sleeved green cotton shirt and ran some gel through her hair before leaving.

*   *   *

"God, it's good to see you, Lisa. You have no idea," Amy said, getting into the rental car. She was dressed in a pair of baggy jeans and a gray Puma T-shirt.

"Good to see you, too." Lisa drove out of the Shell parking lot.

"Where are we going?"

"It's called the Black Velvet." She caught Amy's reaction out of the corner of her eye. "It's safe. It's a very discreet gay bar on the other side of town."

Amy asked how Lisa had been doing and how things were in Indianapolis. Lisa thought it was curious that baseball was the farthest thing from Amy's mind, but she was afraid she knew why.

They arrived at the bar. Lisa had been here a few years ago, and it hadn't changed much. The music was at a tolerable level when they entered. She recalled that it didn't get loud until about ten. Lisa didn't intend to be there that long.

They found an empty table and ordered a couple of beers and some sandwiches. Lisa was checking out the sparse crowd when Amy said, "You look great, by the way."

"Oh, thanks. You do, too." Lisa hesitated before continuing. "I have some good news for you, or at least I hope you'll think it's good."

Amy took a drink from her Foster's. "Yeah?"

"I'll be here for the entire six weeks."

Amy's face lit up. "Oh, Lisa, that's awesome."

A few of the women at the other tables turned toward them after Amy's exclamation.

"And I'll be covering you all next summer for Minor League.com."

Amy sat back in her chair. It seemed to Lisa like she was about to cry. "I don't know what to say, except you have no idea how happy I am right now."

Lisa squeezed Amy's arm.

Amy took another drink of her beer and blinked away her tears.

Lisa wanted to get out of there and be alone with Amy, somewhere… anywhere. It was as if Amy could read her mind.

"I'd like to go somewhere quiet with you. Is that asking too much?" Amy said.

Lisa's heart skipped several beats. "No, it's not."

The server brought their food at that moment. Lisa peered up at her. "Can we get to-go boxes for this?"

The server's gaze shifted from Lisa to Amy and back to Lisa. "Sure, champ. I'll bring them right out." She picked up their food from the table and gave Lisa a wink before walking away with a half smile.

"Guess she's got us figured out," Amy said.

Lisa chuckled. "I guess so."

Lisa paid the bill despite Amy's insistence that they go Dutch.

"Where did you want to go?" Amy asked, getting into the car.

Lisa stared at the dashboard before turning to Amy. "Would you like to go to my hotel?" She held her breath, waiting for Amy's answer.

"I'd like that very much."

Chapter 11

Lisa flipped on the room lights. She pointed to the table against the far wall surrounded by cushioned chairs. "Why don't you set our dinners down over there and make yourself comfortable. I'll run to the ice machine." She picked up the ice bucket. "Do you want a Coke or something?"

"I'll take a Coke."

As Lisa walked down the hall, she thought about what it meant to ask Amy to her room. This wasn't a casual thing for Lisa. They had agreed to take it slow, but the time felt right. The ice machine spat out the cubes in fits and starts; she fed the dollars into the Coke machine and picked up the two cans. She cradled the cold Cokes against her body in the crook of her arm on her way back to the room.

Lisa slid the key card in the slot. Amy sat at the table in front of her open Styrofoam box. She looked extremely hungry.

"I'm sorry, Amy. I know you must be starving. You could have started without me, you know."

"No. We agreed to a dinner date, didn't we?"

"Yes, we did." Lisa took the wrappers off the glasses, dropped some ice in them, and carried the glasses over to the table with the Cokes. "Guess this isn't too romantic, huh?" Lisa asked, sitting down across from her.

Amy gave Lisa an intense stare. "Actually, I find it extremely romantic."

Lisa's stomach fluttered with excitement. Amy's desire was evident. She tore herself away from Amy's gaze and took a bite of her hamburger.

After they finished, Lisa picked up the Styrofoam containers and used napkins and tossed them in the trash. "How's it going with the guys on the team and with Reed?" She turned back to Amy to find her wiping away tears. Lisa quickly walked over to the bed and sat down on it in front of Amy's chair. "What've they done?"

"Nothing. I mean nothing physical. It's that they…"

"Hey, you can talk to me." Lisa took hold of Amy's hands.

"They ignore me. Totally. I've tried talking to them, but it's like there's this unspoken code to freeze me out. The only guy who talks to me is the second baseman, Henderson. He doesn't care what kind of flak he gets from the others." Amy sighed. "It doesn't help that they think I'm getting preferential treatment with my own apartment. Not that it's a fancy place or anything. It's a studio for God's sake. But the fact I'm the only one without a roommate, for obvious reasons, has gotten under their skin even more." Her face clouded over. "And…"

Lisa's body tensed. "And?"

"I heard a couple of them when they walked by my locker say, 'fuckin' cunt.'"

Anger rose from Lisa's gut. The "c" word was the ultimate insult for a woman. She never used the word. Never. "Goddammit."

Amy now held Lisa's hands gently in hers. "I knew this crap was coming down. I should probably get used to it here at the bottom rung."

Lisa jumped to her feet and paced the room. "No. Don't ever get used to that. Ever." She spun around and walked back to Amy's chair. She stood there, almost physically feeling Amy's pain, fearing that this was only the beginning for her. She wanted to protect her. "Promise me," Lisa whispered, lightly caressing her face. "Promise me you'll never get used to being insulted and disrespected."

Amy tenderly kissed the palm of Lisa's hand. "I promise. For you."

Lisa brought Amy to her feet. "No. For you, Amy. Never forget who you are."

They stood there, staring, anticipation hanging in the air between them. Lisa moved even closer. She sought out Amy's lips, and their tongues touched. The kiss deepened with each passing second. Lisa drew away from Amy. Silently, quickly, they undressed. Lisa pushed Amy back onto the bed and placed kisses along Amy's neck. She lightly brushed a hand over Amy's breasts and brought her mouth to where her hand had just touched.

Lisa could tell Amy was ready. She dipped her hand below and explored and discovered all of Amy's soft, wet places, finding what gave her the most pleasure and taking her to the edge of ecstasy. Lisa moved with Amy, feeling Amy's thigh muscles tighten against her own when Amy exploded into her climax.

Lisa fell back onto the bed and took in several labored breaths.

Amy rolled to her side. "That was incredible," she whispered, caressing Lisa's breasts. She took her time, worshipping Lisa's body with her hands, her lips, her tongue, until Lisa gave in to her own orgasm.

* * *

A couple of hours later, they lay there, exhausted and sweating, but relishing the quiet contentment. Lisa spoke, regretting that it would break the mood. "Do you have a curfew?"

Amy jerked. "Oh, crap, what time is it?" She rose up on her elbows to check the digital clock beside the bed. "Good. It's only ten-fifteen. I need to be in the room by eleven." Lisa stretched her long legs. Amy ran her fingertips lightly across Lisa's naked body. "Don't do that, Lisa, or you'll get me in a world of trouble with Reed."

Lisa shivered at Amy's touch and pretended she didn't know what Amy was talking about. "Really?"

"Really. I could have you all over again."

Lisa heard the want in Amy's voice, and it sent an instant throbbing between her legs. "I wish we had more time."

"Me, too." Amy sighed. "But I need to get going." She pointed toward the bathroom. "Mind if I take a quick shower?"

"Not at all." Lisa propped herself up to watch Amy walk across the room. She heard the water start in the shower and lay back onto the bed.

She smiled in satisfaction, but ugly thoughts soon intruded and brought her back to the real world. It hit her. Is this how it will be? Stolen hours of ecstasy, but never an entire night in the arms of her lover? Could she do this? Did she even want to?

"You're getting way ahead of yourself," she whispered and sat up to get dressed. She pulled on her clothes, but deep down she knew it was already too late to be getting ahead of herself.

Lisa heard the water shut off. Amy stepped out, rubbing her hair with a towel. Seeing Amy's naked body glistening with water made Lisa want her all over again.

Amy grinned. "I know that look. I'd like to again, too, but I've got to get back." She gathered her clothes and began dressing.

"You're right, but you can't fault a girl for trying."

"No, you can't." Amy laced up her shoes.

Lisa snatched the keys from the dresser. Before she opened the door, she gave Amy one last kiss. The cool night air greeted them when they stepped outside.

The drive to the Shell station was over too soon. Lisa stopped the car and turned off the engine.

"I enjoyed tonight," Amy said.

"Me, too."

"Maybe we can get together again before the first game?"

"Yeah, maybe we can."

A couple passed by the car on their way into the convenience store. They glanced over at Lisa and Amy. To Lisa, it was nothing more than harmless glances. But Amy's panicked expression said she saw it as a threat. She was out the door, slamming it behind her before Lisa could say another word. She took long strides back toward the apartment complex.

Lisa stared out her windshield.

"Fuck!" She slammed the heel of her hand onto the steering wheel. She turned the key in the ignition, backed out of the lot, and merged into traffic. She wanted to go to Amy's apartment, pound on her door, and tell her how demeaning this all was.

Instead, she kept driving.

Chapter 12

On Monday night, a capacity crowd filled HoHoKam Park. Groups of young girls in their Little League uniforms were scattered throughout the stadium. They craned their necks to find Amy on the field. They all wore their oversized caps and their mitts, ready for any balls hit their way. The temperature had dropped considerably since the sun lowered. Soon the sun would dip below the horizon completely, but the last rays still lingered, filtering through part of the western bleachers.

The Solar Sox were out on the field taking grounders and tossing the ball around in the outfield to warm up. Amy was at first base taking throws from the guys in the infield. A makeshift box area for the photographers had been erected beside the Solar Sox dugout. It was like a World Series game; they were stacked three deep. All cameras focused on Amy, and not only the ones in the press area. Flashbulbs pulsed around the stadium like running lights at an airport.

Lisa sat in the cramped press box with the other reporters. The ballpark clearly wasn't built for something like this. Sarah was beside Lisa, talking to a local reporter from the Phoenix paper. He told her this wasn't the norm in either crowd size or publicity. It was a good draw if 400 attended a game, but that rarely happened. It helped that they had moved the game time to 7:05. The Arizona Fall League usually scheduled their games in the afternoon, but tonight was an exception because of Amy Perry's unprecedented debut.

Lisa didn't pay much attention to Sarah and the other reporter, only catching bits and pieces of the conversation.

"I haven't had a chance to see her in full-game action, but Lisa here has. Haven't you?" Sarah asked. "Lisa?"

Lisa shook free from her thoughts.

"Yes. I saw her in Indianapolis when the Indians played Perry's baseball team."

"And?" Sarah gestured with her hand. "Come on. I wasn't

there. How was her play that night? What's your take on her making the majors? I know you and I talked, but Steve here"—she tilted her head toward the *Arizona Republic* reporter—"would like to know what you think."

"She's an extremely talented ball player who happens to be a woman," Lisa said. If it had been only her and Sarah, she would have said, "who happens to have tits" instead of "be a woman." She added, "And she's got a legitimate shot to make the bigs."

The field below was a colorful sight. Players wore the uniform of their major league affiliate, but their hats represented their respective Fall League team.

After two quick outs in the top of the first, the Surprise Rafters got a man on by a walk. The Solar Sox pitcher was a lefty with a sneaky move to first. Amy took the throws from him with ease, tapping the Rafters player with her glove each time he dove headfirst into the bag. One throw was off and got past Amy. The runner started to second. Amy grabbed the ball and fired it to the second baseman, stopping the Rafters player in his tracks. A run-down ensued, and Amy handled it perfectly, finally putting the tag on him for the out. They trotted into the dugout, and the second baseman tapped gloves with Amy. Lisa smiled; Amy was right about Henderson.

In the bottom of the inning, Amy came up with one on and two out. She was patient as the opposing pitcher threw repeatedly to first. She worked the count to 2-2 and hit the next pitch right to the spot vacated by the second baseman because the coach had signaled for the hit-and-run.

Amy asked for the ball, a souvenir of her first hit as a member of a professional men's team. The next batter popped out to end the inning.

The rest of the game passed quickly, with both teams' pitchers throwing well. It was scoreless entering the bottom of the eighth. With one out and runners at second and third, Amy waited on deck. The catcher stood and held up four fingers. They were walking the batter to get to Amy.

Lisa relished the upcoming moments of the game. The other team was underestimating Amy.

Amy stepped into the box and scuffed the dirt. The third base coach flashed her the sign. The infielders played regular depth, ready for the double play. Amy got behind in the count 1-2. She asked for time and stepped out of the box to take a couple of practice swings.

The next pitch was a fastball up in the strike zone, but Amy adjusted her swing to protect the plate. She lined a single over the leaping shortstop. One run scored. The third base coach waved the trailing runner around third. The throw to the plate was high. Amy attempted to advance to second on the play at home. The catcher's throw to the covering second baseman was to the left of the bag. Amy adjusted her headfirst slide to hook her hand around the outside part of the bag. The second baseman smacked his glove down on her hand in an effort to knock it off, but she held on. The umpire called her safe. With her batting helmet sitting cockeyed, Amy raised her free hand at the umpire to ask for time.

The crowd rose and cheered. She stood and dusted off her uniform. Lisa gauged the reaction of the other reporters in the press box. Sarah acknowledged Lisa with a knowing smile. The other reporters were busy typing on their laptops, but Lisa overheard some of their comments.

The next two batters struck out to end the inning. Amy headed to the dugout. Lisa was sure that Amy assumed no one would bring out her hat and glove, which was normally the common courtesy. But Henderson came trotting out of the dugout with both in hand and gave them to her. She seemed to have an extra bounce to her step heading to the first base bag. She tossed the ball to the third baseman for the start of infield warm-ups. Maybe that's how it'll be, Lisa thought. Maybe she'll earn the respect of one player at a time.

The game ended with the Solar Sox on top, 2-0.

Lisa got up to go downstairs for the interviews. Outside the clubhouse, she listened to the guys joking with each other while she waited for the other reporters to show up.

They arrived as a group. Lisa entered the clubhouse with them; they found Amy standing at her locker, still dressed in her dirty uniform. Some of her teammates had towels around their waists, some wore only their jocks. Lisa didn't flinch. She'd seen it all before. She wondered if they were perhaps testing Amy by having her suit up with the rest of the team. The reporters converged on Amy.

She took their questions in stride. She was a natural when it came to speaking to the press. Why did Lisa ever think she might have trouble with this?

"Are you ready for the coming weeks in the league, Amy? Have the Reds let you know where you might go from here?"

"Yes to your first question, and no to your second."

The reporters laughed.

"What about the game-winning hit?" Lisa asked.

Amy gave Lisa her typical blank expression. Lisa had to keep her body from jerking at the impersonal treatment.

"It was a fastball that was up a bit, but I wanted to get the ball up enough to clear the infield. It was a good pitch for me to swing at." Amy went on to the next reporter.

Lisa listened to the other questions, scribbling down a few quotes. Then she extricated herself from the pack. She wanted to see Reed again one-on-one before the others arrived for their interviews. He was digging the chaw out of his mouth when she walked into his office.

"Oh, sorry. Gotta get off this stuff sometime. My wife never stops harping on me about it."

They took their seats.

"What do you think, Coach Reed?"

"You can call me Curt. It's Lisa, right?"

Lisa couldn't hide her surprise.

"You thought I totally blew you off last week, didn't you? I paid attention. To answer your question, Amy Perry has as much talent as some of these other prospects down here and more talent than others. I think she'll do good."

Lisa glanced up from her notebook. "How good?"

Reed pushed back in his chair, propped his feet up on his desk, and put his hands behind his head. He furrowed his brow as if to remember some ballplayers of the past. "She'll make it, and not because the Reds want to make money off of her. She'll make it because she's that good. She knows the fundamentals. She works her ass off. And she has that thing that a lot of these other players will never have. She has a gift. You can't teach that. She has the swing. It's effortless."

She agreed with him. She'd seen that swing the first day at practice in Indianapolis, and it blew her away.

Reed dropped his feet from the desk and sat up in his chair. He tapped his finger on the desk. "This next shit's off the record."

Lisa flipped her notebook shut.

"You and I know what kind of horseshit she'll have to go through. It may get ugly. I know the players on this team aren't giving her a chance. I know you believe that I could stop that, right?" he asked.

Lisa didn't answer. Reed continued as if she had. "You're right. I could. But that could build up more resentment that she's getting special treatment. My instinct tells me that if they see how good she is, some of them will come around. They'll have to admit that, yeah, she's that good. The other ones? They're too pigheaded to ever see the writing on the wall."

Lisa settled back in her chair.

"I'm from Mississippi." Reed's jaw jutted out. "I see some blacks treated like shit by some people when I go home. Some jerks will never come around. It'll be the same for her, no matter what she does." He leaned back in his chair again. "I'll have to admit it pissed me off when they assigned me to be her manager. I sure as hell didn't want to be a babysitter, which is what I figured I'd be here. I thought, fine, I'll put in my six weeks if it means they'll move me up in the minors."

He gave Lisa a crooked smile. "I was a total prick at my first meeting with her. No more. Not after seeing her practice and hustle on every drill this last week. And believe me, I was brutal with her compared to the rest." He waved his hand in the general direction of the field. "Seeing her out there tonight? She's got nothing more to prove to me."

His eyes glinted. "And if any of the players on this team give her trouble in the way of sexual harassment, I'll want to know. That won't be easy since teammates don't rat out another teammate. Unfortunately, it's part of the game, and I realize Amy might not come to me. But if I do find out about any harassment, I'll fucking do something about it."

He stared at Lisa intently from behind his desk, but she projected emotionless calm.

"One more thing," Reed said. "What she's gone through to get here in the instructs and what she'll go through in the future will make her that much better than the next player." He rocked in his chair, causing a rhythmic squeak.

"She'll be with the Reds by September when the others are called up," he said flatly, leaving no doubt how firmly he believed this. "Maybe she'll be in Indianapolis at the beginning of the following year for some more seasoning, but she'll be with the Reds permanently when she's called back up later that spring." Lisa flipped open her notebook to scribble down the quote, but he tapped the desk again. "That's off the record, too. I don't want the brass coming down on me for making up their minds."

Lisa shut the notebook again. "It won't go any farther."

"They'll have her work out with someone from the Reds over the winter. She should be in Chattanooga in the spring. They'll probably give her an invite to the Reds camp before that to have her get a look-see at big league pitching. After that, she'll be off to Tennessee." He stood up and tugged his jersey out of his uniform pants. "Now, if we're through here, I'd like to hit the showers."

Lisa stood and held out her hand. He grabbed it and gave her a full-gripped squeeze.

"Thanks, Curt. I know I'll be seeing quite a bit of you these next few weeks."

"Hope we won't get too tired of each other." He started out the door with her, but the other reporters converged on him immediately. "Ah, hell."

A familiar voice stopped Lisa on her way past the reporters.

"Smooth move, Collins."

"What can I say, Swift? When you got it, you got it," Lisa said, raising her hands, palms up.

"Yeah, whatever!" Sarah shouted at her back before entering Reed's office.

As Lisa left the clubhouse, Reed's words came back to her. September. What he had confided to her was that Amy would be called up for the customary "cup of coffee" offered to deserving minor leaguers at the end of the season. It never guaranteed anything, but it definitely paved the way for a quicker trip to the majors.

She glanced at her watch. She had time to get the article in that night. As she drew nearer to her car, she saw Amy waiting there. Lisa had parked her car with the rest of the press corps and out of sight of the main parking lot—no doubt a safe place, in Amy's estimation.

"Boys won't let you shower?" Lisa asked, only half kidding.

"They're finishing up, and then I'll get in there."

"Good game tonight."

"Thanks."

Lisa unlocked the car and set her laptop on the backseat.

"Do you want to get a beer at that bar tomorrow night?" Amy asked. "We start having day games tomorrow, and I'll be free in the evening. I think they had pool tables in the back, too. I'd love to take you on again."

"Oh, really? Take me on at pool or take me on at..."

Amy's body language changed, and she glanced around the parking lot. "I'd like to take you on at both," she said in a low voice.

A slight shudder ran through Lisa's body. "Want me to pick you up at the same place at, what, seven again?"

"Seven's good. I'll see you tomorrow."

"See you then, Aim."

Chapter 13

Lisa proofed her article one more time before sending it on to her editors via e-mail. This one pleased her as much as her initial article from the night before. Amy's afternoon game had concluded a few hours earlier. The Solar Sox lost 5-2 to the Rafters, but Amy had a solid day at the plate and in the field.

Lisa stretched and checked the time. It was six, which made it nine in Indy. She wanted to get a shower before she left for her date with Amy, but she needed to talk with Frankie. She picked up her cell phone from the table and punched in Frankie's number.

"Hey, you," Frankie said on the other end.

The husky sound of Frankie's voice gave Lisa a sense of comfort, sort of like coming home when she didn't even know she'd been wandering around lost.

"Hey, Frankie."

"How'd Amy do? Her first game was yesterday, right? I haven't had a chance to get online. It's been pretty hectic at the bar."

"She's playing like I knew she was capable of. She has to put up with bullshit from all but one of the guys, but she's hanging in there."

"How's everything else going?"

"It's going okay. I'm getting ready to pick up Amy again tonight."

"Again, huh?"

"Yeah. We went out last Thursday when I got here."

"How'd that go?"

"Okay, but…"

"But…"

"It's the closeted thing, Frankie, like I told you before. Now that we'll be seeing each other, I—"

Frankie interrupted her. "This is more than casual dating?"

"Yeah. I don't really know how I'll handle this. I do

understand that she'll have to stay in the closet this coming year. It'll be tough enough with all the other crap."

"I'm sure you're right. I know how proud you are of who you are. I guess you need to see it from her perspective like we talked about."

"I know. How's everything with you?"

"Fine. How's your writing coming?" Frankie asked abruptly.

"It's good. That's one thing that doesn't go away, thank God."

"Good. Well, I need to take a shower in a few and get to bed so I can get to the bar early in the morning. I'm glad you called."

"Good to talk to you, too. I'll try to keep in touch while I'm down here."

"I'd like that."

"Take care, Frankie. I miss you."

There was silence on the other end.

"Frankie?"

"Miss you too, Leese."

The click on the other end of the line left Lisa cold. She stared at the phone, trying to figure out Frankie's mood. She checked the clock again; it was time to get ready to meet Amy. She stripped and stepped into the water. She placed her hands flat against the tiled shower wall and let the water roll over her back, while her thoughts returned to home. She finished her shower and tugged on a pair of jeans and a long-sleeved T-shirt.

On the drive to pick up Amy, Lisa couldn't deny that she felt almost dirty sneaking around. Amy was waiting for her with a wide grin plastered on her face. It made Lisa temporarily put all her negative thoughts on the back burner. Amy talked about the game all the way to the bar.

After they were seated, Amy said, "Geesh, tell me when to shut up. I didn't even ask how you were."

"It's okay. Honest. And I'm fine."

"Good."

They ordered their sandwiches and beer, finished their dinner, and shot some pool.

"I can remember the first time we played. I was so nervous around you," Amy said while lining up a shot.

"You sure couldn't tell, especially when you kicked my ass."

"Oh, come on, it wasn't that bad. It's not like I ran the table or anything." Amy muffed the next shot.

"True." Lisa lined up her shot and knocked in two solids.

Amy took a swig of beer. "Don't go getting cocky on me."

They played three games, best two out of three, with the loser buying the winner another beer. The place filled up, and the music became louder and louder. They danced for a while, sometimes slow, sometimes grinding out a faster tune, their bodies hot and tight against each other.

Amy pressed her breasts into Lisa's and said into her ear, "Let's go back to your room. We have time."

Lisa led her off the dance floor and outside into the car. They arrived at the hotel, and Amy rushed out her door. She was about ten feet ahead of Lisa, already starting up the steps before Lisa locked the car. Lisa made it to the room and found a playfully smug Amy, waiting, arms folded and shoulder propped against the wall by the door.

"What took you so long?"

Lisa slid the key card into the slot. She kicked the door shut after they entered the room, already reaching for Amy. They tossed their clothes on the floor, bounced on the bed, and giggled. Lisa kissed Amy's lips, then her neck, then her breasts, making her way down until she reached her soft center. She took her time, relishing in giving Amy pleasure and feeling her respond to each touch of her lips and tongue. Lisa prolonged her assault until Amy grabbed hold of her hair, tensed her legs, and cried out. Lisa kissed her way back up her body until she lay next to Amy.

"This is where, if I smoked, I'd say I need a cigarette," Amy said between heavy breaths.

Lisa chuckled. They lay there for a few minutes, not speaking. Amy glanced over at the clock.

"I really do need to get back. Reed calls at eleven on the dot for bed check."

"Okay." Lisa tried not to let Amy hear her disappointment.

They got dressed. Amy pulled Lisa to her for another kiss before they stepped out into the night air. Driving back, Amy talked about the series they would be starting the next day with the Phoenix Desert Dogs. Amy had sat down with Reed after the day's game to go over the pitchers she'd be facing.

"He likes that I always want to learn more," Amy said.

Since her attention was out the side window, she couldn't see Lisa's pleased expression. *You have no idea how impressed he is with you, Amy.*

Lisa turned into the convenience store lot. Amy seemed more

at ease than she had the night before. No one was entering or leaving the store when she stepped out of the car. She leaned down to face Lisa.

"Guess I'll see you tomorrow?"

"I'll be there, doing my job," Lisa said.

"Have a good night."

"You, too."

Lisa backed out and drove to the hotel. She thought about her conversation with Frankie and making love to Amy. She was lonely and homesick… and she didn't even know why.

Chapter 14

The black earth of the farmlands below her told Lisa they were close to Indiana.

She had taken the earliest flight out. The plane landed shortly after eight, and she hurried to the restroom to change into her sweats. With her overnight bag slung over her shoulder, she rushed to the roundabout and hailed a taxi.

She leaned over the seat to address the driver and felt like she was in a grade-B movie when she said, "As close as you can get me to the IUPUI campus. There's an extra twenty in it for you if you get me there in ten minutes." The only thing missing was, "And step on it."

The driver maneuvered around the interstate traffic in the short distance to the campus. The barricades loomed up ahead and police directed traffic.

"This is good," she said and handed the money to the driver before hopping out of the taxi. At least it was a beautiful fall day for the Susan G. Komen Race, with temperatures in the mid-sixties. She jogged over to the group of runners and walkers milling around in the park across from the law school. She searched the crowd, trying to find Frankie and the crew from the Watering Hole. Finally, she spotted the bright purple T-shirts of the bar and hurried over. Frankie was the only one wearing a pink T-shirt, signifying she was a survivor.

"I don't know, man. This is my first time." Billie, one of the other bartenders, was talking to another woman standing nearby. She tugged one of the T-shirts over her black tank top. She was as butch as they came. Burr haircut, no bra, usually dressed in tight jeans with a noticeable bulge in the crotch, and cute as hell with dimples and bright blue eyes.

After Billie pinned on her number, she raised her head and grinned. "I'll be damned. Lisa Collins is here," she said in a loud voice.

Lisa was out of breath when she reached them. *This better be a leisurely walk, or I'm screwed.*

Frankie seemed genuinely touched. Lisa didn't know how Frankie would react, but the instant she saw Frankie's tears, she knew she had made the right decision.

"You came," Frankie said.

"I haven't missed one since we became friends, and I sure as hell wasn't about to start now. I took the earliest flight from Phoenix this morning." Lisa set her shoulder bag on the ground.

Frankie embraced her. "You'll never know how much this means to me," she whispered.

Lisa held her tight. "I'm glad I'm here, Frankie."

The race began, and the crowd surged forward. Lisa picked up her bag again. The runners moved into the fast lane. Frankie, Lisa, and the rest of the group moved over to the walkers' lane.

"You went for your annual, didn't you?" Lisa asked. Frankie scheduled the exam around the race every year.

"Yes. Two weeks ago. Dr. Hodges says everything's good. I had my mammogram and got the results Wednesday."

"And?" Lisa asked anxiously.

"It was clear."

"Great, Frankie. God, that's good to hear."

The only sound was of their shoes slapping against the pavement before Frankie spoke again.

"Amy doing all right?"

"Yeah, she is. She's hitting the hell out of the ball and making plays left and right on the field."

Lisa felt Frankie's stare.

"And you two?"

"We're doing okay." Lisa kept her eyes averted.

"Good."

For the remainder of the walk, they trudged along, chatting intermittently. Frankie waved and said hello to a few friends along the way. They crossed the finish line and picked up cups of water from the tables that lined the area.

"When do you go back?" Frankie asked after she finished her water and tossed the crushed cup in a nearby trash can.

"My flight leaves at nine tonight. It was the latest one I could get."

Frankie's face fell. "I thought you'd at least stay overnight. We're having a get-together at the bar around eight."

"I'm sorry. I can't make it. You have to get to the airport so early now." Lisa sensed Frankie's disappointment by her body language. "But I can come to the bar and visit with you before I go."

Frankie perked up. "I'd love that. I can take you to the airport, too."

"No. Stay at the bar and visit with everyone."

Frankie gave her the look that always ended their disagreements. "You're not paying for another taxi, and that's it."

"Alrighty then."

"Sorry I have to get tough with you sometimes."

"No, you're not," Lisa shot back.

Frankie patted her shoulder. "Not really. How about we drive over to the bar now?"

"Do you mind if I get a quick shower?"

"Nope. You can take it at my house. Come to think of it, I could stand to take one, too."

* * *

Fresh from their showers, they sat at one of the bar's empty tables.

"I still can't believe you're here," Frankie said.

"I hope you know how much you mean to me."

"You mean the world to me, too, Leese, but this is different. This is so personal for me and to have you..." Frankie's voice faltered.

Lisa took her hand. "I wanted to be here for you."

"Thank you."

Lisa squeezed her hand before letting go and taking a drink of her Coke.

"We didn't get into it that much when we talked at the race, but you said you and Amy are doing okay?"

"Yeah." Lisa wondered if her voice gave away her doubts.

"Do you want to talk about it?"

Lisa stalled, wiping away the sweat trickling down her glass.

"Lisa?"

"She doesn't want to be seen with me. After we... well, you know." Lisa couldn't bring herself to say "make love."

Frankie held up a hand. "You don't have to say anymore. I get it."

"I drop her off at this convenience store so I'm not seen taking her to her apartment."

"And you agree with that arrangement?"

"No," Lisa answered with exasperation. "It's like we're doing something wrong. I enjoy being with her, but the other stuff kind of gets in the way."

"Can you see her side of it?"

"I can, but it doesn't make it any easier."

"No, I don't guess it would," Frankie said. "Hang in there. You'll be fine. I hope you know you can always talk to me."

"I do. Thanks."

The next few hours evaporated as she and Frankie caught up on everything that had happened since she'd been gone. Lisa saw the time on the illuminated Colts clock hanging behind the bar.

"Guess I gotta catch a plane."

Frankie stood up with her. Lisa said her goodbyes to everyone before they left. The drive to the airport was too short. This brief visit home only made Lisa realize how much she'd miss Frankie in the coming weeks.

* * *

There was a pattern to the remaining four weeks. Lisa attended the games, sitting in the press box, chatting with Sarah. She'd head to the clubhouse for interviews with the players and with Reed and back to the press box to file her article.

Occasionally, she and Sarah would go out for a few beers. Sarah never asked about her and Amy. The only time Amy's name came up was to critique her play on the field, and her skills were improving with each game.

The Sunday before Amy's last week, Lisa asked her if she'd like to take a trip up to the Grand Canyon. It'd be a long drive getting it done in one day, but Amy was enthusiastically in favor of it.

Lisa picked her up at their usual spot. Amy was dressed comfortably in worn jeans and a jeans jacket with holes in the elbows. Lisa wore a pair of her favorite baggy jeans and an old, faded IU sweatshirt. Driving to the canyon would take about four hours. They left early in the morning so that they could spend at least a couple of hours there before driving back to Mesa.

They talked for a while. A few miles down the highway, Amy's eyelids drooped, and she yawned.

"Oh, hey, Aim. I keep forgetting you haven't had a break in games since April. You must be exhausted after these past five weeks. Why don't you rest until we get closer?"

"You don't mind?"

"No, not at all."

"Thanks," Amy murmured, pushing her seat back and closing her eyes.

Lisa glanced over at her. She'd heard the Reds would have someone work with Amy during the winter months, but at least there would be a break from the games.

The sunrise was gorgeous, streaming through the windows, with pinks and purples spread across the sky. The colors bled into the orange of the desert on either side of the highway. Lisa took a deep breath and let it out slowly. She was glad Amy was asleep. It was nice to have these quiet moments to enjoy God's handiwork.

Lisa wanted the trip to the Grand Canyon to be special. They wouldn't see each other much in the coming months. Amy would be in Florida working out, and Lisa would be in Indianapolis freelancing for the paper. They'd definitely get together at some point during the winter, but they wouldn't be seeing each other every day and sharing their evenings together.

Lisa drove into the mountains of Flagstaff, and Amy stirred awake. Her nap seemed to have refreshed her and made her more talkative. At first, she only talked in generalities, but then she started opening up about the team. A few more of the guys had begun talking to her over the course of the short season. Some were still jerks, but she was learning that she could and would earn the respect of the men who played baseball.

Amy fidgeted excitedly in her seat the closer they got to the South Rim of the canyon. Lisa parked the car. Amy got out and strode ahead of her, but Lisa didn't mind. She enjoyed seeing Amy act like a little kid in her anticipation.

Lisa caught up with her, standing directly behind the barricade that overlooked the vast expanse before them. The expression on Amy's face was one of pure wonderment. The wind whipped up from the canyon below and gently blew through their hair. Amy's eyes glistened in the sunlight.

"Thank you for suggesting this." Amy shook her head. "I don't have the words to tell you how I feel."

They gazed out at the canyon, saying nothing for several minutes. Lisa stood close to Amy, close enough that their shoulders touched. She wanted to take Amy's hand and hold it. Hold it tight. The other couples strolling around the lookout gave her pause, though.

They drove to some of the other lookouts, but Lisa made a decision to forgo the long trip to the North Rim.

"Why don't we head back?" she asked Amy. "That way you can rest tonight before your last week of the season."

"Oh, thanks. I could use the down time."

On the drive back, Amy took Lisa's hand. It was the touch that Lisa had craved only a couple of hours earlier. It meant something, but it mostly served to emphasize the difference between them in showing affection.

Amy held Lisa's hand until she fell back asleep. Lisa glanced over at her. Her face was peaceful, and she appeared much younger than her twenty-seven years. She stirred, murmured something, and withdrew her hand. Lisa brushed a stray curl off her forehead.

It had been a good day.

* * *

"You'll stay in touch, right? I can fly up to see you? I plan to see my mom for Thanksgiving and Christmas, but could I see you the week between Christmas and New Year's at least?" Amy sounded genuinely worried that once Lisa got on the plane to Indianapolis, she'd never see her again.

"I'd love to have you to myself for that week. We'll stay in touch by phone, and you can let me know when you'll be in town."

They were standing in the concourse. Lisa gave Amy a hug, but broke it off quickly.

"I'll call you when I get to Indy," Lisa said, starting for the security area.

"I'll be waiting to hear from you." Amy stayed behind the ropes, raising her hand toward Lisa. Lisa waved to her before leaving for the gate.

On the flight, Lisa worked on her last article covering the Fall League. She wrote a column about her own thoughts on Amy's experience, the progress she'd made, and the promise for her future. She detailed how Amy had honed her skills and how much she'd learned under Curt Reed's tutelage. The Mesa Solar Sox finished last in their division, but it didn't matter. What mattered was that Amy was ready for the next step. In Lisa's last conversations with

Reed, he assured her he had relayed this to the Reds management.

* * *

After the plane landed, Lisa called Frankie. She waited patiently until Frankie's black behemoth appeared around the corner of the passenger pickup area. Lisa set her suitcase on the backseat along with her laptop and carry-on bag. She stepped up into the cab.

"God, Leese," Frankie said. "What'd you do? Lay out in the sun the last month you were down there?"

Lisa didn't realize how much sun she'd gotten until she saw the contrast between her own darkened hands emerging from her jacket and Frankie's pale hands gripping the steering wheel.

"You know I worked like a son of a gun down there."

"Yeah, but I've never seen you this dark before. And your hair? It's as light as I've ever seen it."

Lisa flipped down the visor mirror. Okay, Frankie had a point.

"What? You didn't believe me?" Frankie asked, lightly punching Lisa's arm.

Lisa playfully punched her back. "I did. I just didn't notice it in Phoenix."

"How'd Amy's last week go?" Frankie asked while pulling out onto the interstate.

"It was good. She'll skip Single-A and jump up to Double-A in Chattanooga next spring. I can guarantee it."

"I'm glad to hear she did well."

Lisa studied Frankie's face. It was beginning to hit her again how much she'd missed her. The last four weeks was the longest period she had been away from Frankie since they met.

Frankie glanced over at Lisa. "What? Did I grow another head or something?"

"No. I'm glad to see you. Is that a bad thing?"

Frankie smiled. "No. It's not. It's good to see you, too, Leese. I've missed you."

"Missed you, too."

They pulled up in front of Lisa's apartment building. Lisa hopped down. She reached in to grab her bags out of the back, and Frankie stepped out of the truck to help.

"I can get this, Frankie."

"I can help you take your stuff upstairs. No reason you should be struggling with all of it." Frankie waved her hand toward the truck before they entered the apartment building. "Is that safe where it's at?"

"You've got your blinkers on. You'll be fine."

After they stepped off the elevator, Frankie carried her luggage into the apartment and set it by the bedroom door. Lisa put her carry-on and laptop down on the couch. The apartment smelled stale. Lisa cracked the windows for some fresh air despite the temperature being only in the thirties outside.

She walked over to Frankie and gave her a hug. "Thanks again for picking me up."

"You're welcome." Frankie withdrew from the embrace. "I'd better get to the bar and get things ready for tonight. It's karaoke night. You know how crazy that is."

"Yeah." Lisa walked her to the door. "If I'm up to it later after resting, I'll come over."

"I hope you do. I know the gang will love to see you. Billie's working tonight with Stacy and has been bugging the hell out of me, asking when you'd be back." Frankie wagged her finger at Lisa before leaving. "First, you get some rest, you hear?"

"Yes, ma'am." Lisa shut and locked the door behind Frankie. She shivered. She closed one of the windows, leaving the other open a crack. She flipped on her laptop and read her column a few times, making some small changes. After establishing wireless connection, she logged onto the Internet and sent the article on to New York. She included a note, thanking them again for giving her the opportunity to cover Amy.

Lisa stretched and gazed longingly at the bedroom. She didn't even bother to take off her clothes. She threw off her shoes, curled up on her bed, and pulled the comforter over her. Soon she fell into a deep sleep.

* * *

It was seven-thirty when Lisa awoke, shivering. Cold, cold, cold. She padded into the living room and shut the window. Leaving it open had seemed like a good idea at the time.

She turned the heat up a couple of notches on her way to the bathroom. After she took a hot shower, she dressed in a pair of old jeans and a Colts sweatshirt. The November cold that greeted her when she stepped outside caused her to zip her jacket even higher. After the warm temperatures of Arizona, the cold cut right through her. On the short drive to the bar, a pang of excitement made her stomach flutter. She was looking forward to seeing her friends again.

Chapter 15

Lisa opened the door to the Watering Hole and immediately ran into the karaoke crowd. She pushed her way to the bar, took the only stool available, and draped her jacket across the back before sitting down. She waited for Billie to make her way down to her.

Billie stuck out her hand, and Lisa took it in a buddy shake.

"Jesus, Lisa, it's good to see you. And, man, Frankie said you got a lot of sun, but damn, woman! You're as dark as a Native American."

"You guys are so full of it. But believe me, I didn't miss the cold here."

"Well, we sure as hell missed you." Billie lowered her voice. "Especially the boss. She's been moping around here for the past four weeks. She was okay when you first left, but the longer you were gone, the more miserable she got."

"Really?"

"What? Didn't think she'd miss you?"

Lisa blushed. "No, it's that…"

Billie poked her in the arm. "Didn't mean to embarrass you there, but she really did miss you. Hell, we all did."

Billie left to take care of drink orders. Stacy stepped up to the cash register to make some change.

"Hey, Stacy."

She came down the bar to Lisa. "Welcome back. We missed you around here." She pointed in front of Lisa where her beer normally would be. "Did Billie leave you dry?" Without even waiting for an answer, she popped the lid on a cold Michelob. "It's on me." Before she got too far away, she said, "I'm glad you're back, but I'm especially glad for Frankie."

After a few minutes, someone lightly gripped Lisa's shoulder from behind. She swiveled to see Frankie.

"Whatcha so serious about?" Frankie asked. "You're sitting in my bar drinking your favorite beer. You should at least act happy to be here."

"I'm fine. Got my Michelob, and I'm enjoying my friends."

Frankie patted her on the back. "Good. You're not paying for any of those tonight, by the way. But don't overdo it, because you drove, right?" She waited for Lisa's answer.

"Yes, I drove."

"Good. Didn't want to have to give you a lecture on your first night back."

"Frankie!" someone called.

Lisa recognized a woman from Frankie's softball team motioning her over to a table with her friends.

"It's good to have you back, Leese." Frankie squeezed Lisa's shoulder again before walking over to the table.

The music got louder in preparation for karaoke. Lisa waved at Davey, the DJ, who was setting up his equipment.

"How you doing, Davey?" she asked when he came to stand beside her.

"Oh, my God. It's been so long since I've seen you in here on karaoke night." He gave her a hug and a kiss on the cheek.

She hugged him back and returned the kiss. "Good to see you, too, sweetie."

"You will sing tonight, right?"

"Well..."

"Come on, at least one song."

"Maybe," Lisa said reluctantly.

"Maybe, hell. I'll get you up there." Davey didn't wait for her response and went back to his equipment.

Lisa sat at the bar, content to nurse her beer and talk with Billie when she had time. Frankie stepped behind Billie, lugging a crate of liquor from downstairs.

"Do you need help with that, boss?" Billie asked.

"Nope. I'm good."

Billie turned back to Lisa. "Frankie filled me in on Amy and her baseball. I tried to read your articles online but didn't keep up with all of them. She sounds like a hell of a player." She mixed two drink orders without missing a beat.

"She is. She's going to make it, too."

"She taking any shit from the guys on the team?" Billie asked.

"Some of them were assholes, but by the end of the season, she'd made a couple of friends."

With a disgusted look on her face, Billie swiped the bar in front of Lisa. "That sucks, you know? What difference does it make? Just because she doesn't have a dick."

Lisa put on a serious face and saluted Billie with her beer. "Good observation there, Billie."

Billie's expression quickly changed from anger to amusement. "Why thank you. I've been known to have some intelligence." Billie leaned over the bar. "What about the two of you? Word got around that you had a couple of dates with her while she was in Indy."

"Word got around?"

"Hell, you can't keep a secret around here, especially when you're seen dancing with her in this very bar. Did you two get together any down in Arizona?"

Lisa again felt the heat rise from her neck up to her face.

"I take that as a yes." Billie poked Lisa on the arm again. "So, will we see her in Indy anytime soon?"

Lisa shifted uncomfortably on her stool and took another swallow of beer.

"Oh, come on. You've met all the women I've dated since you've known me."

Lisa almost choked on her beer. She was about to say she wouldn't call what Billie did—sleeping with a woman for a couple of weeks and then moving on to the next one—dating. But she refrained.

Billie grinned. "I sure as shit know what's going through that mind of yours. You're right, it may not be dating, but at least you met them. I'd like to meet your woman."

"Okay, okay. Lord, you're like a lawyer sometimes with these questions."

"And?"

"She's staying with me the week between Christmas and New Year's."

As the words left Lisa's mouth, Frankie abruptly stepped around the bar and walked over to rejoin her softball buddies at their table.

What's up with that? Lisa turned to watch her retreating back.

"Sounds extremely interesting."

"What?" She turned back to Billie.

"I said it sounds extremely interesting."

"I don't know what you mean."

"Don't try to tell me you don't know what to do with your time while she's here."

Lisa sighed. "Let's drop it."

"You sure? I can give you some pointers if you need them."

"Billie…" Lisa gave her a cold stare.

Billie threw her hands up with her palms facing Lisa. "I was only trying to be helpful."

"You can be helpful by bringing me one more Mich."

"Okay."

Lisa took her time with the second beer.

Davey boomed over the loud speakers, "All right, everybody, another fifteen minutes, and we'll get started. Get your names and song titles up to me, and we'll put them in the order we receive them. Songbooks are on every table. No excuses for not singing." Davey played some more music before adeptly singing the first song of the night.

When he finished, he said, "And now, everybody, give it up for my buddy, Lisa!"

Lisa jerked at the sound of her name.

"Lisa, come on up here," Davey shouted.

Lisa was out of practice, but resigned herself to the task. She made her way through the other couples packed in around the tables.

"What do you want to sing tonight, sweetie?" Davey asked.

"I don't know. You got me into this."

"How about some Bob Seger? You always like to sing his stuff."

"All right." A quick image shot through her mind of her shooting pool with Frankie while listening to his Greatest Hits. She thought Davey would pick out one of his fast tunes. Her stomach did a flip flop when "We've Got Tonight" flashed across the big plasma screen. She was about to ask him to change it, but the music started before she had the chance.

At first, Lisa merely read the lyrics, making certain she hit all the notes. She soon found she was putting everything she had into the song, sounding as raspy as Seger did in the original recording.

Thunderous applause greeted her after she finished. Davey took the mike. He kissed her on the cheek and hugged her. "That was beautiful, honey."

"Thanks." She returned the kiss. Lisa pushed her way through the crowd. The route she had taken to come up to sing was blocked. She turned to wend her way around the edge of the floor. She was stuck behind a group that wasn't too intent on moving from where they were planted. She heard Frankie's friends laughing. The group of women parted to reveal Frankie staring at her. Lisa's heart skipped a beat. She felt like she was falling into Frankie's dark brown eyes.

Lisa stood there, lost in the moment.

"Excuse me! Do you mind moving?" a tall woman with a crew cut shouted at her.

The way had cleared, except now she was the one blocking the path for others to get past. "Oh, sure. Sorry." She walked back to the bar and picked up her jacket from the stool.

"Leaving?" Billie shouted over an off-key rendition of "Girls Just Want to Have Fun."

"Yeah." Lisa started for the door, once more weaving her way through the crowd.

"Have a good one," Billie shouted again.

Lisa made it out to her car and leaned against the side. She took a deep breath of cold air, trying to clear her mind. She didn't know how long she stood there, watching women enter and leave the bar. She unclipped her cell phone from her jeans, flipped it open, and punched in Amy's number. Lisa checked her watch. It was ten, maybe too late.

"Lisa? God, it's good to hear from you." Amy's soft voice came through loud and clear.

"Hey. I wanted to give you a call. I thought it was too late at first, but now I remember. You're still in Phoenix, huh?"

"Yeah. I'm flying out tomorrow for Florida. They have me staying at the Reds' spring training camp. They even have me set up for a studio apartment for the winter. I guess I won't be alone. I've found out there'll be a few other players there who they want to work with."

Lisa was quiet on her end.

"Lisa? You there?"

"Yeah. I'm here."

"You sound kind of funny."

"I'm fine. I needed to hear your voice."

"I'm glad you called."

"I'm glad I did, too," Lisa said. "Well, I'll let you go. I'm heading home to get some rest."

"You're not home now?"

"No. I came over to the Watering Hole for a few beers and to catch up with my friends."

"I bet they're glad to get you home."

"Yeah. They are."

There was another awkward silence.

"You're sure you're okay?" Amy asked.

"Yes. Just tired. Like I said, I'm going home now."

"Good. Sleep well, and I'll call you tomorrow when I get into Florida."

"Have a safe flight."

"Take care."

"You, too."

Lisa flipped her phone shut. As she started her car, snow began to fall. The beams from her headlights illuminated the small flakes drifting into view. What was she doing in Indianapolis watching snowflakes when Amy was in Phoenix, soon to be headed for Florida?

Chapter 16

Jack was happy to have Lisa back at the paper covering high school sports, and he proved it by keeping her more than busy. She still posted her occasional column for the website on Amy's progress in Florida.

Thanksgiving came and went with Lisa turning down Frankie's invitation to join her for dinner at her house. She asked Lisa every year, and every year, Lisa begged off. Frankie's family would be there. It wasn't that Lisa didn't like her family, but it was painful for her to see the interaction between everyone. It made her miss her mother even more.

A few days before Christmas, as Lisa entered her apartment and threw her keys on the table by the door, the phone rang.

"Hello?"

"Lisa, glad I caught you."

"Oh, hey, Frankie. I just got in from covering a girls' basketball game."

It was quiet on the other end for a long moment.

"I know how the holidays are for you," Frankie finally said.

Lisa's throat tightened. It was like Thanksgiving. Christmas at Frankie's house was full of love and laughter and kids with happy faces running around, not caring who they hugged. And like Thanksgiving, it was something Lisa avoided.

"I think I know what you're about to ask, but I'm going to hang out here," Lisa said. "I might volunteer to cover the holiday tourney. Jack always has trouble finding correspondents to work this time of year."

"It's different this Christmas. I've asked the family to move the celebration to Christmas Eve day. That way, you can come over for a nice quiet dinner and visit that night."

"Oh, um…"

"I'm not trying to put you on the spot, but I hate it that you're alone every year. You've never given me the reasons you can't

94

make it, but I think it's because seeing me with my family makes you feel really alone."

Lisa didn't respond.

"Am I right?" Frankie asked.

"Yeah."

"At least think about it. No matter what you decide, I have the evening free. I'll leave it up to you if you want to come over. But I'd really love to have you here."

Lisa looked to the end table and fixed her gaze on a framed photo of her mother and her. She was six at the time. Her mother was bent over and had her arms draped around Lisa's neck. She had a big smile on her face, and Lisa was looking up at her, giggling.

Lisa blinked at the burning in her eyes and tried to stop the tears before they started, but failed. "I'll come over," she said softly.

"Oh, I'm so glad." Frankie sighed. "I'll let you get off the phone because I caught you just walking in."

"Yeah. I struggled a little with the article tonight. Took me longer than usual."

"How does six-thirty or seven sound? We'll have a nice dinner. We'll get a fire going, and we can shoot some pool, maybe even watch a movie. Then we'll exchange presents around midnight."

"Seven's good for me."

"I'll see you then."

Lisa hung up the phone and picked up the photo. She wiped away the tears rolling down her cheeks. No matter how many times she thought she'd healed from the loss of her mother, something would happen that brought it all back for her.

With shaking knees, she sat down, unable to keep the dark memories of her past from flooding over her. Lisa had been working in Ohio when she received the phone call. She feared something was terribly wrong from the sound of her mother's voice, but she wouldn't tell Lisa over the phone. She drove home trying to convince herself that everything was fine, but the dread only increased with each mile.

Her mother met her at the door. Lisa had almost collapsed when she saw her stricken expression. Stage IV ovarian cancer. The words echoed in her mind. In the end, when pain wracked her mom's body and she was incoherent with morphine, Lisa did the hardest thing she'd ever done: she told her mother it was okay to go.

Lisa hugged the photo to her chest. "I guess I'll never get over it." Each word nearly choked her.

* * *

"Come on in, Lisa."

Frankie, dressed in a red sweatshirt with Winnie the Pooh wearing a Santa hat, greeted her at the door.

"Nice sweatshirt." Lisa set her gift under the lit tree.

"It's a gift from Andy, my youngest nephew." Frankie peeked out the door. "Looks like we've already gotten a couple of inches."

"They said the snow should stop by midnight. Guess all the people who love a white Christmas will be happy."

"It's nice, providing you don't have to drive in it." Frankie hung up Lisa's coat. She turned back to Lisa and pointed at her chest. "You're in the Christmas spirit, too."

Lisa ran her fingers over the appliquéd Christmas tree on her gray sweatshirt. "I figured you'd get a kick out of it."

"It's you." Frankie gave Lisa a warm hug.

"Your tree's beautiful, by the way."

"It's the only Martha Stewartsy thing I can do. Would you like a beer or an eggnog?" Frankie took a step toward the kitchen and stopped in midstride. "I'd say that look means eggnog is out."

"Am I that obvious?"

"Just a tad."

Lisa followed her into the kitchen, where Frankie stood in front of an open refrigerator.

"What'll it be? I have Bud, Coors, and some crap called Michelob."

"Hmm. I'll take the crappy beer."

Frankie grabbed a bottle and popped the lid before handing it to Lisa. "How'd I know you'd say that?"

"Gee. Must be because you know me so well." Lisa exaggerated tilting her nose in the air and sniffed. "Whatever it is you're cooking smells delicious. Turkey?"

"We have the works tonight. Turkey, stuffing, mashed potatoes, gravy. I could go on and on." Frankie opened the oven door and basted the turkey. "This is about done. In the meantime, why don't you go to the den and rack 'em up. We can get in a quick game."

"You're right. It won't take me long to beat you again." Lisa was almost to the den before she heard Frankie's reply.

"You're lucky I love you or you'd be on your way back home

right about now."

"Love you, too, sweet cakes." Lisa racked the balls.

A couple of minutes later, Frankie joined her. "I'll let you break this time," Frankie said.

"You're making a big mistake." Lisa rolled the cue ball back and forth on the table.

"Just hit the damn thing."

Lisa bent over and brought her cue back. The balls spread out across the table. Two solids dropped into the far pockets. "That'd make you stripes, not that it matters."

Frankie took a swig from her Coors. She motioned with her hand for Lisa to keep playing.

Lisa made a run until she had two solids left on the table.

"Finally," Frankie huffed. She pointed with her cue to the recliner in the corner of the den. "Go ahead and get comfy, 'cause you're not getting another chance."

Frankie kept her word and ran the table. She called the eight ball and knocked it in with ease.

"Ta-da!"

Lisa stood up and took long, slow steps, shuffling her feet along the carpet. "Guess I gotta say congratulations."

"Oh, now you sound like Eeyore."

"What's with this fascination with Pooh characters?"

"Trust me, when you've got eight nieces and nephews, you catch on quick."

The comment was meant to be lighthearted, but it struck Lisa the wrong way. She blinked away unexpected tears.

"Damn. I'm sorry, Leese. I didn't mean…"

"Please don't apologize. You didn't do anything wrong. It's that time of year for me, I guess. I'm too sensitive." Lisa stared at her shoes.

Frankie moved closer to stand in front of her. She lifted Lisa's chin with a gentle touch.

"You feel whatever way you need to feel. You never have to pretend around me."

Lisa took comfort in Frankie's words. "Thanks."

"How about we have some turkey?" Frankie walked to the kitchen.

Lisa lingered behind for a moment and then joined Frankie. She helped her load up the dishes with food from the stove. They worked in silence as they made several trips carrying the food into the dining room.

Lit tapered candles adorned the middle of the table. Fine china that Lisa had never seen before was laid out, along with silverware that caught the glow of the candlelight. A bottle of wine completed the festive look. "I don't know, Frankie, this is pretty Martha Stewartsy, too."

"I guess," Frankie said from the kitchen. "Think I can get on her show?"

"Well..."

"Don't answer that. I'm sitting closest to the carving knife. You finished your beer, right?"

"Yeah."

"Do you mind mixing beer with wine? I thought we'd have a glass with dinner."

Lisa picked up the bottle and checked out the label. She didn't know wine, but she could tell this one wasn't cheap. "Wow. You've gone all out here."

Frankie came in with the dressing. "Only the best for my best friend. Can you get the turkey and bring it in?"

Lisa stepped into the kitchen, picked up the platter of turkey, and carefully put it by Frankie's place setting.

"Take a seat and observe a master at work," Frankie said. She proceeded to slice each piece with ease.

"I'm duly impressed, Ms. Dunkin."

"Why thank you."

They passed the serving bowls back and forth between them.

"How about enjoying a fire and then watching a movie before we open gifts? What about the *Fellowship of the Ring?* I know you love that stuff."

"You're right. I haven't seen it in a while, either," Lisa said with a mouthful of food. "God, this turkey's out of this world. I'm making a pig of myself here."

"You eat all you want."

Which Lisa did until she felt like her jeans would pop open if she took another bite. She pushed away from the table. "That's it for me. I'm full."

Frankie began clearing the table. Lisa started to help, and Frankie shooed her away. "No. I've got this. Why don't you pour us another glass of that wine and get the fire going in the den?"

Lisa rubbed her belly. "You trust me with matches?"

"I trust you with anything." Frankie's voice trailed behind her.

Lisa poured the wine, carried it into the den, and set it on a table. Now the fire. She made sure she arranged the logs the way Frankie had showed her on earlier visits. After a few minutes, the fire crackled to life. She stood there, transfixed by the flames, until Frankie came up behind her.

"Here's your wine."

Lisa took the offered glass.

"I should've done this before dinner, but how about a toast?" Frankie raised her glass.

Lisa held hers up to Frankie's.

"To five years of friendship and many more years to come," Frankie said.

They clinked glasses and took sips of their wine. Lisa watched the firelight dance across Frankie's face. They stood there, seemingly unwilling to move, the fire crackling and popping beside them.

Frankie broke the silence. "How about that movie?"

"Sure." Lisa sat down on the plush couch that faced the TV. Frankie started the DVD player and joined Lisa. Lisa had seen the movie three times, once at the movie theater and twice at Frankie's house. She still easily got lost in the fantasy world of J.R.R. Tolkien.

Lisa felt sleep coming on at the two-hour mark of the movie. She tried to fight it, but the wine and food were winning the battle. She made the mistake of lying back against the cushion. That was the last thing she remembered before succumbing to slumber.

* * *

Lisa stirred awake and tried to focus on the fire that had died down to smoldering embers. She had moved in her sleep, and her head now rested on Frankie's shoulder. Frankie held Lisa against her body. Lisa had draped her right arm around Frankie's waist in a protective embrace.

Lisa didn't want to move, but Frankie stirred and jerked awake. "Oh, Leese. I'm sorry. I fell asleep." She yanked her arm off Lisa's shoulder.

Lisa sat up. "It's okay. I did, too." She was afraid to look at Frankie, but took the chance.

Frankie glanced at her briefly before standing up. "Oh, wow, it's almost midnight. I can't believe we were out that long." She went to the fireplace, picked up two logs, and dropped them on the fire. She pushed the poker around until the fire started going stronger. "How about we open those gifts?" Frankie kept her back to Lisa.

Lisa went into the living room, picked up her gift to Frankie, and found Frankie's gift to her under the tree. Frankie was sitting on the couch when Lisa reentered the den. She handed Frankie her gift and sat down beside her.

"You first," Frankie said.

"You tickle me every year. I always have to go first."

"It's a tradition then, and you know we can't break with tradition."

Lisa ripped back the bright green and red paper to find her first article for Minor League.com framed in beautiful dark wood. "I love it, Frankie," she said softly. "Thank you."

"I know how you always act like it's no big deal, but it is to me."

Lisa waited for Frankie to open her package. Frankie tore the paper away. Her stunned look was just what Lisa had hoped the gift might bring. It was a large framed watercolor of the Watering Hole. Lisa had asked a local artist, who was also a friend, to paint it.

"Oh, Leese, I don't know what to say. It's beautiful." Frankie ran her fingers over the glass as if to touch the colors. She wiped away her tears.

"I had that done months ago," Lisa said. "You don't know how many times I almost broke down and gave it to you early."

"It's the best Christmas present I've ever gotten. Thank you."

Lisa tapped the glass of the picture frame. "Mine, too. Thank you." The chimes from the mantle clock rang out. "Listen. That means it's midnight. Merry Christmas, Frankie."

"Merry Christmas, Leese."

Lisa set her gift aside on the table. Frankie did the same and held out her arms. Lisa fell into them for an embrace. Contentment flowed gently over Lisa, and she relaxed her body in Frankie's arms. But something else stirred deep inside, something that hadn't been there before.

Desire.

She tensed up and felt Frankie do the same. They pulled apart. Lisa searched for a reaction from Frankie, but Frankie jumped to her feet. She walked to the window and pushed the curtain aside.

"There's a lot more out there than they said we'd get, and it's still coming down."

Lisa stayed on the couch, struggling with her emotions. When Frankie did face her again, her eyes offered no window into what she was thinking.

Lisa stood up. "I'd better start for home."

Frankie frowned. "There's at least a good six inches out there. It's not letting up, and it's blowing like hell. Why don't you stay here tonight?"

"I... I don't know..."

"In the spare room," Frankie hastily added. "Stay here tonight in the spare room."

Lisa hesitated, but she dreaded the drive home in her little Toyota.

"Okay."

"Good. I'll grab you an extra quilt and get you a nightshirt." Frankie left the den.

Lisa went to the window to watch the snow fall and tried desperately to understand her feelings. She didn't know how long she stood like that until Frankie's voice shook her from her reverie.

"Lisa?"

Lisa turned. Frankie stood at the entry to the hall.

"Your bed's ready."

"Let me go to the bathroom, and I'll be right there."

Lisa finished and found Frankie waiting for her in the spare room. There was a nightshirt lying on the queen-size bed. It was an oversized, long-sleeved Kentucky Wildcats T-shirt.

"Trying to be funny?" Lisa asked.

Frankie gave her an impish grin. "It's all I got."

"Yeah, right."

Lisa stepped up to the bed and fingered the shirt.

"I'll let you get to sleep."

"Thanks." Lisa waited for a response, but the door shut behind Frankie with a soft click. Lisa stripped down to her panties and put on the T-shirt. She switched off the bedside lamp and climbed under the soft sheets and hand-stitched quilt.

She lay there with the covers tucked under her chin, staring at the ceiling. Now she was wide awake.

"What the hell just happened?" she whispered.

Chapter 17

Lisa waited at the railing at the top of the stairs and scanned the passengers until she saw a grinning Amy approaching her from the concourse. Her flight arrived on time at 8:05 in the evening. Lisa thought she had held her own tan until she saw Amy. Amy's bronzed skin was even darker than it had been in Arizona.

"Good to see you again," Lisa said. She gave Amy a quick hug.

"Good to see you, too."

They started downstairs to the baggage carousel. "Did you bring much with you?"

"Nah. Only one suitcase and this carry-on."

Silence hung between them while they waited for the suitcase to make its appearance. They had talked frequently on the phone, but it had been almost two months since they had last seen each other.

"There it is." Amy pointed at a red suitcase.

"Here, let me get it." Lisa lifted it off the carousel… and nearly broke her arm. That's what she got for trying to be butch. "Damn, Amy. What do you have in here?"

"Oh, it's not that heavy."

Lisa grunted. "If you say so."

They walked to the garage. After they settled into the car, Amy took Lisa's hand and squeezed it. "I've missed you."

Amy's hand on top of hers felt different. And it wasn't because of the rough skin which was even more calloused since Lisa saw her last. It was something else. "I've missed you, too." But Lisa's heart wasn't in it when she said the words.

On the drive to the apartment, Amy told Lisa about the training in Florida.

"Bob Stoltz is the guy who's been helping me with my hitting, trying to get me to pull the ball more on inside pitches. He keeps saying, 'You've got power there, Perry, don't be shy in using it.'"

Lisa smiled, hearing Amy's imitation of what she assumed was

Stoltz's baritone voice.

"And Stan Kubler's been working on getting my footwork right at first base, mainly to know when to let the second baseman take the grounder. He's always telling me to get familiar with whoever I'm playing with and find out what their range is."

They arrived at the apartment, and Lisa pulled into her numbered slot. She jumped out of the car to grab Amy's suitcase. She set the luggage down just inside the apartment door. Amy brought her hands to Lisa's jacket zipper and tugged it down.

Okay, I wasn't prepared for this.

Lisa let the jacket fall off her shoulders while Amy tore off her own jacket.

Amy grabbed Lisa by the shoulders and pushed her onto the couch. She greedily sought out Lisa's lips and pushed her tongue inside. Amy ran her hand under Lisa's sweatshirt and cupped her breast through her bra.

Amy unsnapped Lisa's jeans and yanked the zipper down. She pushed her hand into Lisa's panties. Lisa tried to get lost in the moment.

But she couldn't.

She willed her body to respond and strained to reach orgasm. The only thing she felt after she climaxed was relief.

"Want more?" Amy moved her fingers again, but Lisa stopped her.

"No," Lisa answered.

Amy withdrew her hand and lay beside Lisa, pulling Lisa against her chest.

Lisa clung to Amy's arm that was wrapped around her tightly. Jumbled thoughts filled her mind. She never had a problem reaching orgasm with Amy before, never had to try. Like the feel of Amy's hand on hers on the drive from the airport, something was different.

"What are you thinking?" Amy whispered against her hair.

Lisa flinched at the words.

"Hey, you okay?"

"Yes. I'm sorry I'm a little quiet."

"Tired? I know you've been working long nights at the paper."

"Yeah. That's probably it."

A few minutes went by before Lisa disengaged from Amy's arms. She zipped up her jeans and caught Amy staring at her.

"You really want to be doing that?" Amy asked.

Lisa ignored the comment and attempted to move the

conversation on to something else. "I'll fix you something to eat. I bet you haven't eaten in a while."

Amy gave her a sheepish grin. "Come to think of it, I haven't."

Lisa went into the kitchen. "You know the only thing I'm good at cooking, right?"

"Frozen pizza?" Amy asked from the living room.

"Funny." Lisa opened the door to the refrigerator. "Breakfast. I'm good at breakfast."

Amy came up behind her and wrapped her arms around Lisa's waist, nuzzling her lips against Lisa's neck. "I'd say you're good at breakfast... lunch... dinner... I could have you anytime."

Lisa tensed at Amy's touch and wondered if Amy felt it, too. She gently lifted Amy's arms away from her waist. "Hey, I need both hands to do this. You go sit over there at the table and relax."

Amy sighed. "You're no fun." She stretched. "I'd like to freshen up some. Where's your bathroom?"

"Right around the corner there," Lisa said. "I'll be fun here in a minute when I have eggs, bacon, fried potatoes, and fresh toast on a plate for you." She yelled so Amy could hear her.

A few minutes later, Amy returned from the bathroom to sit at the table. "I get it. You convinced me to be a good girl."

"Why don't you tell me more about Florida and how you're doing? Have they told you where you're going in the spring?" Lisa tried to keep her voice light. She turned down the flame under the bacon.

Amy's voice was full of enthusiasm. "They're inviting me to the Reds' spring training camp, but then sending me on to Chattanooga."

"Good for you. I'm glad they're giving you a chance to see big league pitching before you move on to the Lookouts' camp."

"Guess what else? Curt Reed has been promoted to Chattanooga. Can you believe it?"

Lisa remembered Reed's words in Arizona about hoping the Reds would move him up in the minors.

"I'm glad for you. He's a good manager." And he was the perfect manager to take care of any signs of trouble.

Lisa finished preparing Amy's food and set the plate in front of her. "I know you don't eat like this often, and you need to stay in shape. But tonight, you can have whatever you want."

"What? Aren't you joining me?" Amy asked between bites.

"No. I ate earlier, and I have trouble keeping the weight off, especially in the winter."

"I hope you know you've got a hot body, but if you need me to show you again, I'd be glad to."

Lisa blushed. "Stop. And eat."

"You don't have to twist my arm. You really can cook breakfast."

After Amy finished every morsel on her plate, they went back into the living room to channel surf. Amy put her arm around Lisa, and Lisa fought the urge to tense up again.

* * *

"Why don't we go to bed?"

Lisa jerked awake. "Wh-what time is it?" she asked, rubbing her eyes.

"Eleven-thirty."

Lisa stood up. "I'm going to take a quick shower before I do."

"How about I join you?"

"If we do that, I'll have to take two showers." Lisa tried to play down Amy's question.

"All right, all right. You said you're tired."

Thank God. She finally took the hint.

They started for the bedroom. Amy stripped down to her bra and panties. Before she took them off, Lisa went into the bathroom and undressed there. She ran the water and tested it before stepping into the shower. She tried to clear her mind while she bathed. After she finished, Lisa entered the darkened bedroom. She grabbed a nightshirt from the dresser and put it on.

She sat gingerly on the edge of the bed. Amy was snoring softly. Lisa lay down, lightly touched Amy's back, and found she was wearing a nightshirt. Lisa didn't have the energy or the inclination to question why she felt only relief when her fingertips brushed against the cotton.

Chapter 18

While Amy was in Indianapolis, Lisa tried to set aside her personal life and focus on her job. Whenever she flashed back to Amy making love to her that first night, she pushed the image out of her mind.

Amy accompanied her to a girls' basketball game one night. A few teenagers straggled up the bleacher stairs and sat down in front of them. One of them, an athletic-looking girl, came up to get Amy's autograph.

"What's your name?" Amy asked the girl.

"Terri."

Amy signed her name on the program.

"I want... want to." The girl stopped and started. "I want to be like you, Amy."

"Yeah? Do you play softball or baseball?"

"I fought the athletic director and the school board to get on the boys' baseball team." The girl stood up straighter with the words.

"Good for you." Amy handed the program and pen back to the girl. "What's your last name?"

"Montgomery."

"Well, Terri Montgomery, I hope to see you featured on ESPN in the future. Keep holding onto the dream."

The girl blushed and mumbled her thanks. She stepped down in the bleachers to sit with her friends. They scooted forward to talk to her and giggled. A few minutes later, Terri turned back one last time and smiled at Amy.

"You have people reading your articles, Lisa." Amy gestured to the girls. "There's proof."

"I guess so, huh?" The only thing that mattered to Lisa was that Amy was getting recognition. She didn't care where the readers got their information, providing the story was accurate and well written.

The game ended. Amy remained in the bleachers while Lisa visited the respective locker rooms. She got her typical quotes from the coaches and players. Lisa had attended high school with one of the coaches and had played with her on the school's softball team.

After completing her interview, Lisa and the coach chatted a while about Amy and their own efforts to play on the boys' baseball team. Unlike Amy, they hadn't gotten the chance to argue their case with the school board. The athletic director shot it down before it even got that far.

Lisa was lost in thought as she walked through the locker room corridor, remembering things that she'd left in the past. She reentered the gymnasium.

Amy lifted her long legs off the metal bleacher in front of her and made her way down the steps. "What?" Amy asked when she got to the floor. "You're thinking about something."

"The coach and I were talking about how we tried to make the boys' baseball team and weren't allowed. I honestly had forgotten about all that." They started for the exit.

"I told you about the fight I had in getting them to go along with it."

"You'll inspire a lot of girls around the country, Amy, even the world. I don't know if you realize the impact you'll have," Lisa said as they reached the parking lot.

"I honestly haven't even thought about all that. Having that girl ask for my autograph made it hit home a little, but it won't really sink in until I'm playing on that field."

"It'll happen, and I'm not even sure you can prepare yourself for it." They were standing by Lisa's car. "Why don't I take you back to the apartment while I file my story?"

"Can you drop me off at that bar you go to? I want to shoot some pool. You can come down there when you're done."

"Okay." Lisa hadn't taken Amy to the Watering Hole since she'd arrived. She'd left Frankie's house early Christmas morning. Since that day, she and Frankie hadn't seen or talked to each other. Lisa didn't know if she was the only one who had felt the physical attraction that night. She also didn't know what she would do about it.

Lisa dropped Amy off at the bar and drove on to the newspaper office. She entered the sports room, found a free computer at an empty desk, and inputted her stats. She blocked out the conversations of the other sportswriters working around her and typed her article rapidly. After she proofed the copy, she saved the article and said goodnight to Jack in his office before leaving.

* * *

Lisa walked through the Watering Hole door and searched for Amy. She was at a pool table, playing a game with Stacy.

"Hey, Lisa. Your usual?" Billie asked.

"You got it."

Before Lisa could ask, Billie said, "Frankie's in the office going over receipts."

Lisa took a drink from her beer.

"And your woman's over at the pool tables kicking Stacy's ass," Billie said. "The only reason I know this is because Stacy keeps yelling, 'You're such a bitch.'"

They laughed.

"Lisa," Amy shouted, "please come over here and tell Stacy I'm not a bitch."

As Lisa neared their table, she said, "Stacy, Amy's not a bitch unless she's kicking your ass in pool."

"Hey." Amy playfully shoved Lisa.

Lisa took off her jacket, grabbed a cue, and chalked it. "Who am I playing? Whoever won the last game?"

"That'd be me," Amy said. "But why don't you and Stacy play?"

"You up for another ass-kicking, Stacy?"

"Bring it on, Collins."

"Bring it on? You actually said 'bring it on'?" Lisa strutted around the table to break.

Lisa and Stacy played a spirited game as Stacy and Amy talked. Stacy paid more attention to Amy than to her game, occasionally flipping her dark hair off her shoulders. Was she flirting with Amy?

They finished the game with Lisa coming out on top.

"Up for another?" Lisa asked Amy.

"No, I'm ready to call it a night."

Stacy looked disappointed.

Lisa and Amy went to the bar. Lisa was pulling on her jacket when Frankie stepped out of her office.

"Frankie, I don't know if I ever formally introduced you to Amy." Lisa turned to Amy. "Amy Perry, this is my best friend, Frankie Dunkin. She's the owner of Frankie's Watering Hole."

Frankie offered her hand. "Nice to finally meet you, Amy. You have no idea what it means to me and my friends to have you do what you're doing." She held onto Amy's hand, but Frankie's smile seemed forced.

"Thanks. Having Lisa's support has meant the world to me."

"Lisa's a very special person." Frankie's dark eyes focused on Lisa and not on Amy.

Lisa broke away from Frankie's gaze and noticed that Amy was staring at Frankie.

"You guys are coming here New Year's Eve, right?" Billie asked.

"I don't know," Lisa said. "I had planned for us to celebrate at my apartment."

Amy took Lisa's hand. "Oh, come on. It'll be fun. I'm flying back down to Sarasota on Monday and would like to have a special night with you before I leave. I even brought some dress clothes."

Lisa felt a pang of guilt after seeing the hopeful look on Amy's face. "I guess we'll be here."

"Good," Billie said. "Right, boss?"

"Right. Well, I need to get back to the receipts. Amy, nice to meet you. Good luck the rest of the way if I don't get a chance to talk to you again."

"Thanks. Will we see you Saturday night?"

"I'll be here, but I'll be busy making sure everything's running smoothly. We'll have dinners going and special drinks."

"Hell, Frankie, you make it sound sooo exciting," Billie said.

Frankie glared at Billie. "Sometimes you're such an ass."

Lisa caught Amy's eyes darting back and forth between Lisa and Frankie. There was an uncomfortable pause.

Lisa cleared her throat. "I think we'll be leaving now. Have a good night." Lisa and Amy neared the door.

"You, too," Billie said. "And don't do anything I wouldn't do, which pretty much means you two will have a hell of a night."

Lisa stiffened her back at the comment. They walked out the door.

Chapter 19

Lisa and Amy entered the Watering Hole at nine on New Year's Eve. The place was packed. Lisa guided them to their reserved table. They had decided they wouldn't have dinner there, only drinks, and would dance until midnight.

They each wore white tux shirts, black jackets, and black slacks. Amy received quite a few stares as they made their way to their table. Lisa could understand why. She was quite handsome with her tan even more pronounced against the white of her shirt.

Lisa looked for Frankie after they took their seats, but didn't see her.

"Want to dance?" Amy asked.

"Yeah. That'd be nice."

It was a fast dance. Lisa moved to the music with Amy. They waved at Stacy who was dancing with a blonde. Lisa kept her attention on the bar and on the office door, but still no Frankie.

They danced to a few more songs that ran together in a mix before Lisa decided she needed a break.

Stacy walked over to them. "Hi, you two."

"Hey," Amy said.

"Hi, Stacy. What happened to your date?" Lisa asked. The blonde had moved on to someone else.

"Oh, Cheryl? She's a friend. She called to ask if I'd be coming. I told her it wouldn't be too cool if I didn't come since I work here."

"Speaking of which…" Lisa was about to question the working arrangements for the evening.

"Billie and I are taking turns at the bar. We've asked everyone to go up there to get their drinks. We knew how many would be here based on the reservations."

Lisa turned to Amy. "Why don't you and Stacy dance a while? I'll grab us some beers."

Amy and Stacy went back out on the floor when another fast song started.

Approaching the bar, Lisa got a better view of Billie's attire. She was wearing a white tuxedo jacket. Instead of a regular tie, she had on a black T-shirt with a painted-on white bow tie and sewn-on sequined buttons.

"You're stylin', girl." Lisa shouted over the music.

Billie finished pouring a beer from the tap. She set the glass down on the bar where a brunette scooped it up. "You like?" She put her hands on her hips and did a spin.

"Smooth. You're too damn smooth."

"What can I get you?"

"A Foster's and a Michelob."

Billie popped the lid on Lisa's Michelob and poured the Foster's in a glass.

"Thanks," Lisa said while taking the beer. She glanced over to see Amy and Stacy still on the dance floor. She waited until Billie walked down to her again after mixing a couple of drinks. "Where's Frankie?"

"She was in earlier, but she had a headache. Said she'd try to get back by ten."

Lisa checked the time on the clock behind the bar. It was nine-thirty. She brought the beers to their table, and Amy came over from the dance floor.

"Thanks for the beer," Amy said.

"You're welcome."

"Where's Frankie?"

"Billie said she'd be in around ten."

Something behind Lisa drew Amy's attention. "Oh, she's here."

Lisa turned around to see Frankie walk through the front door. Lisa's heart skipped a beat at Frankie's appearance. She was wearing a full tux—black jacket, black slacks with satin stripes down the sides, a white tux shirt with cuff-links, and a black bow tie. She had gelled and spiked her salt-and-pepper hair.

Frankie waved at them, but to Lisa's disappointment, she didn't come over. She instead went to the bar where she had a few words with Billie and then disappeared downstairs.

"Wow," Amy shouted. "She looks sharp."

Lisa said nothing, but stared at the basement door.

"Let's finish our beers and do some more dancing," Amy said.

Lisa didn't reply.

"Lisa?"

"Sure." Lisa took her by the hand, and they stepped onto the dance floor again. Lisa noticed Frankie emerging from the basement carrying a case. She went behind the bar and restocked the liquor. Frankie took over filling drink orders, and Billie left to join a table of her friends.

"Do you want to go talk to her?" Amy yelled into Lisa's ear.

Lisa jerked at the question.

"I don't know. She seems busy."

"Go on over. I'm sure she has time for you."

Lisa thought she heard sarcasm behind Amy's words. Lisa ignored it and left for the bar. Amy danced toward Stacy and Cheryl.

Lisa waited for Frankie to approach her.

Frankie tilted her chin up at Lisa. "What do you need?" she asked.

"I wanted to tell you Happy New Year and... and... that you look fucking hot tonight." Lisa knew her face was bright red. *Oh, my God. Did I just say that?*

"Th-thanks, Leese. You look damn good yourself. Happy New Year."

Someone yelled from the end of the bar and interrupted the moment. Frankie left to take the drink order.

With the surge of customers, Billie rejoined Frankie to help. When Frankie started to put the bottle back on the shelf, she bumped into Billie. The bottle slipped out of her hand and shattered across the floor.

"Damn it!" Frankie leaned over and started picking up the glass.

Lisa hurriedly stepped behind the bar to help.

"Hey, you guys, don't do that," Billie said. "Let me get a broom before you cut yourself."

"Shit!" Frankie held up her hand. Blood dripped from her index finger. "Shit!"

Lisa snatched up a towel by the sink and wrapped it around Frankie's finger. "Come on. Let's go to your office so I can check this out."

"Lisa, it's a cut. It's not even that big."

"Stop arguing, and let's go."

Frankie relented, and they moved toward the office. "Get a mop to clean that up," Frankie said over her shoulder.

"Got it covered, boss." Billie brought a mop out from the back room. The overwhelming odor of ammonia overtook the strong smell of whiskey from the shattered bottle.

"Where's your first-aid kit?" Lisa asked, following Frankie into the office.

"Over there on the back shelf." Frankie sat down behind the desk.

Lisa opened the tin box. It held a small bottle of peroxide and some bandages. "Let me see."

"This really is no big deal." Frankie squirmed in her chair.

"Damn it, Frankie, give me your hand."

Frankie stuck out her hand for Lisa to inspect. Lisa gently unwrapped the towel. The bleeding had slowed, but there was a gash in the top part of Frankie's index finger. Lisa opened the bottle of peroxide.

"Put your hand over the wastebasket."

Frankie dutifully obeyed.

Lisa poured the peroxide on the cut. Frankie jerked, but Lisa kept hold of her hand.

"Damn, that stings."

"Don't be a baby. It'll help keep the infection out." The peroxide dried and the bleeding stopped. Lisa fumbled with a Band-Aid strip before freeing the bandage. She held onto Frankie's hand while carefully wrapping the Band-Aid around the cut.

"Here. Let me kiss it to make it all better," Lisa said with a smile. She brought Frankie's finger to her mouth and gently kissed the Band-Aid. She raised her eyes, and her heart jumped to her throat. Frankie was staring at her. Hard. Lisa's smile slowly faded, and she pulled her mouth away. She kept hold of Frankie's hand, but she could see that her own hands were trembling.

The office door swung open.

"Hey, boss, I was checking... oh, sorry." Billie stood in the doorway, her attention shifting from Lisa to Frankie. "Wanted to make sure you're okay."

Frankie shook free from Lisa's hands. "I'm fine. Like I said, it's only a cut. It wasn't worth all this fuss." She stood up, and Lisa joined her. Frankie brushed past her and Billie, who was still in the doorway.

Lisa felt Billie staring at her. She found her voice. "You know how she is. Never wants anyone to baby her." She quickly left the office. She rejoined Amy at their table.

"How's she doing?" Amy asked.

"What?"

"Frankie. I heard the bottle crash and saw she cut her hand."

"Oh that. She's fine. The cut's just a little one." She avoided meeting Amy's eyes.

Around eleven-thirty, they took to the dance floor again. Some slow songs filtered in between the techno music. Amy pulled Lisa close. Lisa allowed her body to press against Amy's, but didn't really feel the contact. She wished she could ask Frankie to dance to this music. Lisa could no longer see the bar. They spun back around, but Frankie's back was to her.

Lisa and Amy danced until almost midnight. Then everyone stopped to watch the big screen TV, tuned to the channel covering the ball falling in Times Square.

"Five... four... three... two... one... Happy New Year!" everyone yelled.

Amy touched her lips to Lisa's for a kiss. Lisa kissed her, but without passion.

After a few more dances, Lisa was ready to go. She forced herself to refrain from searching for Frankie again before they left the bar.

* * *

Amy pulled off Lisa's jacket and undid the top two buttons of her shirt.

Lisa took hold of her hands. "Do you mind if we go to bed? I'm really tired." She couldn't let Amy make love to her, just as she couldn't make love to Amy. Things had changed, and Lisa couldn't go back.

"What is it?" Amy asked with one hand on her hip.

"What?"

"You. What's wrong? You've been acting strange since I got here. And what's with Frankie?"

"I don't know what you mean." Lisa's face felt like it was on fire.

"You guys can't keep your eyes off each other."

Lisa was about to protest, but knew she had no excuses. "I'm not sure what's going on."

"Have you and she..."

"What? No, no, we haven't. For all I know, this is only me."

"Trust me, Lisa, the way she looks at you is more than just as a friend. There's a lot more to it. And you? You've never looked at me the way you look at her."

"I'm sorry. I never meant for this to happen. But since I've been away, I didn't realize how much I missed her. I didn't realize how much I…" Lisa swallowed. "I love her."

Amy's shoulders slumped and tears welled in her eyes. "At least you're honest now," she said hoarsely.

"I was honest before. This is all new to me. I never meant to hurt you. Never."

"And here I thought we'd be together while I'm in Chattanooga."

"I'll be there, Amy. That hasn't changed."

"That's where you're wrong. Everything has changed." Amy stalked off to the bedroom.

Lisa followed her.

"I'm going to take an earlier flight back to Florida," Amy said, haphazardly tossing clothes into her suitcase.

Lisa knew she should protest, but she also knew Amy was right. Lisa walked to the living room and fell onto the couch. She drew in a deep breath. She sat in the dark, waiting half an hour before going to the bedroom. The lights were off, and Amy was in bed, her back to the door. Lisa silently undressed, put on her nightshirt, and lay on the other side of Amy, careful not to let their bodies touch.

God, what a difference a couple of months made.

Chapter 20

Amy and Lisa stood outside the security area at the airport. Amy wouldn't meet Lisa's eyes.

"I want to be there for you," Lisa said. "I'll be working, but you'll still have my support."

"I need to get back to Florida and sort through all of this. Let's not talk about it now. We'll talk when you come down to Sarasota."

Amy's flight was announced for boarding. Amy lifted up her chin to acknowledge the call. "That's me."

They stood there uneasily. Finally, Lisa took a step toward Amy and gave her a quick, but tense hug. After Amy passed through security, she picked up her carry-on bag from the conveyor belt. She didn't turn around to acknowledge Lisa. Soon, she was obscured by others hurrying to their gates.

On her drive back to town, thoughts cascaded through Lisa's mind. She rubbed her forehead, trying to will her worries away. She didn't even remember exiting I-70 onto city streets and was oblivious as to how slow she was going.

A car full of teenage boys passed her. "Get it off the road, grandma!" one of the kids yelled out the window.

Lisa did just that. She pulled into an empty parking lot of an office building and sat there in the silence of her car.

* * *

Over the next couple of weeks, Lisa deduced that Frankie was avoiding her. Lisa would go to the Watering Hole only to have Frankie leave on an errand. Lisa called her, but would get her voice mail. She would pop over to Frankie's house, but Frankie wouldn't be there.

Lisa had a Thursday night off from covering the boys' and girls' high school basketball tourneys. She dropped by the Watering Hole to see if she could catch Frankie working.

She opened the door, and the typical, blaring music throbbed under her feet when she entered the bar. Billie was working frantically filling drink orders, her forehead glistening in sweat. Lisa scanned the bar and saw that Billie was alone. "Billie!"

Billie hurried over to Lisa. "Shit, man. Stacy's sick with the flu and couldn't make it tonight. Is there any way you can—"

Before she could finish, Lisa said, "I can work tonight. I'm not covering anything for the paper."

"Oh, thank God. You're a lifesaver."

"Where's Frankie?"

"She went downstairs to bring up more vodka. It's been crazy tonight."

"I'll go to the office and change."

Frankie was a stickler for employees to wear matching denim shirts with the Watering Hole logo, an embroidered image of a woman with a fishing pole, pulling a rainbow-colored fish from a pond. Lisa opened the door to the office and found the cardboard box where the shirts were stored. She had taken off her shirt and was standing there in her bra when Frankie walked in.

Frankie jumped back. "Oh, Lisa, I'm sorry. I didn't know you were in..." Her voice trailed off as her gaze dropped to Lisa's breasts. Her face reddened.

"I... uh... I need to get some register tape," Frankie stuttered. She walked to the file cabinet and opened the drawer, but kept her face turned away from Lisa.

Lisa fumbled with the shirt, dropped it, bent over to get it, and stood up.

Frankie closed the file drawer, turned, and ran right into Lisa, pinning her against the wall.

They stood there with their bodies pressed together in the cramped space. Lisa held the shirt to her chest like a security blanket. Frankie's body tightened against hers, and a surge of desire throbbed between Lisa's legs.

Oh, my God. This is real, and it's not going away. She tried to gauge Frankie's reaction.

Frankie pulled away. She hesitated, made a move toward Lisa, then quickly took a step back. It happened so fast, Lisa almost didn't catch it.

"I'd better get back out there with this." Frankie waved the cash register tape in her hand.

Lisa stepped forward. "Frankie."

Frankie started for the door with a pained expression on her face.

"Frankie, wait," Lisa said to her back, but Frankie didn't stop.

Lisa stood there with the shirt in her hands, her chest moving up and down with each deep breath she took. She put her arms through the sleeves of the denim shirt and deliberately buttoned it, trying to clear her mind and slow her breathing before she reentered the bar.

She pushed the door open. Frankie and Billie were taking the drink orders shouted their way, but Frankie's back was to the office. Lisa asked Billie where to take the four drinks that sat on the bar.

"It's that table back there," Billie shouted and pointed to four women in the corner.

Lisa put the drinks on a tray and hurried over to the table. "Here you go, ladies."

"You're new here, aren't you, love?" one of the women asked, leering at Lisa.

"No. I only fill in when they need help. One of the bartenders is out sick tonight."

"Honey, you can bring these to me all night long so I can watch your tight little ass on the way back to the bar." The cute brunette jiggled her drink in the air, causing it to splash onto the table.

Lisa blushed.

The bleached blonde at the table patted Lisa's arm. "Don't pay Molly any mind. She's just drunk and horny." The crowd at the table burst out laughing.

Lisa hurried away and bussed a nearby table. Although she was busy, her mind was on Frankie. Everything came back to her like frames in a movie. *I'm so damn clueless.*

"Hey! Hey!" A thin woman with dark curly hair grabbed Lisa's arm.

Lisa jerked.

"Didn't you hear me?" The woman scowled at Lisa.

"I'm sor—"

"Don't be sorry. We need four more Miller Lites." The woman went back to talking to her friends.

Lisa carried the tray up to the bar. "Four Miller Lites." Billie hurriedly popped the lids on the four beers and plopped them on the tray.

Lisa stared down at Frankie at the end of the bar. Look at me, Lisa silently pleaded. Turn around and look at me. As though

Frankie had heard her, she turned and faced Lisa.

Lisa didn't hear the music. She didn't hear the din of the room. She didn't hear anything. She felt she was seeing Frankie—really seeing Frankie—for the first time.

"Yo. The beers are there on your tray, man."

Lisa didn't move.

"Lisa!"

Lisa finally realized Billie was yelling at her. "Sorry." She picked up the tray and took the beers to the women.

Davey sang his first song of the night. The next singer followed. The music blared through the speakers and seeped into her brain. The edge of a headache that had plagued her earlier blossomed into a full-blown migraine. But she didn't want to leave Frankie and Billie to handle the crowd at the Watering Hole alone. Billie joined her, taking orders on the floor while Frankie stayed behind the bar.

Lisa lost count of how many trips she made back and forth to the bar. She also lost count of how many times her butt had been pinched and smacked while she passed by the tables full of women. Given the pain she was in, if another woman touched her, Lisa was going to slap her upside the head.

Lisa gave Frankie the drink orders, but Frankie wouldn't meet her gaze. She mixed the drinks, poured the beers from the tap, or popped the lids on the bottles, all without looking her in the eye.

Lisa came to the bar with a tray full of empty glasses to fill another drink order. She plunked the tray down, causing the glasses to crash into each other. She rested her elbow on the bar and rubbed her forehead.

"Leese, are you okay?" Frankie asked with a furrowed brow. She placed more drinks on Lisa's tray.

"Mostly."

"One of your headaches?"

Lisa nodded and winced at the pain shooting through her temple.

"Why don't you go home?"

"No. I can't leave you guys tonight."

"Lisa..."

"I need to deliver these drinks. These women are vicious tonight." She walked away before Frankie could argue with her. Thinking about Frankie and her feelings only added to the pain in her head. What it was doing to her heart would have to wait until she could sort it all out.

Thankfully, Frankie announced last call. Lisa picked up the final orders and took them to the tables. She had gotten decent tips for the night. Some of the women had tucked the bills into Lisa's front jeans pockets, allowing their fingers to roam freely. Lisa had glared at them and quickly stepped away.

The bar emptied out at one. Clearing the tables, she vaguely wondered if any of these women had day jobs.

She took another tray full of glasses up to the bar. Frankie was there to take it from her. Their fingers touched in the transfer of the tray. Despite the pain throbbing in Lisa's temples, she couldn't ignore the warmth that coursed through her body at the touch. Frankie dumped the glasses in the sink and came back to Lisa.

"Go home. Please."

"Okay." Lisa wasn't going to argue anymore. She stumbled on her way to the office to get her jacket when another pain shot over her left eye.

Frankie must have noticed. "I'll follow you home to make sure you're okay."

"You don't have to, Frankie."

"This is where I say don't argue with me. And this is much more serious than a damn cut finger."

Lisa's head and body hurt too much to object.

"Billie, I'll be right back after I make sure Lisa gets home."

"No problem, boss." Billie was emptying ashtrays and wiping down tables.

Light snow greeted them upon stepping outside. Lisa took in a deep breath to try to ease the pain. Frankie followed her to the apartment. Lisa adjusted her rearview mirror to deflect the truck's headlights behind her. She stepped out of her car and told Frankie, "I can make it into the apartment from here."

Frankie stared at her.

Lisa held her hand up in the way of an apology for even suggesting such a thing. After the ride up in the elevator, Frankie followed Lisa into her living room.

"Really, I'm all right. I..." Another sharp pain pierced Lisa's skull like a knife. The familiar, lurching sensation slammed into the pit of her stomach. She sprinted to the bathroom and made it to the toilet right before she threw up. She stayed on her knees for a long time until the nausea subsided. Since she hadn't eaten anything since lunch, there wasn't much to come up. But it didn't help the queasiness in her stomach. She gagged a few more times.

She moaned, leaning onto her forearm, and feeling the cold porcelain under her fingers that gripped the commode. Eventually, her stomach quieted down enough for her to attempt standing up.

"You all right?" Frankie's muffled voice came through the closed door.

"Yeah." Lisa's throat was burning. She ran cold water at the sink, brushed her teeth, splashed her face a few times, and toweled off. She took one of her prescription pills for migraines. She downed the pill quickly with water, trying to avoid the nausea again.

Lisa came out of the bathroom. Frankie had already pulled back the covers on the bed. She hadn't switched on the lamp by the bed, but the streetlight reflecting off the snow outside the window cast a soft white glow in the room. Lisa turned off the bathroom light and got to the bed.

"Come on, Leese, let me help you out of your clothes," Frankie said gently, holding out her hand.

Those words would have been so welcome to Lisa at any other time, but tonight, Frankie was only there to nurse her.

Lisa sat down on the edge of the bed and fumbled with the top buttons of the denim shirt.

"Just unbutton it enough to slip it off," Frankie said. After Lisa undid the top two buttons, Frankie tugged the shirt off, and their eyes met. Frankie slowly rose up.

"Frankie." Lisa tried to stand, but stayed seated when a wave of dizziness washed over her.

"Easy."

Frankie spoke the word with such kindness that it brought Lisa to tears. She took hold of Frankie's hand. "We need to talk," she whispered.

Frankie squeezed her hand. "Yes, we do, but right now you need to sleep."

"But..."

"Shh." Frankie gently pushed her back on the bed. She slipped Lisa's jeans off her without speaking and brought the covers up to her chin. "I'll let you take care of the rest later." She left the bed for a moment.

The throbbing pulsed through Lisa's temples, and she prayed that the medicine would kick in soon. She heard Frankie beside her again and felt a cool, wet cloth over her eyes.

"This should help some. Try to sleep. I'll stay with you tonight."

Lisa lifted the washcloth. "You will?"

"Yes. I'll call Billie and ask her to close." Frankie put the cloth back over Lisa's eyes. "Now rest."

The pain eased with the coolness of the wet cloth and the knowledge that Frankie was staying. "Thank you, Frankie." The last sound Lisa heard was of the door creaking shut.

Chapter 21

Sunlight filtered through the slats of the shades in Lisa's bedroom. She woke up with her head buried beneath a pillow. She tossed the pillow aside, propped herself up on her elbows, and squinted at the bright light, slowly taking it in. The covers were twisted tightly around her legs. Trying to untangle them, she quickly became frustrated. She reached down and yanked them off with one swift tug.

The last time she woke up like this, she was hung over from a rowdy night of drinking. She lay back on the bed, stretched, and attempted to focus on the digital numbers of the bedside clock. Jesus. Ten-thirty.

She remembered that Frankie had told her she was staying overnight. She picked up her jeans and the Watering Hole staff shirt from where they lay folded neatly on a chair in the corner. She went to the bathroom and then slipped into her clothes before entering the living room. Frankie was on the couch, her elbow against the arm with her chin on her fist, apparently lost in thought.

Frankie finally looked up. "How are you feeling this morning?"

Lisa sat down on the couch beside her. "Better. Thanks for taking care of me last night and for staying."

"You don't need to thank me."

Lisa took a deep breath. "Frankie, I need to tell you how I've been feeling. About us."

"You don't need to, Leese. I know you're with Amy."

Lisa was startled at how forcefully Frankie said the words. "No, I'm not. Things pretty much ended between us the night before she left. I'm hoping she and I can still be friends, but I know Amy needs some time to think things over. And..." Lisa stopped. "God, I'm babbling. I'm sorry."

She took Frankie's hand.

"When I went down to Arizona, I didn't know exactly where things were going with Amy. I didn't know until I was there that we'd start a relationship." She waited for Frankie's reaction, but Frankie offered none. "And I also didn't know how much I'd miss you when I was there. I came back here, and in the two months that I hadn't seen Amy, it made me realize how much I..." Lisa swallowed. "How much I love you, Frankie. I've always loved you, but this is different. I know now that I'm in love with you."

Frankie took a few seconds before she spoke. "I don't know how to tell you this." Her lower lip trembled. "Since my break-up with Sherri and my mastectomy, I haven't dated a lot of women." She gave a harsh laugh. "I've been on a lot of first dates. The truth is that I've been afraid of intimacy."

"Frankie."

"No, let me finish." Frankie jumped to her feet and went to the window. She kept her back to Lisa. "Sherri promised me over and over how she'd be there for me during the surgery and the recovery afterward, through the chemo. Through everything. She said how much she loved me." Frankie took in a shaky breath. "I found out later she was seeing a friend of ours. It was after the surgery when I started chemo." Frankie spun around to face Lisa. "I should have known. When she saw the scar..." Frankie's voice broke.

Lisa hurried over to her. "I'm so sorry." She took Frankie into her arms, and held her while her shoulders shook with sobs. "I'm so sorry, Frankie."

Frankie let Lisa hold her for a while, but then ended the embrace. "The look on Sherri's face..." Lisa saw the pain that Frankie tried to conceal from everyone around her. "It was disgust. She was disgusted. She tried to hide it, but it was obvious what she really thought. It wasn't long after that she started seeing Mel. She moved out during my first round of treatment."

Lisa had never hit someone else in anger, but at that exact moment, she wanted to hurt Sherri.

She lifted her hand to Frankie's cheeks and gently wiped away her tears. Frankie leaned her face against Lisa's palm for a moment. Lisa edged closer, but Frankie broke away.

"I can't, Lisa." The same anguish returned to Frankie's face that Lisa had seen in her office the night before. "I love you. I fell in love with you not long after we met. But I was afraid to tell you."

"Oh, Frankie."

"It was never an age thing for me. Never. It was this." Frankie put her hand on her chest. "How could you possibly love me? How could you possibly want to make love to me?" Frankie struggled with her breath, her cries becoming more ragged. "And when you started seeing Amy, I knew then there wasn't a chance."

"Oh, God." Lisa again took a step toward Frankie.

"No," Frankie cried. "Can't you see? Can't you see what I'm trying to tell you?"

This time, Lisa wouldn't let Frankie stop her. She stepped forward until she was within inches of Frankie and took her face in her hands. "I love you. I love everything about you. Everything. Do you understand?"

Frankie still seemed doubtful. Lisa wanted to erase the doubt, but wasn't sure how. So, she did what felt natural. She pressed her lips to Frankie's and kissed her gently. Lisa slowly pulled away and caressed Frankie's face.

"What about the intimacy?" Frankie whispered. "You're saying this now, but you don't know how you'll feel later."

Lisa kissed her again, and Frankie relaxed against her body.

"What I do know is I've been a fool these past five years. You're my best friend. We've already worked through the hard stuff. A lot of couples never have what we already share. Do you know that? I'm ready to love you in every way I can with everything I am. But if we need to take this slow, we will. I can wait on the physical part."

Frankie didn't seem as uncertain now. Then her face clouded over. "What about Amy? She needs you. This won't be easy for her."

"I know it won't be. I'll do my best to be there for her, but as her friend. I'll talk with her when I go down to Florida. Don't worry about that." She ran her fingertips over Frankie's cheek. "I know I've always loved you. But now I've fallen in love with you. And I can't go back. I don't want to go back." Her voice broke. "Please, please don't ask me to."

Frankie pulled Lisa close, and they shared another tender kiss. Frankie smiled. "I won't."

* * *

The night before Lisa was to leave for Sarasota, Frankie came over and visited with her while she packed. Lisa placed her clothes in her suitcase, but stopped when she saw Frankie's sad expression. Lisa knelt between Frankie's legs and leaned her elbows on Frankie's knees.

"Do you know how much I'll miss you?" Lisa asked as she looked up to meet Frankie's dark brown eyes glistening with tears.

"I think so."

"I'm not going back to Amy. You do know that, don't you?"

Frankie nodded slightly.

Lisa ran her hand across Frankie's thigh. "I love you. I told you I can't go back to just being your friend, and I meant it. I want to show you how much I love you, but I'll wait until you're ready. I want to spend the rest of my life with you, as your best friend and your lover." She kissed Frankie. "I'm not Sherri."

Frankie grabbed Lisa and held her tight. "I'm sorry. It's that…"

"I know. You don't need to explain." Lisa squeezed Frankie's shoulders.

In the morning, Frankie took Lisa to the airport. She drove up to the passenger drop-off and helped Lisa get her luggage out of the truck. She held Lisa for a lengthy embrace. "Call me when you get there. I love you."

God, that was so good to hear. "Love you, too, Frankie." Lisa reluctantly withdrew from Frankie's arms and pushed through the automatic doors. She turned one last time to catch a glimpse of Frankie still standing by her truck and then started for the counter to get her boarding pass.

* * *

The bright Florida sun felt good on Lisa's skin. She stood curbside at the airport, waiting for the shuttle to take her to her rental car. She slipped her sunglasses on and was glad she had dressed lightly in a short-sleeved cotton shirt and khakis.

Lisa felt someone staring at her. There was a tan blonde in shorts and a T-shirt peering at Lisa over the top of her magazine. Their eyes met briefly. The blonde quickly went back to reading. Lisa couldn't resist a half smile. Must be the local lesbian greeting committee. She flipped her cell phone open, dialed Frankie's number, and left a message when it clicked over to voice mail.

The shuttle dropped her off to pick up her rental. She drove to the hotel to check in, knowing she couldn't make it to the ballpark in time to catch the day's practice session. She slipped on some shorts and a tank top and stretched out in a poolside lounge chair. While the sun baked down on her, she replayed in her mind all that had happened in the past few days. She drifted into that dream state when all the images from the day somehow swirled into one before she succumbed to sleep.

She awakened at six-thirty and tried Amy's cell number.

"Yeah?"

Okay, I deserved that tone of voice. "Can we talk?" There was a long pause. "Amy?"

"Yeah, I guess. Come on over." Amy gave her directions from the hotel to her apartment.

With trepidation, Lisa knocked on the door.

Amy, dressed in a Cincinnati Reds T-shirt and baggy gray shorts, opened it and stared at her, then moved aside to allow Lisa to enter. "Have a seat," Amy said and joined her on the couch.

There was a long, clumsy silence. Then they both talked at once.

"Amy, I'm sorry—"

"I know you didn't—"

"You go first," Amy said.

"I'm sorry I've hurt you. I didn't see this thing with Frankie coming. I was away from her those weeks, and when I got back, it hit me."

"I won't lie to you, Lisa, it does hurt. It'll take some getting used to this new you and me now." Amy's eyes were wet with unshed tears. "But you and Frankie? I suspect you've had these feelings long before I entered the picture. I guess it takes someone else to come into our lives to help us realize where our heart was all along." She stared at her feet. "I only wish it'd been me."

"I know it isn't the same, but I'll still be in Chattanooga to support you anyway I can. Don't doubt that, Amy." Lisa patted her leg for encouragement.

"I'll try not to."

"How are things going here so far?"

"Hang on while I recover from the whiplash," Amy said with a grin.

"What?"

"From the change in subject."

"Oh, well..."

"Baseball. You're right. Baseball's a safe thing to talk about. Since I got here, I've learned more about the fundamentals than I thought was possible. I learned a lot during the winter down here, but this is even more intense. Most of the guys are assholes. Only difference between here and Arizona is some of them are assholes with money." She gave a sarcastic laugh.

"I'm sorry I missed the first few practice sessions. I had to finish covering the girls' basketball tourney this last weekend."

"They haven't let me slack off any, that's for sure. Murphy told me I'll be batting sixth while I'm here. It's a good spot for me in the line-up. Not too much pressure, and I can get some RBIs."

"I'm glad the Reds did the right thing and hired Max Murphy."

"Yeah, he's a good manager."

They talked until almost ten, finishing off a couple of Cokes as they caught up on things. Amy stretched and yawned.

"I think that's my cue to leave," Lisa said. She stood and Amy accompanied her to the door. Before Lisa put her hand on the doorknob, Amy spoke.

"Frankie's a lucky woman."

Lisa's throat tightened at the comment. "I'm the lucky one. I have her as my partner, but I hope I still have you as my friend." She waited a couple of heartbeats for Amy's answer.

"Like I said. It'll take some getting used to, but we can give it a try."

"That's all that I ask." Lisa stepped out into the warm air. "I'll catch you tomorrow at the ballpark."

Lisa took a couple of steps.

"Hey, Lisa?"

Lisa stopped and turned.

"Thanks for being honest with me."

"You deserve it."

Amy quietly shut the door.

*   *   *

Lisa entered her hotel room, feeling her cell phone vibrate at her side. Frankie's name registered in the display.

"Hey." She fell back onto the mattress and grabbed another pillow to prop herself up.

"Sorry I didn't answer earlier. Today's supply day here. We had some mix-ups on our orders and what the guy brought us."

"It's good to hear from you. I miss you already."

"Miss you, too." Frankie didn't say anything for a few seconds. "Did you get to talk to Amy?"

Lisa could hear the worry in her voice. "Yeah, we talked."

"How'd it go?"

"It wasn't easy, not that I really expected it to be."

"How does she feel about us?"

"Not exactly doing backflips over that bit of news."

Frankie chuckled. "No, I guess not, huh?"

"Uhh... no."

"But she understands she has your friendship and support?"

"Absolutely."

"As long as she knows it's only friendship." There was a slight edge to Frankie's voice.

"Trust me, she knows."

There was silence on Frankie's end.

"You do trust me, don't you, Frankie?"

"It's not you I'm worried about," Frankie answered.

"It'll be okay. Like she said to me, it'll take some getting used to." Lisa tried to stifle a yawn.

"You should get to bed. You've had a long, tough day."

"You're right about that." Lisa stretched out her legs. "I'm going to strip down and climb under these sheets. I'll be home soon enough. I can't wait to take you in my arms and kiss you again."

"Me, too. They'll give you a break before she starts the season, right?"

"I've already talked to Sean. He knows I'm taking a couple of weeks off before Amy reports to Chattanooga. I won't need to be there until the first game."

"Good. I didn't want to have to fly to New York and have a little discussion with your baby editors."

Lisa laughed. "I could see you doing that, too. God, I love you. You're so good for me."

"We're good for each other."

Lisa yawned again.

"We really do need to get off the phone," Frankie said. "Sweet dreams."

"If you're in them, they'll be sweet enough for me." At first, Lisa thought she had lost her signal when there wasn't a response. "Frankie?"

"You know just what to say," Frankie said in a throaty whisper.

Lisa swallowed to stave off the tears. "I love you."

"Love you, too."

* * *

Lisa stepped onto the field with the other reporters and waved at Max. He was beaming like a kid with a shiny new bicycle.

"How the hell are ya, Lisa?"

"Max, it's good to see you. I was thrilled when I heard you were named skipper for this team."

"Thanks. Got my work cut out for me, but I wouldn't want to be anywhere else. I'm ready to manage this group, but I'll have to make some tough decisions in the coming weeks. That's the part of the job I don't like."

"How do you see this year going?" She watched the team warm up. Amy was tossing a ball with a player who was maybe in his early twenties. A few players from the Indians roster were on the field, but not many veterans. The Reds were definitely in a rebuilding year.

"What do you think?" Max asked, gesturing to his team. "Don't you agree we'll be a bit on the young side?"

A stray ball dribbled to Lisa's feet. She tossed it back to the second baseman while continuing to listen to Max.

"But I've worked with a lot of these kids. They know me, and I know them. That'll help." He nodded in Amy's direction. "Guess you're here for her."

"Yeah, there's just a little interest." Lisa motioned to the other reporters.

"She worked on a lot of stuff with the guys down here over the winter, and she hasn't let up since camp broke last week. She's impressed the hell out of me. I don't know if it's because she's a woman about to make history or because she loves the work. It's probably a little of both."

"I think you're right. How do you see her abilities?"

"You know, I saw her play in Indianapolis. She was good, but was it just one great night? Then I kept track of how she did in Arizona and went to some games. I also checked with the coaches to see how she did this winter." He shifted his attention to Amy and then turned back to Lisa. "Seeing her in practice this past week or so?" He shook his head. "She's got it all. The good thing is Amy knows she'll be sent down to Chattanooga's camp in a couple of weeks, and she understands the reasons. It's one less trip inside my office to break the bad news. The really good news is next time I see her, it'll be in the Show. It may not be until September, but I know she'll make it this year."

"Listen, I'll let you get back to work. I'll be here until Amy's sent to Chattanooga's camp."

"Enjoy the sun and the games. I'm always around to talk."

"Thanks, Murph. Again, I'm glad the Reds finally got smart and hired you." She stuck out her hand.

Murphy grasped it in a firm handshake. "Thanks, Lisa."

"Good luck."

Max rejoined his coaches. Lisa watched Amy work out. Someone called to her from behind.

"Hey, Collins." Sarah approached her.

"Swift, we have to quit meeting like this."

Sarah laughed and then gestured toward Amy. "She keeps moving up, huh?"

"She doesn't give them much choice."

"How was your winter?" Sarah asked.

"Technically, it's still winter."

"Oh, shut up. You know what I mean."

"It was good. Yours?"

"You're a piece of work, you know that?"

Lisa folded her arms across her chest. "I've been told that from time to time."

The team was practicing the fundamentals, hitting the cutoff, perfecting the rundown, and bunting. Lisa and Sarah talked about baseball in general and who they felt would be tough that year, including the pitching and hitting strengths of each major league team.

The afternoon ended, and they made plans to get together for lunch the next day. One more practice session remained before the first game of spring training. Lisa wondered who was more anxious to see Amy hit against major league pitchers, she or Murphy and the rest of the Reds organization.

Chapter 22

Lisa sat down next to Sarah in the press box. She couldn't suppress her pride in seeing Amy, dressed in a full Reds uniform, trot out to first for warm-ups with the infielders. Without the Solar Sox hat from the Arizona Fall League, she looked that much more like a big league ballplayer. The red hat with the white "C" stitched on the front polished off the image perfectly.

The Reds scored two runs against the Marlins starter in the bottom of the third. The Marlins scored twice in the top of the sixth to tie it. Amy came up in the bottom of the sixth, hitless in her first two at-bats. She had struck out and grounded out to the first baseman. There was a runner on second with no outs. Would Amy go for the hit or play fundamental baseball and move the runner to third?

The Marlins reliever threw the first two pitches for strikes on the inside corner of the plate. Amy glanced back at the umpire on the last call, but she didn't argue. She stepped out of the box, unsnapped and snapped her batting gloves and settled back in. The next pitch was a high fastball off the outside part of the plate, a clear ball. But Amy adjusted her swing and hit it deep between the first and second baseman. The second baseman quickly recovered and threw her out at first, but the runner moved over to third on the play. A sacrifice fly would score him.

Max slapped Amy on the back when she came down the dugout steps. Only a couple of her teammates came over and gave her high fives, and they weren't veterans on the team. She was 0-for-3, but accomplished what she needed to do to get the runner in with less than two outs. The next batter hit a deep sacrifice fly to score the runner from third.

The score remained 3-2 in the bottom of the eighth. Amy came to bat again, this time with runners on second and third. The count was 2-0 after two inside pitches. The next pitch was on the outside corner of the plate. Amy went with the pitch and lined it down the first baseline. It barely hooked foul. She trotted back toward the plate, took the bat from the batboy, and stepped back in. The pitcher toed the rubber, checked the runners, reared back, and fired a high and tight fastball aimed right at her head. She fell away from the pitch and landed flat on her back. The pitcher stepped off the mound and stared in at Amy while he rubbed up the baseball. She stood, dusted herself off, and got right back into the batter's box.

His next pitch was a slow curve on the outside part of the plate. Amy went with it and lined the ball just out of the reach of the leaping first baseman down the right field line, scoring both runners. She slid into second well ahead of the tag from the second baseman. She got to her feet and dusted herself off again. The pitcher stepped behind the mound to retrieve the rosin bag, bouncing it up and down on his pitching hand. He glared at Amy. Amy slapped her hands together, causing little puffs of dirt to fly up, and glared right back at him.

"Guess knocking her down wasn't too smart," Sarah said.

"Nope."

The game ended with the Reds on top 5-2. Lisa followed the rest of the reporters down the steps. At times, it felt like a parade: up to the press box, down to the clubhouse, and back to the press box again. She interviewed Max and a few of the players about the game and their impressions of Amy. Max was happy. Most of the players Lisa interviewed expressed indifference.

Lisa stood with the group of reporters surrounding Amy. She asked her about giving up a chance for a hit in order to move the runner to third.

"That's part of winning baseball." Amy pointed at another reporter for the next question.

* * *

The days flew by like they often did when Lisa covered the game she loved. Two weeks later, the Reds announced that Amy would report to Chattanooga's camp.

Lisa called her and asked if she could take her to dinner. Amy hesitated, but agreed.

* * *

The waiter handed them their menus. "This is on me tonight,"

Lisa said.

"No argument from me. I'm not exactly rolling in money."

"Yet." Lisa checked out her menu.

Amy stared at her for a long moment. "It's good to know you still believe in me."

"Of course I believe in you. You're that damn good."

They talked about baseball. Amy settled back into the booth and munched on the peanuts the waiter had placed on their table. She told Lisa what Murphy and the coaches had asked her to work on in Chattanooga.

"They want me to pull the ball unless the situation calls for me to hit the other way or if the ball's on the outer half of the plate. They have a lot of confidence in my power. Or at least they're confident I'll hit a hell of a lot of doubles."

"I agree with them. I saw that power with that 300-foot fly ball you hit in the first practice I attended. We all know that doubles eventually lead to homers, right? It's the progression of a good hitter." Lisa reached over and grabbed a handful of peanuts. "And you're the very definition of a good hitter."

Amy smiled. "Thanks."

The waiter arrived with their meals, and conversation shifted to other topics. After they finished dinner, Lisa drove Amy back to her apartment. They pulled into the complex and talked a while in Lisa's parked car.

"I guess I'd better get in and pack my stuff," Amy said. "I'm leaving in the morning with a few of the guys. After camp breaks, I'm flying back home to pick up my car for the summer."

"Then I'll see you on April fifth, the day before your opening game in Chattanooga."

Amy chewed on her lower lip and didn't make any move toward leaving the car.

Lisa took Amy's hand. "You'll be fine, Amy. I told you before, you shouldn't ever doubt that."

The light cast by the streetlamp captured the worry in Amy's eyes. "You think so?" Her voice was shaky.

Lisa squeezed her hand. "I know so." She tried to convey her reassurance in her touch.

"I'll see you in a couple of weeks, right?"

"Right."

Amy leaned across the gearshift to hug Lisa before getting out. Lisa lowered her head to be able to see Amy, who held on to the open door. "Take care, Amy."

"You, too."

Lisa waited until Amy made it safely into her apartment and then started the drive back to her hotel. She thought about the past months and all that had happened to Amy, to Frankie, and to her. Mainly, her thoughts drifted back home and to a certain bar owner.

*   *   *

Lisa spotted Frankie across the security ropes at the airport. She was hopping up to peer above the passengers' heads. Lisa cleared the security area, and Frankie greeted her with one of her bear hugs.

"It's good to have you home. I've missed you so much," Frankie said.

"Missed you, too."

"How's Amy doing?" Frankie asked after releasing her and helping with her bags.

Lisa shot a glance over at her.

"What?" Frankie asked.

"I know Amy isn't necessarily one of your favorite topics."

"I can wish her well in baseball, even if I don't wish her well where you're concerned."

Lisa playfully bumped shoulders with Frankie.

As they crossed the walkway to the parking garage, they dodged the shuttles darting in to pick up passengers. They act like they're on a mission from God, Lisa thought while stepping into the safety of Frankie's truck.

"You really have two whole weeks here before you go to Tennessee?" Frankie asked. "I know I keep asking, but I don't trust your baby editors sometimes."

"Yes. The whole two weeks."

"Good." Frankie tapped her thumb on the steering wheel. "Hey, do you want to come over for dinner tonight? I'm taking off early from the bar."

"You never take off early."

"I do now that you're here."

A warm tingle ran through Lisa's body.

"I'd love to come over. Do I need to bring anything?"

"Nope. I already know what I'm fixing. How does spaghetti and meatballs sound?"

"Like I'll be having seconds."

* * *

They arrived in front of the apartment building and jumped down from the truck cab at the same time.

"I can get my luggage myself," Lisa said.

"I swear if you tell me that one more time when I drop you off, I'll..."

"You'll what?"

"I'll show you when we get upstairs."

After stepping off the elevator, Frankie picked up Lisa's suitcase, and Lisa carried her laptop case. She unlocked the door, and Frankie took the suitcase to the bedroom. Lisa set the laptop down on the table and flipped through the mail she had retrieved on her way through the lobby. She looked up again to find Frankie leaning against the hallway wall, arms folded, staring at her intently.

"Something wrong?" Lisa asked.

"I told you I'd show you when we got up here." Frankie came to the table and took the mail from Lisa's hands. She brushed her lips against Lisa's and dipped her tongue into her mouth.

Lisa pushed her tongue against Frankie's. She put her hand to the back of Frankie's neck and tugged her even closer. She moaned as desire coursed through her body. The kiss lasted for a while longer before Frankie drew away.

Lisa tried to catch her breath. "God, Frankie, you can kiss."

Frankie pecked her cheek and playfully tapped Lisa's nose with her index finger.

"That's because you're kissing the right woman." Frankie backed up toward the door. "Dinner tonight's at six."

"I'll be there."

Lisa tried to slow down her breathing after Frankie left. She opened her laptop and punched the power button. As she waited for it to power up, she ran her fingertips across her lips. When she started writing her article about Amy's promotion to Chattanooga, she couldn't keep her mind on what she wanted to say.

Dinner with Frankie seemed much more interesting than baseball.

* * *

The door swung open, and Lisa handed Frankie a bottle of wine.

"You didn't need to bring anything."

"I wanted to, and I remembered the wine from Christmas Eve."

Frankie flipped the bottle around and checked the label. "You sure did. This was too much."

"I wanted to do something special, and I knew you liked it."

Frankie gave her a quick kiss. "It's perfect. I'll shut up now and say thank you."

"You're welcome."

Frankie walked toward the kitchen. "Take off your coat and make yourself at home. Dinner's almost ready."

Lisa hung her coat in the closet.

Frankie hollered from the kitchen. "Why don't you get a fire going since it's freezing outside?"

"You got that right," Lisa said while entering the den. "I left temperatures in the low eighties for this shit."

"All the more reason for a fire."

Lisa started the fire and stoked it with the poker until she heard Frankie's call from the kitchen.

"Dinner's ready!"

Lisa stepped into the kitchen and lifted the lid off the pan that held the thick sauce. "Smells wonderful."

"You've had my spaghetti and meatballs lots of times."

"Yeah, but I can still say the sauce smells wonderful. I'm beyond hungry."

"Then get yourself in there, sit down, pour us some wine, and I'll bring you your dinner."

"You don't have to tell me twice."

Lisa opened the wine and poured two glasses. Frankie had changed the seating arrangement to make it more intimate. Frankie's chair was at the head of the table, but Lisa was to her left rather than at the opposite end. As they had done on Christmas Eve, lit tapered candlesticks adorned the center.

Frankie brought the food out. "Don't be shy. Eat all you want."

"I'd like to make a toast first," Lisa said. She picked up her glass, and Frankie raised hers. "This time, let's toast to starting a new chapter of a long and lasting relationship, one full of love and laughter." Lisa held her glass up higher. "To my life partner."

Frankie blinked away her tears as she clinked glasses with Lisa.

Over dinner, they talked about work. They also discussed how often they could get together while Lisa was in Chattanooga. They decided it'd be easier for Frankie to travel down to Tennessee on occasion. There would rarely be a break in the Lookouts schedule long enough for Lisa to make it home.

Frankie stood, and Lisa picked up her plate to help her clear the table.

"No. You go rack 'em up, and let me do this. I'll be there in a few."

Lisa took a step toward the den.

"Take the wine in there, and we'll finish it," Frankie said.

Lisa picked up the bottle and carried her glass with her. After pouring another full glass, she set the bottle down. She took a long drink before moving to the pool table. Frankie came in shortly after Lisa had racked the balls.

"Time to give you another lesson in how to win at pool." Frankie chalked her cue and leaned over to break.

"How was it decided that you get to break?"

Frankie stared up at her. "I fixed dinner."

"Ah. I see. Proceed then." Lisa took another sip of wine.

Frankie hit the cue ball and scattered the balls. A stripe dropped in.

"Might as well chill out over there and savor your wine."

"Just play, Ms. Dunkin."

By the time Frankie missed a shot, Lisa had nearly polished off the rest of the bottle. She didn't realize how tipsy she was until she bent over the table for her first shot.

"Damn, what kind of wine is that again?"

"It's not the wine, Lisa. It's how fast you drink it."

"Now you tell me." Lisa drew her cue back and muffed her first shot.

Frankie jumped to her feet. "Well, hell, if I'd known that all it took was a little wine to knock you off your game, I'd have plied you with it long ago."

Lisa saluted her with her glass before draining the rest of the wine.

Frankie finished the game in less than two minutes. She bit her lip, motioning toward the couch. "Do you maybe want to sit down now?"

"I'm fine." Lisa was unsuccessful in her attempt to put her cue in a slot.

Frankie stepped behind her and took it from her hand.

"Allow me, m'lady."

Lisa teetered to the couch, and Frankie followed. Lisa leaned her head against the cushion.

"You all right?"

"Yeah. Let me get my bearings here for a minute." Lisa swung her head toward Frankie. "I want you to know I'm not drunk."

"Whatever you say."

"Seriously. Don't go telling the gang at the Watering Hole that Lisa Collins got schnockered on wine. I'd never hear the end of it. Besides, I'm fine."

"Right."

"Are you patronizing me?"

"No."

"'Cause it sounds like you are."

"Never."

"Good. I'm glad we've got that settled."

Frankie's body shook beside her, causing the cushion of the couch to move with each tremble.

"Oh, go ahead, Frankie. I know you're trying to hold it in."

Frankie laughed raucously. "You're so cute on wine, do you know that?"

Lisa turned to face her. "I hope you know you can't have your way with me just because I'm a tiny bit tipsy."

Frankie's laughter faded.

"Because…"

"Yes?" Frankie asked, staring at Lisa's mouth.

Lisa scooted closer and kissed Frankie. "Because you could have your way with me regardless."

Frankie pushed her onto her back, captured her lips, and thrust her tongue against Lisa's. The more the kiss intensified, the more Lisa's desire built. She tore her mouth away in a rush. "Make love to me, Frankie," she whispered.

Frankie stood up and took hold of Lisa's hand, leading her to her bedroom. It was dark, but there was enough moonlight streaming through the window for Lisa to see Frankie's face. Lisa brushed her short hair back with her fingertips and then slowly undressed.

Frankie drew nearer. She lightly ran her fingers along Lisa's shoulders, down her arms, and along her sides. Lisa shivered when Frankie's hands trailed up her stomach to stop below her breasts.

Frankie gently cupped each breast and gazed into Lisa's eyes.

The love that Lisa had always seen there had deepened into something more. These were the eyes of her lover now. Frankie brought her mouth to Lisa's and pushed her tongue inside.

Lisa groaned and became weak in the knees. Frankie reached behind her and threw the covers back, then lay Lisa down on the bed. Frankie pressed her body against Lisa's, but Lisa wanted more. She gripped Frankie's arms and gazed at her with a longing she couldn't hide.

"Please, Frankie. Please let me feel you against me. All of you."

Frankie's arms tensed under Lisa's fingers, and her face instantly grew troubled. She moved to the side of the bed, but not before Lisa could see the tears that Frankie tried to hide. Lisa sat up and ran her hand back and forth across Frankie's back.

"I'm sorry," Lisa said. "I shouldn't have."

"You have every right to."

"No. No, I don't. I told you I could wait, but here I'm asking you to do exactly what I said I wouldn't."

Lisa brushed away a tear that trickled down Frankie's cheek.

"I wish I could take this pain away," Lisa whispered. "But know I love you. Nothing will ever change that. Nothing." Lisa lay down on the bed again. She held out her hand. "Come here and lie beside me."

Frankie took Lisa's hand and lay back. It was quiet in the room for a long while before Lisa broke the silence.

"Touch me."

Frankie rolled onto her side and brought her hand to Lisa's breast. Lisa pushed herself against Frankie's fingers. Lisa was throbbing.

"Touch me, Frankie," she said again. She took Frankie's hand and pushed it lower into her wetness. Lisa's whole body trembled.

"Oh, Leese." Frankie kept her hand still at first.

"God, the way you feel inside me is so wonderful," Lisa said in a shaky voice.

Frankie moved her fingers slowly. Lisa pushed her hips up to meet her and got lost in Frankie's tender touch. She cried out, the pleasure mounting and rushing through every nerve of her body. They kissed, and their tongues met, causing Lisa to moan. She ran her fingernails down Frankie's back and tensed her legs until she climaxed.

Frankie took Lisa into her arms and lightly stroked Lisa's hair.

"You okay?" Frankie whispered.

"I'm perfect." She patted Frankie's stomach. "And you're perfect."

"Glad you think so." Frankie kissed the top of Lisa's head.

"Oh, I know so." Lisa rose up on her elbow to face Frankie. "I love you."

Frankie brushed the back of her hand against Lisa's cheek. "Love you, too, Leese."

Lisa lay down again in Frankie's arms. She snuggled even closer and sighed.

Chapter 23

Over the next two weeks, Lisa spent almost every night with Frankie, usually at Frankie's house. Some nights Frankie made love to her. Other nights, they were content to sleep in each other's arms.

On the Wednesday before Lisa was to leave for Chattanooga, she covered her last high school game and filed her article at the *Gazette*. She met with the correspondent who would take over her Indians beat for Minor League.com and discussed the team. She said her goodbyes to Jack before driving home to her apartment to get a jump on packing.

Lisa checked the time. She had told Frankie she'd drop by the bar and would stay overnight at her house. After a quick shower, Lisa put on a red IU sweatshirt and faded blue jeans. The weather was nice enough that she could walk to the bar, but she decided against it, remembering Frankie's frequent lectures about walking alone at night. She drove to the Watering Hole at ten and encountered a large crowd when she entered the bar. She maneuvered around the women.

Lisa searched for Frankie, but didn't see her. She took a seat on an empty stool.

"What it'll be, chief?" Billie asked, placing a napkin in front her.

"A Coke."

Billie brought her the soft drink.

"What's with the crowd?" Lisa asked.

"It's dollar well night. Frankie's trying something new. Hey, I keep meaning to ask you. How's Amy?"

"Playing the hell out of the game like I thought she would. She'll be moving up," Lisa said, sipping her drink.

"And the two of you?"

Lisa hesitated. No one at the bar knew about Frankie and Lisa yet, but she could at least tell the truth about Amy. "I told her I thought we should just be good friends."

"Really?"

"Yeah, and I'm hoping that's what we'll be."

Lisa turned away from Billie and scanned the bar.

Billie pointed toward the office. "She's in there."

Lisa entered to find Frankie doing paperwork.

"Busy?" Lisa asked.

"Never too busy for you," Frankie said.

Lisa bent down to kiss her on the cheek.

"Mmm. You smell good." Frankie nuzzled her nose into the nape of Lisa's neck. "I'm glad you could make it tonight. I know things have been hectic for you at the paper."

"This place is my refuge." Lisa took a seat in the chair in front of the desk and stretched out her legs. "You're my refuge."

Frankie looked up from her paperwork and smiled warmly. "I feel the same way."

"If I recall the last time I was in here, I got nervous as hell when you came in and caught me in my bra."

"You weren't the only nervous person in the room."

There was a knock at the door.

"Yeah?" Frankie shouted.

Stacy popped in. "Frankie, I need—" She stopped. "Oh, hi, Lisa. Didn't see you come in."

"Hi, Stacy."

"What'd you need?" Frankie asked.

"Some Smirnoff from downstairs. I don't have my keys."

Frankie moved toward the door, but said to Lisa, "You can stay in here a while if you want."

Lisa stood. "Nah. I'll take my little Coke out front." The music was definitely louder when Lisa reentered the bar. She took her seat again and nodded at a couple of her friends.

A cute, long-haired blonde sat down at the stool beside Lisa that had just emptied.

"I think she's coming right back," Lisa said, motioning to the drink of the woman who had been seated there.

"Oh well." The blonde flipped her hair off her shoulders. "Can I buy you a drink?"

"No, thanks. I've got a Coke." Lisa held up the glass.

"How about I buy you one of those?" The woman moved closer.

"No, thanks." Lisa said staring straight ahead. Then she felt a hand on her knee, slowly making its way up to her crotch. Lisa pushed the hand away. "And no to that, too." She glared at the blonde.

"Okay, okay, sheesh." The woman left and stood at the edge of the dance area.

Frankie had come back upstairs with the liquor and put it under the bar. "Not into blondes, huh?" she asked with amusement.

"That pisses me off. I hate it when someone assumes that because you're sitting alone, you're ready and available for whatever they've got in mind."

"Really? I never would've guessed from your reaction."

"Besides, I'm only interested in one woman."

Billie passed by and jerked to a stop. She glanced at Lisa and then Frankie.

"What?" Frankie asked.

Billie grinned, making her dimples even more pronounced. "Nothing, boss, nothing." She poured a beer on tap. She made her way to the other end of the bar, but cast another glance their way.

"Guess our secret's out," Frankie said.

"Is that a bad thing?"

Frankie smiled. "No."

Frankie got busy again, mixing drinks, and bringing up more beer and liquor when needed. It was getting late, and Lisa was anxious to have Frankie to herself.

Lisa's ears prickled with the opening notes of Sugarland's "Just Might Make Me Believe." She searched for Frankie. She was on the floor, talking to a friend at one of the tables. Lisa jumped down from her stool and made her way over.

She tapped Frankie on the shoulder. Lisa ignored her startled look and took Frankie's hand to lead her out onto the dance floor. Lisa drew Frankie close and swayed to the music. It was a perfect song about believing in your love. When the chorus drifted down from the speakers, Lisa leaned back to see Frankie's face.

"I believe in you," she whispered.

The music stopped. Lisa gave Frankie a gentle kiss. She pulled out of the embrace to find everyone around them staring. Then the bar erupted in cheers and wild clapping.

Lisa blushed, but enjoyed the acknowledgment. Frankie was red faced, but grinning.

"It's about damn time!" Stacy shouted from back by the tables.

"Yeah! What took you so long, boss?" Billie called from the bar.

Lisa gave Frankie another quick kiss.

Frankie then waved her hand in the air. "Now that everybody's had their fun, you can go back to whatever you were doing."

They meandered around the couples to end up in front of the bar.

"Aren't we full of surprises tonight?" Frankie asked.

"I hope I can surprise you for many years to come."

"I'll hold you to that." Frankie gave her a quick peck on the cheek. "You ready to get out of here?"

"You can leave?"

"It is my bar, Lisa."

Lisa hit her on the arm. "I kinda knew that."

"Let me tell Billie she can close tonight."

* * *

Lisa followed Frankie to her house. "I'm going to take a shower," Frankie said when they entered. "You tired?"

"Yeah, I'm a little beat."

"Let's go to bed then."

Lisa undressed and took out her boxers and T-shirt from her drawer in Frankie's dresser. She lay back on the pillow, thinking about how Frankie was comfortable now wearing a nightshirt to bed. But they had gone no further with the intimacy. She heard the water shut off. She sat up to watch Frankie come in, drying her hair. She had on an oversized, short-sleeved, Kentucky Wildcats T-shirt.

"I don't know how you started following that team in the heart of Hoosier country," Lisa said.

"I told you. My parents were from Kentucky. It's in our blood."

"Right."

"What's the problem?"

"You do it to irritate me."

Frankie made a show of acting as though she were giving it a lot of thought. "Maybe."

Lisa threw Frankie's pillow at her.

"Hey!" Frankie picked up the pillow and came over to the side of the bed.

"You're adorable, you know," Lisa said. "You're so cute with your hair all mussed up like that."

"Why, thank you."

"You're quite welcome."

"Do you think we sound like the Disney characters, Chip and Dale?"

Lisa laughed. "Probably, and we probably annoy the hell out of people, too."

Frankie placed her pillow next to Lisa's and smoothed out the pillowcase.

Lisa reached over and intertwined her fingers with Frankie's. "Do you know how happy I am?"

Frankie took in a deep breath. "Me, too."

They stared at each other for a long time.

Lisa's heart throbbed loudly in her ears. She moved across the bed to sit in front of Frankie. She held her hands lightly at Frankie's sides, her gaze never wavering. Lisa stood up and took Frankie's face in her hands. She gently kissed her forehead, her cheeks, and her mouth. When Frankie's eyes fluttered opened again, they were wet with tears.

"I love you so much," Lisa said in a hoarse whisper.

Frankie didn't answer. She stepped away from Lisa, turned her back to her, and pulled off her nightshirt. She crossed her arms in front of her chest and bowed her head. Lisa could see her shoulders shaking with sobs.

Lisa undressed and stood behind Frankie to press her body against hers. She brought her arms around Frankie's waist and enfolded her in an embrace. She kissed Frankie's shoulders, bent down to lay her head against Frankie's neck, and held her tight.

Frankie turned to face Lisa with her arms still folded across her chest. She stood there for a long moment before slowly dropping them.

Lisa took a step toward her. Then she lowered her gaze to Frankie's chest and trailed her eyes from Frankie's left breast to the flat area with a light pink, horizontal scar. She was close enough now that she could feel Frankie's breath against her skin. She touched her lips to Frankie's cheeks, kissing away her tears. She sought out Frankie's mouth. Frankie was tentative at first, but the kiss quickly deepened.

Lisa tenderly brushed the back of her hand across the scar. Frankie flinched, but Lisa continued to caress her. She kissed Frankie's neck and planted light kisses down her chest until she reached the scar. Lisa traced the length of it with her lips, feeling Frankie tremble and grip her shoulders.

Lisa rose up and touched her lips to Frankie's again. She waited for Frankie to open her mouth, and their tongues met. She gently pushed Frankie onto the bed and lay on top of her.

Lisa trailed her lips down Frankie's chest and kissed the scar. "I love you," she whispered against her skin. Frankie raised her hips, and Lisa helped take off her panties. Lisa dipped her hand below and into her softness. She entered Frankie and brought her lips again to the scar. Lisa took her time, relishing the feel of Frankie surrounding her fingers. They moved in perfect rhythm until Frankie soared to her orgasm. Lisa kissed her way up Frankie's chest until her face was inches from Frankie's.

Lisa's tears fell softly to join the ones streaming down Frankie's cheeks. "I love you, Frankie," she said again.

"Oh, Leese," Frankie sobbed.

Lisa held Frankie as she buried her face into Lisa's chest. Lisa rocked her, kissing her hair. "I love you." She repeated the three words until Frankie's cries subsided, and she relaxed in her arms. Lisa felt a peace embrace them that was almost holy. She breathed in and let it flow through her.

"I love you, too, Leese," Frankie whispered in the stillness of the room.

Chapter 24

April fifth dawned. Lisa had already packed everything she needed for her five-month stay in Chattanooga. Frankie was up before the alarm to fix Lisa breakfast.

As Lisa showered, she thought about the past few nights she'd shared with Frankie. They had made love every night since Wednesday, and each time, it deepened the bond between them. It also made Lisa realize how much she'd miss her.

She dried off, dressed, and entered the kitchen. Frankie was taking bacon out of the skillet.

"You didn't need to do all this." Lisa stood behind Frankie and put her arms around her waist.

"I wanted to." Frankie's voice quivered.

"Hey." Lisa gently turned Frankie to face her. She tilted her chin up and saw Frankie was crying. "Oh, honey." Lisa kissed her and drew her close. "I know this'll be rough, but we agreed that you'd come down to see me, right?"

"But it won't be the same," Frankie said into Lisa's shoulder.

Lisa held her tighter. "I know."

Frankie pulled out of her arms. "How about you at least have one good meal before you take off? I know you won't eat right while you're there." She brushed past Lisa with the bacon.

Lisa followed her into the dining room where they ate in silence. She tried to keep her emotions in check before glancing over at Frankie, only to find her wiping away tears, which brought Lisa to tears herself. She stood up and brought Frankie to her feet. Frankie fell into her arms, and they clung to one another for several moments.

Frankie took Lisa's face in her hands and kissed her deeply. She wiped away Lisa's tears. "God, we're a mess, huh?"

"I guess so." Lisa sniffed. She stared at Frankie as though it were the last time she'd ever see her. "Love you."

"Love you, too." They kissed again.

"I'd better get out of here if I want to miss the Nashville traffic." Lisa hoisted her laptop case onto her shoulder. Frankie reached for her suitcase. Lisa grabbed hold of her hand to stop her. "No. I want to say our goodbyes here. I can't take you standing there in the driveway while I leave."

Lisa held her tight one last time before picking up the suitcase and leaving the house. She didn't turn back after getting into the car. She drove toward the interstate, brushing the rest of her tears away to clear her blurry vision.

* * *

The Appalachians surrounded her as she made the steep descent into Chattanooga. It was two-thirty, and she'd made good time. She took the first turnoff into the city, stopped in an empty parking lot, and read the directions again to the condominium complex. After a few more turns, she was there.

She carried everything into the one-bedroom condo. Though small, it had all the essentials she needed for the summer: completely furnished, with a full kitchen and washer and dryer. She took in the living room decor. Granted, some of the furniture wasn't to Lisa's taste, but she couldn't complain. She cracked a few windows to let in some fresh air.

She slumped onto the couch and propped her feet up on the coffee table. She took her cell phone off her belt and called Frankie, leaving a message that she'd arrived safely. Afterward, she found Amy's number on her contact list and hit the button.

"Lisa?" a tired voice said.

"Hi. You sound beat."

"I got settled into my apartment today. I never knew unpacking could be such fun."

"You're further along than I am. My suitcase is staring at me from the doorway where I left it."

"Hope you enjoy it as much as I did."

"Do you maybe want to have dinner?"

There was a slight hesitation before Amy answered. "Can I come over there?"

"Sure. Were you able to bring your car like you wanted to?"

"Yeah. The drive took me a couple of days, but I'm here, and so's my ten-year-old Mazda."

Lisa told Amy the name of her condominium complex and

gave her the address.

"I'll log onto the Internet and get directions on my laptop."

"You really are at home, huh?"

"They pretty much told me that I'll be here for the summer. I figured I'd be ready for the long haul."

"I'm glad you can get directions off the net, because I have no idea how to tell you to get here."

"I'll be there in a few minutes. You want me to grab us a pizza on the way over?"

"Yeah. I didn't realize until just this minute how hungry I am."

Lisa unpacked her clothes and put them into the drawers in the bedroom. She heard a knock at the front door, opened it, and Amy stepped in. Lisa shut the door behind her. Amy set the pizza on the nearby dining room table.

"I don't exactly know how to act," Amy said. "I've got to get used to this friendship-only thing." She shoved her hands in her jeans pockets.

"Why don't we take it one day at a time?"

Amy moved forward, wrenched her hands from her pockets, and gave Lisa a brief hug. "Gee, that went well, huh?"

"It'll get better," Lisa assured her.

"I am glad you're here."

"Me, too. Let's sit at the table while you tell me how the rest of spring training went for you at the Chattanooga camp."

Amy sat down as if she had the weight of the world on her shoulders. She stared at the pizza box, seemingly searching for answers inside the closed cardboard container. "It'll be hell, just like I thought."

Lisa sat down across from her. "What happened?"

"It's the same silent treatment I got in Arizona, except these guys are even more resentful. It was me and six other guys from the Reds farm system on that team in Mesa. All the other players were from around the majors. These guys? I'm competing against every one of them for a spot on the Indianapolis Indians or Reds roster. It's much more personal."

"Have they done anything to you?" Lisa waited, hoping the answer was no, but afraid it would be yes.

"No, only the usual silence and glares."

Lisa relaxed, relieved by Amy's response. She was glad it hadn't gotten out of hand. She hoped it never would. One thing she was certain of. If Curt Reed ever found out about anyone harassing

Amy, he'd address the situation head-on.

"You haven't made any friends yet?" Lisa asked.

"Nope." Amy flipped open the lid to the pizza box and took out a slice. She tore off a bite, swiping away the tomato sauce from the corner of her mouth with the back of her hand.

"It'll happen when you least expect it." Lisa hoped she sounded more convincing than she felt.

"You really think so?"

"Yes, I do." Lisa held her gaze, willing Amy to believe her.

"Okay," Amy said with a sigh.

They discussed the team and Reed's expectations of Amy. She would bat third and would be the everyday first baseman.

"Curt said, 'Perry, if you're not ready for this and you plan on slacking off any, then tell me right now. Because if you aren't ready, I'm not wasting my time on you.'" Amy imitated his Mississippi drawl to perfection. She bit into another piece of pizza. "That guy's always on my ass."

"He has a lot of respect for your talent, Amy."

"Can't tell it from the way he acts."

They finished the pizza and talked for another hour. Amy stretched and yawned. "I'm bushed and need to get back."

They stood. Amy gave Lisa another hug. This one was warmer.

"I'll catch you tomorrow at the ballpark. I can't wait to see you in a Chattanooga Lookouts uni." Lisa walked Amy to the door.

"They're kind of cool." Amy stood outside the condo. "Wish me luck."

"You'll be fine. No doubt about it."

Lisa waited until Amy was in her car and the red taillights had disappeared onto the street in front of the condo. After cleaning off the dining room table, she went to the bedroom to strip the bed. While she waited for the sheets to dry, she checked her e-mail and sports news on the Internet.

She didn't realize how stiff and sore she was until she stood and stretched. It seemed every joint in her body popped in protest. She headed to the shower and let the hot water ease away her aches.

She made up the bed and crawled under the covers. Once again, she picked up her cell phone from the bedside table to dial Frankie's number, pleased when Frankie answered on the first ring.

* * *

The Lookouts' home opener was a day game, and the afternoon was a scorcher. Attendance at games was light anyway, but a workday drew an even sparser crowd. Lisa estimated the ballpark, which held a little over 6,000, wasn't even a third full.

Sarah weaved her way down press row to sit on the chair next to Lisa.

"Can't I ever get rid of you, Collins? Do you have to follow me everywhere?" Sarah plugged her laptop into the nearby outlet.

"Quit being paranoid, Swift. It's mere coincidence."

"You're too funny." The sound of the ball popping into Amy's glove could be heard up in the press box. Sarah cocked her head toward the other reporters who sat to the right of them. "We've got a few more heavy hitters here now."

"I guess everyone figured out this story wasn't going away."

Sarah nudged Lisa with her elbow. "But we knew, huh?"

"Yes, we did." Lisa lowered her voice. "Then again, we're not sexist pricks."

Sarah's guffaws caught the attention of the other reporters. "You're good to have around. Do you know that?"

"So I've been told," Lisa said with a straight face.

Roberto Sanchez, the Lookouts pitcher, fired the first pitch to the plate. Using his wicked slider, he struck out the lead-off batter on three straight pitches. Lisa had followed Sanchez's progress throughout the Reds farm system. He was pegged to be in Indianapolis by next spring, if not this season. Along with the slider, he had a sharp breaking curve that kept hitters off balance. According to the radar gun readout on the scoreboard, his fastball consistently hit the low nineties and occasionally ninety-five. The Huntsville Stars failed to get anything going in the top half of the inning.

The first two Lookouts batters were retired before Amy's first at-bat. The public address announcer boomed out her name, and she strode to the plate.

When he announced her name, most of the small crowd cheered. Two men, however, stood up behind the Huntsville dugout, and because there weren't many fans in the stands, their shouts carried easily up to the open press box.

"Hey! Why don't you go back to wherever you came from, you big lezzie," one of them yelled. His gut hung over his low-riding jeans, and he splashed what Lisa assumed was beer in the air as he shouted.

His skinny buddy joined in. "Yeah, you big lezzie. Why don't you go back to your kind? Go back to your dyke friends."

Lisa flinched with each word. If Lisa could hear them in the press box, Amy most certainly heard their insults. But Amy didn't even look their way. Instead, she took a couple of practice swings and scuffed her front foot in the batter's box before stepping in.

The first pitch was a curve ball on the outside corner of the plate that dropped in for a strike.

"Yeah, baby! How do you like that, lezbo?" Beer Belly shouted.

Amy didn't leave the box, but instead took another practice swing through the strike zone, waiting for the next pitch. It was a fastball on the inside half of the plate. Amy did what the coaches had been asking her to do all winter. She pulled the ball into the left field corner. It hit directly below the yellow line on the outfield fence that signified a home run. The left fielder, who had been playing straightaway, ran over to retrieve it and fired it back into the second baseman, but Amy was already there with a stand-up double.

The two men sat in their seats with their arms folded.

Yeah, screw you, assholes. Out of the corner of her eye, Lisa caught Sarah clenching and unclenching her teeth.

The next batter flied out to deep right. Amy stayed out on the field by first base, but no one brought out her hat or glove. She trotted to the dugout. One of the coaches handed them to her at the top of the steps.

The Huntsville Stars crossed the plate with a home run in the top of the third. The Lookouts' half of the inning started with a pop out to the second baseman. The next batter walked, and the second-place hitter grounded a single into right field.

Amy strode to the plate. The two hecklers instantly came to their feet.

"Hey! Wouldn't you rather be getting some pussy?" Beer Belly shouted.

"Yeah! Go on home, cunt," Skinny Buddy yelled.

Amy was in the batter's box, but with the last comment, Lisa saw her back stiffen, and she stepped out. She leaned the bat against her legs, unsnapping and snapping her batting gloves. Lisa noticed that even the home plate umpire's attention was drawn to where the hecklers were seated.

Amy stepped back in and swung at the first pitch thrown to her. It was a terrible pitch, low and clearly out of the strike zone. Amy made it worse by trying to pull the ball. She barely got wood on it, and it dribbled along the third baseline. Because it was a slow roller, the catcher's only play was to first. Amy hustled down the line. Her foot hit the bag an instant before the ball got there.

The first base umpire saw it differently. He emphatically threw up his right hand in a clenched fist signaling an out. Amy raised her hands, palms up, pleading with the umpire. She wasn't alone. John Rodriguez, the first base coach argued the call.

Reed was out of the dugout like a shot. "What the hell was that, Ron?" Lisa could hear him shouting. "Are you fucking blind?"

The first base umpire kept shaking his head, walking away from Reed. Reed stayed out on the field a few more minutes, kicking the dirt and getting in a few more parting shots before going back into the dugout.

Amy left the field and stomped into the dugout. She shoved her batting helmet into the slot and stripped off her batting gloves. She paced back and forth in front of the bench before sitting at the far end. None of her teammates had congratulated her on her hustle, and no one sat next to her on the bench. Reed walked down and smacked her on the leg before taking his place at the other end of the dugout.

Lisa heard some shouting again in the area above the Huntsville dugout. The two hecklers were arguing with three security guards who were escorting them out of the ballpark. The fans who sat nearby the men stood and clapped as the security guards passed them. One man patted a guard on the back. Apparently, it was okay to shout out homosexual slurs, but using vulgarities had gotten them tossed from the stadium.

The game ended with a loss for the Lookouts, 3-1. Sarah and Lisa joined the rest of the reporters in the clubhouse. Again, the club chose to have Amy's locker in with the rest of the players'.

Amy removed her hat. Her brown curls hung in wet ringlets around her face. Her uniform was dirt-stained from diving for a ball in the sixth inning. She finished the day 1-for-4. It should have been 2-for-4, but the box score wouldn't reflect this.

"How was it, getting the first game in Double-A under your belt?" one reporter asked.

"It's good. I'm ready to get going for the rest of the season now." Amy grabbed a towel from her locker and wiped down her face.

"Were you safe at first, Amy?" Sarah asked.

"If the umpire called me out, I was out."

Lisa liked her answer. Spoken like a true pro.

"Amy, did you hear any of the insults shouted your way from those two fans in the first and third innings?" another reporter asked.

Amy brought the towel to her face again for a long moment. She lifted it and gave the reporter a cool look. "I heard them," she said in a level tone.

"Do you have any comment?"

Amy stood mute, rooted to the spot. The reporter tried following up, but Lisa quickly broke in. "You seemed to be concentrating on pulling the ball for your hit that almost made it out of here, right?" It wasn't even a true question, but it was an out for Amy.

Amy's green eyes softened.

"Yeah. I'll go with the pitch and try pulling it if it's inside on me like that. Curt wants to see me hit for some power."

She took a few more questions. The reporters dispersed to talk with other players and with Reed. Lisa had enough quotes to finish the article she'd started during the game. She made her way to the press box with her notebook in hand. Sarah was already there. The other reporters hadn't arrived yet from the clubhouse.

Lisa sat down beside Sarah who typed away on her laptop. "Do you think that's the way it'll be every game for her?" Sarah asked, not looking up from her computer.

Lisa set her notebook on the desk beside her laptop and opened up her article. "I don't know."

Sarah stopped typing. "I'm sorry. I can't imagine what that was like for you, considering your relationship."

"We're not dating anymore," Lisa said. "But we've remained friends. And you're right. I hate hearing that crap being shouted at any lesbian, but since we're friends, it cuts even deeper."

"She's a good kid. You can see that in the way she conducts herself." Sarah sighed heavily. "Will we ever see the day that a person's sex doesn't mean anything? That instead, we celebrate that a woman can play this sport as well as a man?"

"I hope so. It'll take time, unfortunately."

They concentrated on their articles. After they finished, they met for a beer at a nearby bar. As they settled onto their stools, Lisa's cell phone rang; Amy's name popped up on the caller ID.

"Hey. I want to thank you for cutting that guy off."

Lisa jumped down from the bar stool and walked outside to talk privately. "Are you okay? I know those guys were assholes."

"I'm sure down here I'll be hearing more crap like that. I'm glad you're here, you know?" Amy's voice quivered a little.

"I'm glad I am, too, Aim."

"I'm going to get out of here. I just finished my shower. I didn't realize how much adrenaline I had for this game until it was over. I'm wiped out."

"Go home and try not to let that other stuff bother you."

"I'll try." Amy still sounded shaky. "Thanks again. I'll see you at tomorrow night's game."

"See you then."

Lisa hung up and went back into the bar.

"Was that Amy?" Sarah asked.

"Yeah." Lisa sat down.

"How is she?"

"A little shaken up." Lisa took a sip of her beer.

Sarah raised her bottle in the air. "Here's to a certain first baseman telling the men to kiss her ass all the way to the majors."

"I'll definitely drink to that."

Chapter 25

The cool April days gave way to warmer temperatures in the first week of May. Amy's hot play in most of the games kept up with the rising thermometer.

But a few tough games wedged themselves in between her stellar performances. The night the Lookouts played the Mississippi Braves was one of those down games. She finished the game 0-for-4, with three strikeouts and a groundout into a double play with the bases loaded that had ended the inning.

The rest of the reporters had left the clubhouse. Lisa had gone to Curt's office to follow up on one of her questions. She passed by Amy who stood in front of her open locker, staring straight ahead. Her face was red, and her jaw was tight. Lisa walked over to speak to her.

"Try to shake it off, Amy. You just had a tough night." She said it softly to keep the other players from overhearing. Then she saw where Amy's attention was drawn. What appeared to be a used condom was taped to the back of the locker. Lisa's stomach did a quick roll, and bile rose in her throat.

"Jesus," she said under her breath. She heard some snickers. To her right, two players stood at their lockers trying to hold in their laughter.

"Hey, Collins, I forgot to tell you..." Curt Reed came up behind them. Lisa turned around in time to see him transform into a different man.

"Goddammit!" He kicked the locker beside Amy's, denting it in the process. The same two players, who a moment before were holding back guffaws, visibly paled. "Who the fuck did this? Do y'all think this is funny? Do y'all think this is a fucking joke?" Reed stalked up and down the aisle between the lockers. "I want every one of y'all's asses up here now." He pointed to the open area in front of the lockers.

"I want to know who did this," he repeated. The players kept their heads lowered. "Y'all look at me." Reed's Mississippi drawl was even more pronounced in his anger, and "y'all" had taken on a completely new meaning. This definitely wasn't friendly southern chit-chat. "I'm only gonna ask one more time. I want to know who did this."

The players still wouldn't look at him.

"Well, hell, then. Since none of y'all will own up to it, then every one of y'all's docked one week out of your month's pay."

The players' heads all shot up at the same time.

"I did it, Curt." The left fielder, Bernie Monroe, spoke up. His face was beet red, and he looked as though he'd like to crawl unnoticed under the nearest bench.

Reed stomped over to him. "What the fuck were you thinking, Bernie?"

Monroe shrugged his shoulders and said nothing.

Reed strode back to the front of the group. "Let's get this straight. Amy Perry's a hell of a lot better athlete than most of y'all put together. She just happens to be a woman." He took off his cap and ruffled his hair in apparent frustration. He took a few deep breaths before he started in again.

"Let me tell y'all something. I felt the same as you when they assigned me to manage her in Arizona."

Lisa glanced at Amy who was now sitting on a bench behind the players, staring down at the floor.

"But after seeing her play in the six weeks down there, I got over my macho self and took her for who she is—one of the best goddamn ballplayers I've ever seen."

Lisa studied each of the players' faces. One of them shook his head.

Reed must have noticed because in three long strides, he was in front of Chris Thompson, his right fielder. "What the hell's your batting average, Thompson?"

Thompson didn't raise his head.

"I'll tell you what it is. It's .242. No, wait, it's even worse than that." Reed turned to John Rodriguez, his first base coach, who flipped open a notebook. "John?"

"After today's game, .238."

"And you're our leadoff hitter, which doesn't say much for me that I've left you there." He turned to Rodriguez again. "What's Perry batting?"

Again, Rodriguez flipped through the notebook. "She's at .308, even after today's game."

"I'm not telling you this to embarrass you, Thompson, because we both know you can hit the hell out of the ball. But what I'm telling you is Perry's the real deal." He waved his hand over the group. "I'm telling all y'all this. And she ain't going away." He paced in front of them some more. "You know what that means?" The players were mute. "It means we're going to play as a team, and that includes Perry. You may not like it, you may think it's horseshit, but this ain't a publicity stunt like I've heard some of you say when you think I'm not around."

He walked over to Amy's locker and pointed at the condom. "Monroe, get that crap out of here."

Monroe didn't move.

"Now!"

Monroe hustled over and pulled it out of the locker. Rodriguez took the garbage bag out of the can. Monroe dropped it in the bag, and Rodriguez twisted it shut.

Reed stuck his finger in Monroe's face and pointed with his other hand at the locker. "I expect you to clean her locker from top to bottom with the best goddamn cleaning shit we have here. And you will be docked a week of your pay."

Monroe opened his mouth, but Reed cut him off.

"Wanna make it two?"

Monroe didn't respond.

"Now, apologize to Perry."

Monroe had taken his hat off. He twirled it nervously in his hands, not meeting Amy's gaze.

"You had the balls to put that in there, Monroe. Now have the balls to apologize," Reed snapped.

Monroe finally looked up.

"I'm sorry, Perry."

Amy nodded slightly.

Reed stood in front of the players again. "I never want to see anything like this again, y'all hear? Everybody get your asses on the field at seven tomorrow morning."

There was some grumbling.

"Wanna try for six?"

There was silence.

"Now get the fuck out of my sight."

The players scrambled back to their lockers, hurriedly gathered their belongings, and fled the clubhouse. Only Amy, Lisa, Reed, and

Rodriguez remained.

"You all right, Amy?" Reed asked.

"Yeah, I'm all right."

"Do you want to maybe talk about this?"

"No. I just want to get out of here." Amy's voice was barely audible.

Reed stared at her for a long moment like he wanted to say more. He walked away, but motioned at Lisa to follow him. He stopped outside his office. "Make sure she's okay." His expression was softer now, and his voice was full of concern.

"I will."

Lisa walked back to Amy's locker. She had taken her uniform off, but hadn't stripped down all the way.

"Since they're gone, I can take my shower," Amy said.

"I can follow you to—"

"No. I'm fine."

Lisa started to leave her, but stopped. "Call me if you need to talk."

"Thanks, but I said I'm fine."

Lisa reluctantly left the clubhouse and walked to her car. She put her laptop in the backseat, threw her notebook on top, and slammed the door shut.

Then she kicked the back tire. "Goddammit!"

*　*　*

The next night didn't go much better for Amy. She was forcing her game, and it showed. After she grounded into her second double play for the night, she made a sharp right directly past the first base bag into the dugout. Lisa followed her progress down the steps. Amy tore off her batting gloves and then tossed her helmet into the helmet slot. It fell to the dugout floor. She picked it up and slammed it onto the concrete where it shattered, causing pieces of plastic to fly everywhere. The batboy hurried over and collected the shards, dropping some in his haste to stay out of Amy's way.

Reed came to her and put his hand on her shoulder. She shook him off and stomped down the steps into the hall leading into the clubhouse, presumably to let off even more steam.

"I know she's had a couple of bad nights, but I've never seen her do that before," Sarah said.

Lisa didn't respond. She watched the entrance to the

clubhouse. The Braves recorded the final out. Amy came back up the steps, grabbed her glove, and ran out to her position. She seemed to be firing the ball to the infielders with a little more gusto.

The Lookouts were leading 5-2 in the bottom of the eighth. Amy came up for what probably would be her last at-bat for the night. The first pitch was a ninety-two-mile-an-hour fastball on the inside part of the plate. Amy promptly smacked it over the left field wall. What was left of the crowd stood and cheered. She trotted around the bases, slapped hands with the third base coach, but showed no emotion.

Reed smacked her on the back. She stood in front of the rack of batting helmets after placing her new one in its slot. She didn't take a place on the dugout bench. The other players looked toward her, but no one moved to congratulate her.

After the game, Sarah and Lisa picked up their notebooks to go down to the clubhouse.

"Do you know what's up with her? Is the pressure starting to get to her?" Sarah asked.

"I'm not sure what it is."

"Alrighty, Collins. Whatever it is must be something best left alone."

Lisa walked on.

They entered the clubhouse. Amy was already fielding questions. It was the first time that Lisa heard her snap off her answers with either curt replies or a simple "yes" or "no." Amy turned her back on them, dismissing them without another word.

Lisa interviewed the pitcher and Monroe who had a good night at the plate with three RBIs. As badly as she wanted to punch him in the mouth, she tried to maintain her professionalism. She got a couple of quotes from Reed, went back to the press box to finish her article, and walked out to her car. She drove to Amy's apartment.

Amy's Mazda pulled into the lot about an hour later. Lisa watched as Amy slammed the car door and started up the sidewalk. Lisa got out of the car and came up behind her before she reached the door.

"Amy."

Amy snapped her head around.

"Last night I said I didn't need to talk, and I still don't."

Even in the limited amount of light, Lisa could see the anger etched on her face.

"Yeah, you do."

Amy unlocked the door and blocked the entrance. Eventually, she stepped inside, and Lisa followed her.

Amy threw her keys on the table and stomped into the kitchen. Lisa heard her popping the lid on a bottle before she reentered the living room. She took a long drink of the beer, glaring at Lisa.

"I'd offer you one, but since I told you I didn't need to talk, you won't be staying," Amy said coldly.

"Let's sit down."

Amy took another big drink. "After you." She swooped her hand in an exaggerated motion toward the couch.

"So?" she asked after they took seats on opposite ends of the couch.

"You know why I'm here." Lisa stared at her until Amy started picking at the label on the bottle. "Amy, you need to let this out, and I'm—"

"You're what, Lisa? What exactly are you? You aren't my lover. You want to be friends?" Amy asked. "I told you this would be hard, and it sure as hell is. I'm not one of those lesbians who can be all chummy with her ex." Her eyes darkened in her anger.

"I'm sor—"

"If you say you're sorry one more fucking time, I swear I'll—" Amy slammed her bottle down on the coffee table. Beer sloshed onto the newspaper that was lying there. She leaned her elbows on her knees and looked straight ahead.

Lisa writhed in her seat. Why did I think it was a good idea to come over here? Amy was right. I'm not her lover, and I'm not much of a friend, either.

Amy turned to her with tears running down her cheeks.

"I knew crap like what happened in the clubhouse would come up. That's when I knew I'd need you the most." Her voice cracked.

"But I'm here."

Amy angrily swiped at her tears. "I need more."

Lisa took a deep breath. "What I can give you is what I offered before. I can be your friend. I can offer my support." Lisa waited for Amy to say something, but she remained quiet. "What happened last night was deplorable. Reed handled it the right way, but that doesn't make it any easier for you." Lisa put her hand on Amy's shoulder. Amy tensed. "I'm right here, doing my best to be here for you, however you need me to be."

It seemed those words were what Amy needed to hear before finally letting go. "I only want to play baseball," she said between choked sobs. "That's all. Is that so horrible?" She turned toward Lisa with her face full of pain. "Is that so bad?"

Lisa moved closer and put her arm around Amy's broad back. Amy laid her head down on Lisa's shoulder and let Lisa hold her.

"No. It's not. It should be simple, but all this male ego bullshit gets in the way. I hate that you're going through this."

Lisa held Amy until her shoulders stopped shaking from her crying. Amy raised her head and stared into Lisa's eyes. Then her gaze dropped to Lisa's mouth.

Oh, God, no.

Amy moved her lips to Lisa's, but Lisa jumped up.

"I can't. I can't, and I won't." Lisa stood her ground. "Amy, I love Frankie."

Amy leaned back on the couch and buried her face in her hands. "God, I know. I know!" She took her hands away.

Lisa waited.

Amy met her eyes again. They reflected only resignation. "You can come back over here and sit down. I promise to be good."

Lisa sat on the edge of the couch at the far end.

"Seriously. I do get it," Amy said. "That'll never happen again. I promise."

Lisa was still uneasy.

"I promise." Amy said it more forcefully. "I do need you. It's been a rough couple of days, and I'm sorry. Forgive me?"

"As long as we have an understanding."

"Never again," Amy repeated. She stood up and went into the kitchen. She came back into the living room with an opened beer for Lisa and handed it to her. Amy picked up her bottle and held it up. "Here's to being at least baseball friends?" Amy waited for Lisa's response.

Lisa tilted her bottle toward Amy. "Amen."

Amy joined her again on the couch and took a sip of her beer.

"You do realize that home run was a shove-it-up-your-ass home run, right?"

"Really, Aim? I never could have guessed."

Chapter 26

Over the next few weeks, little by little, subtle changes occurred with Amy's teammates. After a sacrifice fly, they congratulated her when she stepped back into the dugout. If she made a good defensive play on the field, the pitcher or another infielder pointed at her with his glove in acknowledgment.

On a particularly hot and muggy night, Lisa was hoping the game against the Birmingham Barons would be a quick one. Amy came to the plate in the fourth inning. She performed her ritual of unsnapping and snapping her batting gloves before stepping into the box.

The first pitch was a high fastball under Amy's chin. She backpedaled out of the way just in time. The pitcher snatched the ball thrown from the catcher and glared back in for the sign. The next pitch came in at her head. Amy ducked and raised her left arm in a reflexive action. The ball hit directly below her shoulder with a thud heard all the way up to the press box.

The umpire took off his mask and pointed at first base for Amy to take the bag. Lisa thought he was about to warn the pitcher and the dugouts, but instead, he took out the broom from his back pocket and dusted off the plate.

The trainer trotted out of the dugout, but only made it halfway to first base before Amy waved him off. She didn't rub the area where the ball struck her. Standing on the bag, she bent over while Rodriguez put his arm around her shoulder and talked to her.

Amy's teammates edged up closer to the railing. One of them shouted something out to the pitcher, and the pitcher's head snapped around. Lisa saw Willis, the Lookouts pitcher, talking with the catcher. The next batter popped out to the third baseman for the final out.

"Let's see if we have tit for tat here, so to speak," Lisa said to Sarah when the top of the fifth started.

The Barons' power-hitting third baseman led off the inning.

Willis went into his wind-up and zipped a ninety-mile-an-hour fastball behind his shoulder.

When the ball whizzed past the batter, the umpire jumped out from behind the plate, yanked off his mask, and pointed at Willis before issuing warnings to both benches.

Lisa snuck a peek down at Reed who stood with one foot up on the top step. He was glaring at the other dugout.

The next pitch from Willis again was a high and tight fastball that the batter turned away from. It hit him in the back. He made a move toward Willis, but the umpire was quicker. He whipped off his mask again and pushed him toward first. Then he pointed at Willis, threw his thumb up in the air to eject him from the game and made the same gesture to Reed. Before Willis made it into the dugout, he raised his chin in Amy's direction.

The crowd cheered when Reed hopped up the last step onto the field and charged the umpire. He got within inches of his face. "You expect me to sit over there and do nothing while they bean my best hitter? You shoulda tossed Morrison last inning, but you fucking didn't do it."

The first base umpire positioned himself between Reed and the home plate umpire. He started nudging Reed toward the dugout.

Reed pointed at the Barons manager.

"Fuck you, Terry," he yelled one last time before leaving the field.

Sarah spoke up. "You were right. Definitely tit for tat."

Lisa smiled. "Good for them." And good for Amy.

* * *

The first week of June arrived. The Lookouts, like all teams in the Double-A Southern League, had a brutal schedule. In the five-month season, they played 141 games. Reed had been careful with Amy, giving her four games' rest during the first two months, but she hadn't missed a beat. Through fifty-three games, she was batting .305, with 7 home runs, 13 doubles, 4 stolen bases, and 31 RBIs.

Lisa and Frankie had only been able to see each other twice. Lisa's schedule was as brutal as the team's, and traveling only added to the long hours. The Lookouts had an away series in Huntsville, Alabama. When Lisa returned to her hotel room after the first game, the red light was flashing on her phone. Lisa listened to the message. It was Frankie.

"Hey, babe. I remembered where you told me you'd be staying. Thought I'd leave you a cute and corny message telling you how much I love you and miss you. Wish I was there tucking you in at night. Hope to see you in a couple of weeks. Give me a call when you get this."

Lisa speed-dialed Frankie's cell.

"Got the message, huh?" Frankie asked.

"I don't know if I should be offended. You sound awfully giddy there without me."

"Oh, stop. I hope you know how much I miss you."

"I dunno."

"What do I have to do to prove it to you?"

"Well—" There was a knock at the door. "Hang on. Someone's here." Lisa opened the door to find a grinning Frankie on the other side. "Oh, my God." Lisa practically yanked her into the room.

"You do realize I could've been an axe murderer. You need to be more careful and check before opening the door."

"Shut up and kiss me." Lisa pressed her lips to Frankie's.

"I take it you really did miss me?"

"I can't believe it. How'd you find this place?"

"Huntsville ain't exactly a bayou. I got the address off the Internet and double-checked with the desk to make sure you were here. It's only about a six-hour drive from Indy. Not that bad at all."

Lisa took Frankie into her arms and held her.

"Missed you, too, babe," Frankie whispered.

Lisa withdrew from the embrace and pushed Frankie toward the bed. "How about we get reacquainted?"

"You might have to twist my arm on that one."

"Oh, there are definitely more pleasurable things I want to do to you." Lisa shoved Frankie onto the mattress.

* * *

The next morning over breakfast, Frankie shared the good news that she'd be able to stay one more night.

Lisa set down her forkful of scrambled eggs. "This is a nice surprise. You can go to the game with me and finally get to see Amy play."

"I'm not sure if I want to."

"Frankie, you really should see her."

"I know. I'm being totally juvenile about this." Frankie pushed at her pancakes with her fork.

"Hey." Lisa took Frankie's hand. "Look at me."

Frankie raised her head.

"You're not being juvenile. You're being human."

Frankie started to say something and stopped.

"What? You can tell me."

"It's that with Sherri, she and I were friends with all sorts of people, and one of those supposed friends turned out to be who she left me for. It's a struggle to get past all of that crap. I guess a part of me's afraid that if I become friends with Amy, that, oh hell." Frankie threw her fork down. "Shit."

"That somehow Amy and I'd get involved again?"

Frankie barely nodded.

"Amy understands now. It took some time, but we've come to an agreement." Lisa could see she hadn't erased all of Frankie's doubts. "We're friends. Period." Lisa looked into Frankie's eyes. "I can say I know how hurt you were by what Sherri did to you, but the truth is, I can't even imagine how horrible that was. I only hope with each passing day, you'll grow to trust me and see that you're the one I love." She reached across the table and squeezed her hand. "You. No one else." She kept her gaze steady until Frankie's brow was no longer creased in worry.

"Can you keep telling me that?"

"For the rest of my life."

Frankie took a deep breath. "Thanks."

"Don't ever thank me for loving you." Lisa could see Frankie's lower lip trembling. She went back to her eggs. "How's your breakfast? I always say I hate grits until I come to the South and find out how they're really done."

"You never had my mama's grits. Nothing compares to them, although these are pretty close."

* * *

Lisa finished her article after the game, and she and Frankie drove to a nearby bar for a beer before driving back to the hotel. Lisa and Amy had dropped by the bar after some games earlier in the season, so she knew it was a good place to hang out.

"Damn, she's good," Frankie said. "You told me, and I've kept up with her through your articles, but seeing her in person really brings it all home."

"It's kind of like describing the sun going down over the ocean. Unless you're there to take in all the colors, you don't get it." She caught Frankie's smile. "What?"

"You. You're such a romantic."

"If I am, it's because you've made me one."

"Glad I could be of assistance."

"I am, too." Lisa had a view of the door from her seat and saw Amy enter.

Amy made her way over to the bar and sat on a stool.

"What?" Frankie asked. She twisted around and saw Amy and then turned back to Lisa. "Invite her over."

"Yeah?"

"I'm okay with it. Of course, she might not be."

Lisa walked over to Amy. "Hi."

Amy seemed genuinely pleased to see her. "Hi, Lisa."

"Want to join us?" Lisa pointed to Frankie and their table.

Amy's expression changed, and she pursed her lips.

"She won't bite," Lisa said.

Amy gave a nervous laugh. "You sure?" She stood, grabbed her beer, and trailed behind Lisa.

"Hi, Amy," Frankie said evenly.

"Frankie." Amy pointed at the bench where Frankie sat. "Do you mind?"

"Not at all." Frankie moved over. "Have a seat."

Lisa slid onto the booth seat across from them. Maybe this wasn't such a good idea.

"Soooo…" Frankie said. "How 'bout those Cubs?"

* * *

Later, back at the hotel, Lisa held Frankie close after making love to her. She brushed her fingers through Frankie's hair. "Did I ever tell you how soft your hair is?"

"No, I don't believe you have."

"Frankie, your hair's soft."

Frankie poked Lisa in the ribs. "Funny."

Lisa squeezed her shoulder. "You all right?"

"You need to ask that question after what you just did to me?"

"You know what I mean."

Frankie gazed up at her. "I'm fine with you and Amy being friends."

"Good."

"It was a little uncomfortable tonight, and I don't expect us all to be best of friends from now until forever." Frankie ran her fingertips back and forth between Lisa's breasts. "But I can see where she needs you."

"I'll never hurt you intentionally," Lisa said. "Never."

Frankie leaned up and kissed her. "I believe you."

Lisa put her fingers around the nape of Frankie's neck and pulled her in tighter, sharing an even deeper kiss. Frankie trailed her lips down Lisa's throat and lower. Lisa got lost in the feel of Frankie's mouth on her skin and in her sweet, gentle caresses that found all the right places.

"Oh, Frankie," she said in a choked whisper. She gave into the sensations that electrified her body. "You know just what to do."

*　*　*

Frankie returned to Indianapolis the next morning. Their goodbyes were filled with promises for when they'd next be together, which was the middle of July when the teams were idle for the all-star break.

A few weeks later after a Saturday night game, Lisa straddled one of the benches in the clubhouse, flipping through the stats for the team. She heard someone clear her throat and stopped flipping the pages to find Amy hovering over her.

"Everything all right?" Lisa asked.

"Yeah, well, no, well, I mean yeah."

"Something you want to talk about?" Lisa set the binder aside.

"Can we go somewhere?"

Lisa swung one leg over the bench and stood up. "Now?"

"Let me get my shower. Can I meet you at your condo in about an hour?"

"Sure." Lisa waited for more of an explanation, but Amy left for her locker.

*　*　*

About an hour later, Amy was at her door, hair wet from her shower, and dressed in a red Lookouts T-shirt and baggy black shorts. She carried in a stack of envelopes.

"Can we sit at the table?" she asked. "It would be easier."

They went into the dining area and sat across from each other. Amy fidgeted with the rubber band that held the envelopes together.

Lisa asked, "So, you wanted to talk?"

"I've been getting letters."

Lisa straightened in her chair. "Not hate mail, I hope. If that's it, then you need to tell Reed."

"No. It's not always bad, Lisa. This is good. At least I think it is, but I don't know what I want to do about it." She tugged one of the envelopes out of the stack and handed it to Lisa. "Read this."

Lisa took the letter out of the envelope. It was from a sixteen-year-old girl in Virginia who had been following Amy's story. She wrote how much Amy meant to her and how she was an inspiration. She ended the letter with: "I'm gay. There are a couple of us on our fast pitch softball team in high school. They feel the same way I do. What you're doing has made us not be afraid of who we are. We look up to you, and because you're brave enough to go against guys and face harassment, we're not afraid anymore about what others think of us."

Lisa set the letter aside.

Amy pushed the stack of envelopes across the table. "Go through all of them. Every one of them has something like that in them about being gay. I've gotten other letters, but I wanted you to see these."

Lisa picked up twenty of them, finding a similar theme in each one. She laid the last letter down on the table.

"What do you think?" Amy asked.

"It's an honor that these teenagers look up to you."

"I'm talking about them being gay."

"It's good that they feel comfortable enough to confide in you."

"You know what I mean," Amy said with some exasperation. "I'm in the closet, and these teenagers are out in high school. I'm twenty-seven-years old."

"You really want to know what I think?"

"I wouldn't have come over and shown you these if I didn't."

Lisa still hesitated.

Amy waved her hands in frustration. "Say something!"

"All right. If you were to come out at some point, and I'm stressing 'some point' here, you'd be much more of an inspiration than you already are. Every young lesbian struggling with her sexuality would see what you're doing and say, if she can do it, I can, too."

Amy was quiet.

"It's got to be up to you if you ever come out. No one can force you into it. It's your decision to make." Lisa took a breath. "You know I'm out, and it's been a freeing experience for me. But there's a big difference. I'm not a high-profile athlete getting ready to break into what's long been considered a man's game. You've already put up with crap, and you would face ridicule on this, too. For every young lesbian you'd inspire, there'd be someone out there who'd criticize you for who you are."

Amy stared at the table.

"I believe Sheryl Swoopes is the only gay athlete to come out while she was still playing the game," Lisa said. "If it happens, it's usually after the player retires. But when you do make it to the majors…"

Amy met Lisa's eyes.

"And it will happen, Amy. When you make it, and you have someone in your life who you love, that's when it'll be exhausting. You can cover it up by calling her your friend or your roommate when you know she's your lover. The question is how will you feel at that time? You're the only one who'll be able to answer that."

Amy picked up one of the letters. "This definitely has made me look at everything differently."

"It's not something to decide on impulse. Give it some time. You'll know what's right for you."

Amy gathered the letters and stood up. "Thanks. I knew you'd be honest with me."

"Always."

Lisa walked her to the door. Amy gave her the first genuine hug they'd shared in a long time.

"I'll see you tomorrow," Amy said.

Lisa stood there until Amy got into her car and drove away. She shut the door and leaned her forehead against it.

Chapter 27

Lisa finished polishing her article after the first night game in July. Amy didn't have a particularly good night at the plate, but she made some outstanding defensive plays. Lisa paused when Sarah walked up to her. She seemed upset.

"Hey," Lisa said. "What the hell's wrong?"

They were alone in the press box. Sarah sat down beside Lisa, her chest rising and falling in an apparent effort to control her anger.

"Jesus, what is it?"

"I'm telling you this because I know it isn't true, and I know this particular sportswriter is a prick. I'm telling you because I know you'll be able to track this down better than I could."

"What?" Lisa almost shouted. "You're starting to scare me."

"Marty Bender from the *New York Bugle* is coming out with an article next week that says Amy took steroids while playing for the Kansas City Bandits. That there was a lot of steroid use on the team. Basically, he's saying she's this good because she juices."

Lisa saw red. She had heard the expression "seeing red" before. She always thought it was just that, an expression. But a red hue definitely swirled before her eyes. If this is what seeing red did to a bull in the ring, no wonder bullfighters were considered the bravest of the brave.

Sarah grabbed Lisa's arm. "Are you okay? I know this is a shock, but you're white as a ghost."

Lisa tried to control her anger. "There's no way that Amy or anyone on that team ever did steroids," she said, drawing out each word. "No way."

"You know that, and I know that, but we need to prove it. You've interviewed Amy's manager and some of the players, right?"

Lisa's mind raced with scenarios on how this might play out. None of it was good.

"Lisa?"

"Sorry. Yes, I've interviewed them. I'll find out from Amy how to reach them. Where the hell did this Bender come up with this crap?"

"It's my understanding that he contacted a former player, and she told him."

"Do you know who she is?"

"No, but I can try to find out. I know another reporter on that paper. She'll help me. She can't stand this asshole Bender."

Lisa sat back in her chair, her article all but forgotten. "Shit. Shit!"

"I know."

"I need to tell Amy, to prepare her for this. You know how this works. There'll be another reporter who'll catch wind of the article and throw it in Amy's face before the damn thing even comes out."

"I know you'll get to the bottom of this. You're the best damn sportswriter I know," Sarah said. "Get that stunned look off your face, Collins, and don't let it go to your head."

Lisa tried, but couldn't muster a smile. "Thanks for letting me know about this steroid mess."

"I'd never keep something like this from you." Sarah stood up. "I'll contact my source. I'll let you know when I hear something."

Lisa felt sick to her stomach.

"Try not to worry," Sarah said, patting Lisa's shoulder. "We'll straighten this out."

Lisa chewed the inside of her mouth. She wished she could be so sure. She thought of the extensive work Amy had put into getting to where she was. She thought about her raw talent, her gifted swing, as Curt Reed had called it months ago in Arizona. She remembered the first day she had met Amy at practice. Amy had it all, but she was a woman. And now, probably only because of that, someone was trying to tear it all down.

Lisa's stomach churned in anger as she struggled to finish her article. She completed the last line of copy and rushed directly from the press box to Amy's apartment.

* * *

Amy opened the door on the second knock. She was wearing a Kansas Jayhawks NCAA Basketball Champions T-shirt and a worn pair of denim shorts. Any other time, Lisa would have teased her about the shirt.

"Lisa?"

"Can I come in?"

"Yeah, sure." Amy stepped back. "Have a seat." Amy started for the kitchen. "Want a beer or something?"

"No." Lisa sat on the edge of the couch, unwilling and unable to relax.

Amy twisted the top off her bottle of beer. "What's wrong? Are you sick? You look kind of pale." Amy sat down beside her.

Lisa tried to form the right words to say.

"What?" Amy asked again, a little louder this time.

Lisa took Amy's hand in hers. Amy set the beer down. "There'll be an article coming out on Monday in a New York tabloid." Lisa took in a breath before continuing. "The reporter's claiming you took steroids while you were on the Bandits."

The color left Amy's tanned face. She slumped against the cushion of the couch. Tears sprang to her eyes. "You know it isn't true." Her voice was barely above a whisper.

"I absolutely know it isn't true, and I promise you"—Lisa squeezed Amy's hand—"promise you I'll get to the bottom of this."

Tears rolled down Amy's cheeks.

"I won't let this happen," Lisa said.

"It's already happening, Lisa. It's bullshit. Complete bullshit. Who would say this about me? No one's even interviewed me."

"It's someone who was on the team. Do you have any ideas who she could be?"

Amy contemplated briefly. "It has to be Nancy Drake," she said, her voice shaking with anger. She stood and paced in front of Lisa, her long legs taking only four steps to span the living room. "It has to be her."

"How can you be sure?"

"She was kicked off the team. She kept staying out late after games, getting drunk every night, and missing curfew. Coach Tompkins gave her a couple of chances, but she wouldn't listen." Amy stopped pacing. "It has to be her."

Lisa stood up. She put her hands on Amy's shoulders. "It'll be okay."

"You know they'll tear me up in the press. You…" She started sobbing. Lisa held her tight.

"Let me do my job. I'll get the truth to come out." Lisa stroked her hair. "I know it's bad, but you can get through this. You're so strong. Don't you know that by now?"

Amy pushed away. "I don't feel strong."

"Well, you are."

Amy wiped at her tears, but said nothing.

"I'll have to contact Marge Tompkins. Do you have a number I can reach her? I need to find out where they're playing. I'll have to miss a couple of your games while I do some traveling."

Amy picked up her cell phone, found the number, and read it off. Lisa programmed it into her own phone.

"I need to jump on this fast." Lisa gave Amy one more hug and then started for the door. "I'll keep you posted," she said before stepping outside.

She walked away, and Amy shut the door behind her.

* * *

Lisa broke the speed limit to get to her condo. She set up her laptop to type quotes before dialing Marge Tompkins's number.

"Yeah?" Marge's voice was gravelly. "Do you know what the hell time it is?"

Lisa glanced at the clock and cringed. It was ten-thirty. "Coach Tompkins?"

"Yeah? Who's this?" Marge asked, her voice still gruff.

"It's Lisa Collins."

"Who?"

"The reporter from Indianapolis."

"Oh, Lisa. What can I do for you?"

"There'll be an article coming out on Monday claiming Amy Perry was on steroids while she was a member of the Bandits and that there was rampant steroid use by your team. I need to get your input."

"What?" Marge yelled.

"An ex-player of yours has claimed there was steroid use on the Bandits team."

"Goddamn mother fucking son of a bitch!"

Yup. That pretty much summed it up. "Do you know who it could be?"

"I know exactly who it is. It's Nancy Drake. That little, little…"

Marge confirmed the player's name without Lisa prompting her. Good.

"I have to ask this, Coach, but did Amy or any of your

players—"

"Don't even go there, Collins!"

"I'm sorry, Coach, but I needed to confirm it."

Marge sighed on the other end. "Don't apologize. I know you're only trying to do your job. The answer is no. None of my players has ever done steroids or any of that other crap."

"Where's this Nancy Drake now? Do you know?"

"The last I heard she was in a fast-pitch softball league in Kansas City."

"Any idea which league?" Lisa didn't have much time to try to discredit the story.

"Shit, let me think." Marge was quiet for a long moment. "It's the Metro League on the east side. Yeah, that's it."

"Do I have your permission to talk to any of your players?"

"Hell, yeah, you have my permission."

"Where are you guys right now?"

"We're in Chicago. We're playing an exhibition against a men's team on the north side." Marge gave her the specifics.

"I'll fly there first and interview you more in depth and talk to some of your players. That way, when I catch up with Drake, I'll have quotes to give her and hear what she has to say. I'll especially want details from you about what happened with her while she was a member of the team."

"You got it."

"Thanks, Coach. I'm sorry I called so late."

"No. Don't apologize." There was a pause. "How's Amy holding up?"

Lisa had seen Marge in the stands at one of Amy's Lookouts games, so it was evident she was keeping up with Amy's career.

"None of the rumors are true," Lisa said. "She'll come out all right, Coach."

"Good. I'm counting on you to make sure that's what happens."

"Thanks for your time. I'll let you get back to sleep. I should be able to make it up there tomorrow."

"We'll be waiting for you."

After they hung up, Lisa stared at the computer screen. How the hell could she sleep now?

*   *   *

Thursday morning dawned. Lisa walked to the convenience store and bought a copy of one of the national newspapers. She flipped to the sports page, and her heart sank. There it was.

"Reds' Female Phenom Accused of Steroid Use."

She scanned the lead: "A *New York Bugle* article, set to appear in print on Monday, alleges Chattanooga Lookouts' star first baseman, Amy Perry, abused steroids while a member of an all-women professional baseball team." The article ended by stating that the newspaper had been unable to contact Amy for comment.

"Bullshit." Lisa almost sprinted back to the condo to take a shower before driving to the ballpark. She turned into the lot, cursing while maneuvering around the trucks from ESPN and Fox Sports. Sometimes the Internet era truly sucked when it came to immediate news.

She stepped into the clubhouse and pushed her way through the crowd of reporters gathered in front of Curt Reed.

"I'm telling you it's not true, Joe," Reed said to one of the reporters. "The minor league system tests its players as strenuously as the majors. Perry has never, and I repeat never, tested positive for any performance-enhancing substance."

"When can we talk to Amy?" another reporter shouted.

"Y'all can talk to her when I damn well say y'all can." Lisa could see Reed was livid. The veins in his neck bulged, and the muscles in his jaw twitched. And of course there were the "y'alls."

"Come on, Curt, you can't protect her," a reporter from ESPN said.

"I'm not fucking protecting her," he shouted at the reporter. "We're getting to the bottom of this, and when we do, I expect every fucking one of y'all"—he made a sweeping gesture with his hand—"to fucking apologize to her. This fucking shit is leaked without even contacting her? What kind of fucking reporting is that?"

A representative from the Reds whom Lisa recognized from the Indianapolis Indians' exhibition game approached the crowd of reporters and stood beside Reed. He had to be from public relations, and if body language meant anything, he was immensely worried. He held up his hand. "That's it. No further comment."

The reporters grumbled but dispersed.

"You." Reed pointed at Lisa. "In my office."

Lisa followed him. After they entered the office, Reed slammed the door.

"What the hell is this shit?" he asked. "I come into the ballpark, and I'm surrounded by these assholes. You and I know she didn't do this."

"An ex-player from the Bandits is probably the source for the rumors. I'm following leads. I'm trying to gather all the facts by Monday."

Reed stomped around in the limited space of the small office. He slumped down into his swivel chair. The vinyl covering hissed in protest. "Where do you start?"

"I'm flying into Chicago this afternoon to interview the Bandits and the manager. I've already called my editors and booked a flight. Then it's down to Kansas City to find this ex-player."

"If you're half the reporter I know you are, Collins, you'll get this straightened out."

"You can count on me." It sounded like a corny line from an old movie, but it was the best Lisa could do under the circumstances.

"Go do your job. I have to talk to the brass now."

Reed ushered her out of the office and set off to deal with the public relations nightmare this allegation had spawned.

Lisa's stomach was tied in knots as she made her way out to her car.

"Lisa."

Lisa heard Sarah's voice behind her.

"You'll interview the manager and the Bandits?"

"Right. I think I've found out who's the source of all this bullshit."

"I got the name, too. Nancy Drake?"

"Yes." Lisa unlocked her car door and got in. She checked her watch; she had two hours until her flight.

Sarah bent down with her hand on the roof of the car. Lisa gave her a knowing look. "We haven't talked about this, Sarah, but I want to write this article with you. You gave me the information. I'll track down the leads. When I get back, we'll put it all together."

"You don't have to do that."

"It'll be better if it's coming from both of us. I'll be back by Saturday, I hope. When I do get back, I want you to contact this Bender guy. Present the crap to him and get his reaction." Lisa shut the door and buzzed down the window. "Thanks for everything."

"You bet. Good luck."

"See you soon."

Lisa drove to the condo and packed. She called Frankie before she left for the airport. Lisa explained what had come up and told her where she'd be for the next couple of days.

"I believe in you, Leese."

"Thanks, Frankie. That's all I needed to hear."

Chapter 28

Lisa ignored the turbulence en route to Chicago. Instead, she compiled her questions for Marge and the players. While walking through the terminal, she called Marge to let her know that she'd landed. The coach told her all players would be available when she arrived at the hotel.

The cab pulled into the hotel roundabout. Marge Tompkins stood at the entrance. Alongside her was Dee, the shortstop.

"Come on in. Everyone's waiting upstairs in my room," Marge said.

On their way to the room, Dee asked Lisa if she could stop the story before it even hit the New York paper.

"We're going to try."

When they left the elevator, Marge marched ahead. Lisa hurried to keep up. They entered the room where the whole team was crammed inside. Some were on the beds. Others were on the floor. Everyone looked unhappy. They loved Amy, but this was personal for each player; the reporter had also accused them of taking illegal steroids.

"Let's get started." Lisa switched on her tape recorder and fired away with her prepared questions.

* * *

Lisa spent the night in Chicago and flew into Kansas City the next day. She had gotten directions to the ballpark where Nancy Drake played from one of the Bandits who had kept in touch with ex-teammates. They had confirmed that Nancy was indeed on a league team, the Rangers. The team was competing in a tournament beginning Friday night.

Lisa parked her rental in the lot next to the diamonds. She spotted a group of women wearing Ranger uniforms and approached the woman she assumed was the manager.

"Hi, I'm Lisa Collins. I'm a reporter for Minor League.com. Do you have a Nancy Drake on your team?"

"She's over there. The short redhead. Number twelve."

Lisa strode over to her. "Nancy Drake?"

"Yeah?" Nancy spun around.

Lisa stuck out her hand. "I'm Lisa Collins, a reporter from Minor League.com. I understand you've accused Amy Perry of steroid use while she was a member of the Bandits."

Nancy was about to shake Lisa's hand, but withdrew it quickly. Her face flushed, and she shifted her weight from foot to foot. "What of it?" she asked while staring out at the field.

Lisa positioned herself to force Nancy to meet her gaze.

"What of it?" Lisa's blood boiled from witnessing Nancy's nonchalant attitude. She composed herself before continuing. "You've made serious allegations against a member of a minor league baseball team who's on her way to breaking into the majors. I want to know the facts."

"That reporter asked me a question. He's the one who assumed there was steroid use. I didn't come out and say there was."

"What?"

"I said—"

"I heard you." The heat rose to Lisa's face. "You're saying it isn't true?"

Nancy wouldn't look at her.

"Ms. Drake?"

"Like I said, it was an assumption on his part."

"That you didn't refute."

Nancy stuck her chin out in defiance. "I figured if he really checked into it, he'd know it wasn't true."

"I understand you had some difficulties while a member of the Bandits."

"Is that what that old bitch Tompkins told you?"

"Marge Tompkins wasn't the only one. All the members of the Bandits I interviewed confirmed the allegations of your heavy drinking and disruption on the team and that it led to your eventual dismissal."

Nancy didn't offer a quick retort this time, but lowered her head.

Lisa took out her tape recorder. "For the record. You're saying that these allegations against Amy Perry are false? And that no member of the Bandits team ever took steroids?"

Nancy kicked at the dirt.

"Ms. Drake?"

Nancy's head snapped up. "Yes, that's what I'm saying," she said with a snarl. "Amy didn't do steroids or any of that other shit. None of them did."

Lisa punched off the tape recorder. "Thank you." She started for her car.

"I could've made it on a men's team, too, you know," Nancy shouted at Lisa's back.

Lisa stopped and faced Nancy. It had all been about spite and jealousy. Lisa toyed with telling her what she thought of her, but she didn't. Nancy wasn't worth the effort.

*   *   *

The flight into Chattanooga from Kansas City landed Saturday, ten minutes after midnight. Lisa was dead tired, but she dialed Sarah Swift's cell number.

"Yeah?"

"I've got the scoop. Can I come to your place, or do you want to come to mine?"

"You don't know how long I've waited to hear you say those words, Collins."

"Quit bullshitting me, Swift."

"I'll meet you at your place. Give me directions."

Lisa gave them as she drove to her condo. She had barely gotten inside when she heard a car door slam. She looked out the window and saw Sarah striding up the sidewalk. Lisa opened the door before Sarah even knocked.

"You ready to work?" she asked Sarah.

"Yup."

*   *   *

Sarah finished with her interviews Saturday afternoon and met again with Lisa to fill her in on the details. She had contacted the reporter, Marty Bender, and presented the facts to him. He stuttered and stammered his way through all of Sarah's questions about how he had gotten his source.

After concluding the interview with Bender, she contacted the editor of the *Bugle,* whom she had known for years. She told Lisa she had chided him for not following up on his reporter's story. Sarah got him to agree to run a retraction in the Sunday morning paper, apologizing for an article that hadn't even gone to print yet. It would reference the fact that the major sports outlets had picked up the story and run with it on Thursday, Friday, and Saturday. The editor had assured Sarah that the retraction would specifically apologize to Amy, Marge Tompkins, and to all Bandits players, past and present.

"Good work," Lisa said after Sarah relayed the details to her.

They each wrote articles on their laptops and then collaborated on merging the two. They finished at seven Saturday night. Their editors agreed that the article would run jointly on the Minor League.com website and on the *National Baseball Weekly* website with a "Lisa Collins & Sarah Swift" byline. Each publication would give credit to the other. Lisa had argued that Sarah's name should be first, but Sarah wouldn't hear of it. They sent the article through cyberspace and sat back in their chairs, exhausted but pleased.

"You look like shit, Collins," Sarah said with a tired smile.

"But I've never felt better."

* * *

Sunday morning, an article appeared on the front page of the *New York Bugle.* The editor of the paper kept all of his promises. An added bonus was that the newspaper also had suspended Marty Bender a week without pay. Although the accusatory article about Amy never appeared in print, the damage had still been done.

The Reds held a press conference Monday afternoon in the Lookouts' clubhouse. Dan Taylor, the general manager of the Reds, sat between Amy and Curt Reed.

Taylor finished his comments with: "I'm glad we can put this ugly, untrue rumor to rest." He turned to Amy. "Amy will now take any questions."

"How'd it feel hearing these allegations?" one reporter said.

Amy took a deep breath before answering. "It was horrible. I knew it wasn't true, but sometimes that doesn't matter once your name's connected to something like this."

"What'd you think of the Collins/Swift article that came out Saturday night, vindicating you and the Bandits?" another reporter asked.

Amy looked at Lisa as she spoke. "I'm very grateful for

184

everything they put into the article. For them to get the information as fast as they did, I know they must have worked nonstop on it. I can't thank them enough." She tried to say more, but her voice broke.

Overcome with emotion while watching Amy, Lisa averted her moistened eyes. With Amy's reputation now restored, Lisa felt confident no one could ever doubt the ability of the woman sitting at the table in front of them.

* * *

A week later, the furor died down, and the major sports outlets stopped hounding Amy for interviews.

Lisa was getting ready to cover another of Amy's games when her phone rang. The caller ID told her it was Frankie.

"How's it going?" Frankie asked. "Everything quiet down there now?"

"Yes, thank God. Amy's exhausted. It's taken a toll on her, but she wanted to do these interviews to make sure no one else would go through something like this."

"You always said she was a good person. I can see it now."

"Things okay there in Indy?"

"Yes. Uh… I was calling to uh…"

"Yeah?"

"God, I sound like a nervous mother setting her daughter up on a blind date with the handsome lad down the street."

"Huh?"

"Is Amy seeing anyone yet?"

"No. She can't really do that here."

"Do you know if she's up to seeing someone?"

"I don't know. I can ask her." Lisa chuckled. "Who is she, and what are her intentions?"

"Stop it. This is serious."

"All right, then seriously, who is she?"

"Stacy."

Lisa sat down on the couch and propped her feet up on the coffee table. "Really?"

"Yeah. Stacy was nervous when she talked to me, but she didn't want to contact Amy on her own. She knows she's very private, and she understands it."

"You know, I wondered if there was an interest there."

"From Amy?"

"I don't know. I definitely sensed it from Stacy when we were at the bar a couple of times, but I'll say this for Stacy. She's a good kid and didn't try anything while Amy and I were together." Lisa laughed. "Listen to me. Kid. Hell, she's, what, twenty-five?"

"About that. You're starting to show your age there, Leese. What do you think about Amy and Stacy?"

"If you approve, then I do, too."

"How'll we do this?"

Lisa checked the time. "It's not too late to call Amy. Let me do that and get back to you. If Amy's interested, maybe they can get together during the all-star break next week."

"Let me know what she says. I have a nervous employee back at the bar waiting for word."

"I'll call you in a few."

* * *

"Are you sure I look okay?" Amy asked. "Is my hair all right? Does this shirt look nice enough? Do these…"

"I swear to God, Amy, if you're about to ask me if those jeans make you look fat, I'm going to smack you." Lisa briefly took her eyes off the road to glance at Amy.

Thanks to Frankie and Lisa's matchmaking, Amy and Stacy had talked by phone several times during the past week and corresponded by e-mail. Lisa and Amy were on their way to meet Frankie and Stacy in Nashville.

"I'll shut up now." Two minutes later, Amy asked, "But you're really sure I look okay?"

"Stop it. You're fine, and besides that, it's not like you and Stacy have never met before."

"Yeah, but this is different, you know?" With her hands, Amy tapped out a rapid drumbeat on her knees. "This is for something more than friendship."

"You and Stacy will be good together. Hell, she asked to see you, remember?"

Amy let out a heavy sigh. "I know you're right, but I'm still nervous."

"Only a few more miles, and it'll all be over." Thank God, because Lisa couldn't take much more of this.

They arrived at the hotel. Frankie and Stacy were waiting for them in the lobby.

Frankie hugged Lisa. "Every time I see you, I fall in love all over again," she whispered.

"Love you, too, Frankie."

Stacy and Amy were standing nearby. Stacy rubbed the back of her neck, keeping her head down. Amy had her arms folded across her chest and was looking everywhere in the lobby but at Stacy.

Lisa walked over to them. "Stacy McCrady, meet Amy Perry. Amy, meet Stacy."

Stacy barely met Amy's eyes. "Hi," she finally managed to say.

Amy cleared her throat. "Hi."

"There. Was that so awful?" Lisa patted Amy on the back.

The two couples checked in and went to their adjacent rooms. Stacy and Amy hesitated outside their door.

"You're sure you don't mind sharing the room?" Amy asked. "I don't want you to think that I expected... well, expected..."

"You don't have to explain," Stacy said hurriedly.

Lisa suppressed a grin while she and Frankie entered their room. They set their luggage down, and she asked, "Have we created a monster?"

Laughter drifted through the wall.

"I don't know why we even thought this was a good idea. Listen to them." Frankie tilted her head to gesture toward Stacy and Amy's room.

Lisa stopped Frankie from saying anything further by pulling her in for a long, soulful kiss. "You really do need to learn when to keep your mouth shut."

Frankie kissed her again. "Keep me happily occupied, and that won't be a problem."

Chapter 29

The rest of the Lookouts season flew by. Amy finished with a
.323 batting average, 18 home runs, 32 doubles, 11 stolen bases, and
79 RBIs.

The entire sports world was anticipating Amy's promotion. The
expectation was that the Reds would call her up on September
second, along with other players on their minor league rosters, for
the remaining month of their season.

Lisa stood around the clubhouse chatting with some of the
reporters and with players who were cleaning out their lockers.

Curt Reed strode in and stopped in front of Amy's locker,
where she was removing her batting gloves and bats. "Perry," he
said. "In my office. Now." He pointed at Lisa. "And you come,
too."

Lisa followed Amy down the hallway.

Reed shut the door and motioned to the two chairs in front of
his desk. "Have a seat." He nodded toward Lisa. "Lisa, this is
unusual, but I invited you in because you've been covering Amy
since she first caught the Reds' attention."

With those words, Lisa's heart started pounding in her ears.

"Perry, a few minutes ago, I got off the phone with Max
Murphy. You report to Cincinnati in the morning. You'll be the
Reds' starting first baseman tomorrow night against the Atlanta
Braves."

Lisa's eyes filled with tears, and Amy had a smile that defied
anyone to try to wipe off her face.

"I'll never be able to thank you enough, Curt," Amy said.

"Thank me, hell. You did all the work. You'll be up for the
month with the Reds. They want to see how you handle major
league pitching. I think you know how this works. Next spring,
you'll report to the Reds camp, but more than likely you'll go to
Indianapolis for some more seasoning. After that, it's up to you
when you're back in Cincy." He pointed at her. "And don't think I

won't be riding your ass in Indianapolis."

"You're the new manager there?" Lisa asked. There had been a rumor that the Tampa Bay Rays would offer the current Indians manager, who had big league experience, the job for their team. This pretty much confirmed it.

"Yeah, I am. Guess I'll have to see your ugly mug next season, huh?"

"I could say the same."

He laughed. "Point taken." He stood and stuck out his hand to Amy. "I don't have to tell you to make me proud, Amy. You've already proven yourself. Do this for you." He held onto her hand and clasped his other hand on top.

"Thanks, Curt."

"Time to break the good news to the others."

Amy and Lisa stepped out of Reed's office and let him pass.

"I'm so proud of you, Aim."

Amy drew Lisa to her and squeezed her tight in her strong arms. "Thank you, Lisa," she whispered. "Thank you for everything."

Lisa didn't speak, mostly because she couldn't get words past the lump in her throat even if she tried.

* * *

On Friday afternoon, the day of the game, Frankie had called Lisa to let her know that she and Stacy were on their way down to Cincinnati. Stacy was to meet Amy and her mother at the hotel where Amy was staying. Frankie would meet up with Lisa at her hotel after dropping off Stacy.

Lisa heard a tap on the door. "Who is it?" Lisa asked, knowing very well it was Frankie.

"Open the damn door."

Lisa swung the door open.

Frankie stepped inside and shut the door. She grabbed Lisa and kissed her passionately.

Lisa managed to speak. "So, this means you missed me?"

"What do you think?" Frankie gave Lisa another intense kiss. "Do we have enough time before the game?" she asked with a sly grin.

"Umm, let me see."

"See hell."

Lisa giggled as Frankie pushed her toward the bed.

* * *

They arrived at Great American Ball Park and ran into congestion from the TV trucks parked in the press lot. ESPN would televise the game, and all three network stations planned to nationally simulcast Amy's first at-bat.

Lisa led Frankie to her seat four rows up the first baseline, even with the bag. Stacy and Amy's mother had already arrived and were seated two rows below. Lisa waved at Marge Tompkins and what appeared to be the entire Bandits team seated in the three rows behind Frankie.

After getting Frankie situated, Lisa took the elevator to the press box to set up her laptop. She rode the elevator back down again before walking onto the field with the rest of the reporters. She saw Sarah and gave her the lesbian salute.

The teams were warming up. Amy was stretching out on the ground, grabbing her toes, and pulling her long body tight against her legs. She stood, and the flashbulbs went off around her. She waved in the direction of her mother and Stacy, Frankie, and all of the Bandits. Poor health had kept Amy's mother from attending any of the Lookouts games over the summer, which made this night that much more special for both mother and daughter.

Amy smiled at Lisa as she approached. At the same time, she skillfully answered all the questions shouted her way from the mob of reporters surrounding her. She didn't blink at the microphones and tape recorders shoved in her face.

Lisa offered a question none of the other reporters had asked. "What's the last thing your mother said to you before you took the field?"

Amy took several deep breaths and tears came to her eyes.

"She told me she only wished my dad could've lived to see this day. I told her there's no doubt in my mind he's here. I wouldn't have made it this far without his strength. And my mom has given me all her support over the years. It's been unbelievable." Amy paused and met Lisa's eyes. "But I also know I wouldn't have made it without the support of a good, good friend."

The Reds' public relations man approached them and held up his hand. "That's it, folks. Let's give Amy some space. You'll have time with her after the game."

The photographers and other reporters dispersed; Amy walked over to Lisa.

"It's your time, Amy."

"Yeah?"

"Yes, it is. How're you feeling?"

Amy slowly scanned the ballpark. "Like I'm in a dream," she said almost reverently. "I'm trying to let it soak in."

"You deserve all of this."

Amy ducked her head shyly like that first day when Lisa interviewed her on the practice field in Indianapolis. When she raised her head, she nodded toward the stands. "I noticed your woman's here."

Lisa beamed. "Yeah, she is. And I'm glad yours is here, too. I'm especially happy your mom could make it."

"It's all good, huh?"

The players started their wind sprints in the outfield. "Well, it's time to get to work." Amy stopped herself. "Hell, this isn't work. This is a game."

Lisa smiled. She hoped Amy always felt that way. "I would say good luck again, but I know you don't need it."

"Thanks, Lisa."

Lisa went back up to the press box and settled into her seat with her laptop in front of her. Sarah made her way down the row.

"What do you know, Lisa. Seems you were right about Perry all along." Sarah sat down next to her.

They talked about Amy and passed the hour before the opening pitch. The night was warm and sticky, typical for the beginning of September in Cincinnati. All the seats in the stadium had filled. Lisa watched Amy at first base as everyone stood for the playing of the National Anthem. Amy bowed her head, holding her hat over her heart.

The Reds pitcher retired the side in order in the top of the first. Amy was due to hit third in the bottom of the inning. The leadoff man struck out swinging. The shortstop was up next and worked the count to try to draw a walk.

While he was at bat, Amy swung a weighted bat in the on-deck circle. The count got to 2-0. She set the weighted bat aside, picked up her bat, and added more pine tar to the handle. Count on the batter: 2-1. A few more practice swings for Amy. Count on the batter: 3-1. The crowd began to cheer, and probably not for the guy about to get a free pass.

As the shortstop trotted down to first base after drawing the walk, the cheers that had started when the count was 3-1 became a deafening roar.

"Now, batting third, number twenty-two, first baseman, Amy Perry."

Lisa didn't think it could get any louder, but she was wrong. The roar rose several decibels. Flashbulbs lit up the stadium. Lisa was thrilled that the fans embraced Amy once she made it to the majors. It felt much like the roar of the crowd Lisa had witnessed at the Indy 500 when, driving as a rookie, Danica Patrick stormed into first place on the front straightaway to become the first woman to lead the race.

Amy walked up to the plate, adjusted her helmet, then unsnapped and snapped her batting gloves. She took a deep breath.

The Atlanta Braves pitcher fired a fastball knee high on the inside part of the plate. Amy took the pitch for a called strike. The next pitch was a looping breaking ball that appeared to be low, but was again called a strike. The crowd groaned. Amy stepped out of the batter's box, adjusted her batting gloves again, and took a couple of practice swings.

Lisa said a silent prayer. Please, God, please don't let her strike out her first time at bat. She held her breath, watching the next pitch come toward the plate.

It was a fastball, thigh-high on the outer part of the plate. Amy's bat sliced through the thick air and connected with the ball. It left the plate on a line over the second baseman's head, a solid base hit.

The ballpark erupted in cheers. Amy asked for the ball. The first base coach caught it from the umpire and tossed it into the dugout. Amy raised her face to the darkening Ohio sky before turning to where her mother and Stacy were seated.

Lisa presumed they were crying. Why wouldn't they be? She was barely keeping it together herself.

The crowd chanted, "Amy! Amy!" Amy tipped her batting helmet to the clamoring fans around the ballpark. Four rows up the first baseline, Lisa watched Frankie wipe her cheeks with the back of her hand. Lisa smiled through her own tears.

Seeing the woman of her dreams in the seats below her and the woman who had just made history standing at first base, Lisa could think only one thing:

It was a perfect night.

Epilogue

"You're sure you want to do this, Amy?" Lisa asked.

"I'm sure. I've thought about it a lot, and Stacy and I talked it over." Amy turned to Stacy. They were sitting in the living room at what had become Frankie and Lisa's house—ever since Lisa moved in with Frankie just after Thanksgiving.

The four of them—Amy, Stacy, Lisa, and Frankie—were eager for the Indianapolis Indians' opening night, less than a week away. "I need to do this before the season starts," Amy said.

She had turned in a solid performance during her month with the Reds back in September. It wasn't spectacular, but she had shown sufficient promise of what she might do if given the chance. Curt Reed had been right in his prediction that Amy would be invited to the Reds' spring training camp, but she had been sent back down to the Indians' camp two weeks before the start of the season.

"It's not like you can ask for a do-over or take it back if you change your mind," Lisa said.

"I know, but I need to do this. Remember those letters I showed you when you were covering my games in Chattanooga? The club has been forwarding more to me here in Indianapolis. I can't turn my back on what all those young athletes are saying to me. I've given this a lot of thought these past few months. If I ever hope to be completely happy, I've got to take this step." Amy took Stacy's hand in hers. "Being with Stacy has gone a long way toward that, but it's time to stop pretending and to show everyone the real me."

"When will you do it?"

"Tomorrow afternoon. Dan Taylor and Curt Reed will be there. I've told Curt what I want to do, and he supports me completely. The Reds' top management team isn't exactly thrilled, but they haven't told me not to do it either."

Amy looked at the other three women in the room. "I really

want you all to be there with me tomorrow, but especially you, Lisa. You've been there for me since all this began. Can I count on you one more time?"

Lisa patted Amy's knee. "I wouldn't miss it for the world."

* * *

The next day, a crowd of reporters gathered in the Indianapolis Indians' clubhouse. Amy, dressed casually in a pair of khakis and a red Indianapolis Indians polo shirt, sat next to Curt Reed at a table that had been set up for the press conference. On Reed's right was Reds GM, Dan Taylor. Reed nodded at Lisa, who sat in the front row with Stacy on one side of her and Frankie on the other.

Taylor said a few words of thanks to the reporters for assembling on such short notice. He added some complimentary words about Amy. "And now Curt Reed would like to address you."

Reed leaned over the microphone in front of him. "Thank you, Dan. Good afternoon. Amy asked for this press conference. But before she gets started, I want to say how much I respect and admire her." He turned to Amy. "And I'm behind her one hundred percent. She knows that, but I need each and every one of you to know that, too. I'll let her tell you in her own words why we're here. Amy?"

Amy cleared her throat. She met Stacy's eyes and briefly glanced at Lisa and Frankie before putting her mouth close to the microphone.

"Like Mr. Taylor, I also want to thank you all for coming here today on such short notice. It's true that I have my own personal reasons for doing this. But more importantly, I'm doing this for any young woman who comes after me who's faced with the same situation I've been in. I want them to know that it's okay to be an out and proud lesbian athlete."

She took a deep breath. "I know this because I'm gay."

The lead for Lisa's article about the press conference leapt into her mind: Today, Amy Perry hit a grand slam without even stepping up to the plate.

Author Chris Paynter   Photo Credit: Phyllis Manfredi

About the Author

Chris was born in a British hospital and happily lived the life of an Air Force brat for the first thirteen years of her life. She received a Bachelor's degree in journalism from Indiana University with a minor in her true first love, history. She worked as a general assignment reporter and sports reporter before settling into her current position as editorial specialist for a law journal.

She lives in Indianapolis with her wife and their beagle, Buddy the Wonder Dog. She is a voracious reader and continues to work on her own writing.

You can visit her website at www.ckpaynter.com.

Coming soon from Blue Feather Books:

Detours, by Jane Vollbrecht

It should have been a typical day of trimming shrubbery and edging lawns, but Gretchen VanStantvoordt—known to everyone as "Ellis"—first gets caught in a traffic jam and then lands in the emergency room with a badly sprained ankle. Mary Moss, a newfound friend who was caught in the same traffic jam, convinces Ellis that trying to tend to her dog and negotiate the stairs at her walk-up apartment while she's on crutches isn't such a good idea. Without friends or family in the vicinity, Ellis accepts Mary's offer for assistance.

When Ellis meets Natalie, Mary's nine-year-old daughter, she's ready to make tracks away from Mary as quickly as possible, but her bum ankle makes that impossible. Ellis stays with Mary and Natalie while she recovers. Little by little, Ellis develops a fondness for young Natalie... and develops something much deeper for Mary.

Ellis and Mary work out a plan for building a future—and a family—together. Destiny, it seems, has other plans and throws major roadblocks in their path. Ellis is forced to reconsider everything she thought she knew about where she wanted to go in life, and Mary learns that even with the perfect traveling companion, not all journeys are joyous.

No GPS can help them navigate the new road they're on. Come make the trip with Ellis and Mary as they discover that when life sends you on a detour, the wise traveler finds a way to enjoy the scenery.

Lesser Prophets, by Kelly Sinclair

We were the despised, the unloved, the fitfully tolerated, the novelty acts, and in some fortunate places, the embraced and even cherished.

In those safe harbors, we celebrated each stage of our growing emancipation even though others of our tribe were faced with hangman's gallows or less deadly alternatives and dared not show their true faces. We passed as "normal" when possible, and we were penalized when we could not pass. We only had freedom when they said we could be free. That was our world. We knew none other.

But then God, or Fate, or the Omniscient Divine—or merely happenstance—negated all the rules, and our status was forever changed.

This is how the new world began. We were the *Lesser Prophets*, and this is our story.

Coming soon, only from

Make sure to check out these other exciting
Blue Feather Books titles:

Tempus Fugit	Mavis Applewater	978-0-9794120-0-4
In the Works	Val Brown	978-0-9822858-4-8
Addison Black and the Eye of Bastet	M.J. Walker	978-0-9794120-2-8
Diminuendo	Emily Reed	978-0-9822858-0-0
Merker's Outpost	I. Christie	978-0-9794120-1-1
Whispering Pines	Mavis Applewater	978-0-9794120-6-6
Greek Shadows	Welsh and West	978-0-9794120-8-0
From Hell to Breakfast	Joan Opyr	978-0-9794120-7-3
Journeys	Anne Azel	978-0-9794120-9-7
Accidental Rebels	Kelly Sinclair	978-0-9794120-5-9

www.bluefeatherbooks.com

Printed in the United States
148214LV00002B/1/P